My Giant Treasury of
FAIRY
TALES

First published in the USA in 1987 by Exeter Books
Distributed by Bookthrift
Exeter is a trademark of Bookthrift Marketing, Inc.
Bookthrift is a registered trademark of Bookthrift Marketing, Inc.
New York, New York

Prepared by the Hamlyn Publishing Group Limited
Bridge House, 69 London Road, Twickenham, Middlesex TW1 3SB England

Printed in Czechoslovakia
Material in this book previously appeared in *The Giant All-colour Book of Fairy Tales*.

My Giant Treasury of
FAIRY
TALES

Retold by Jane Carruth

Exeter Books

NEW YORK

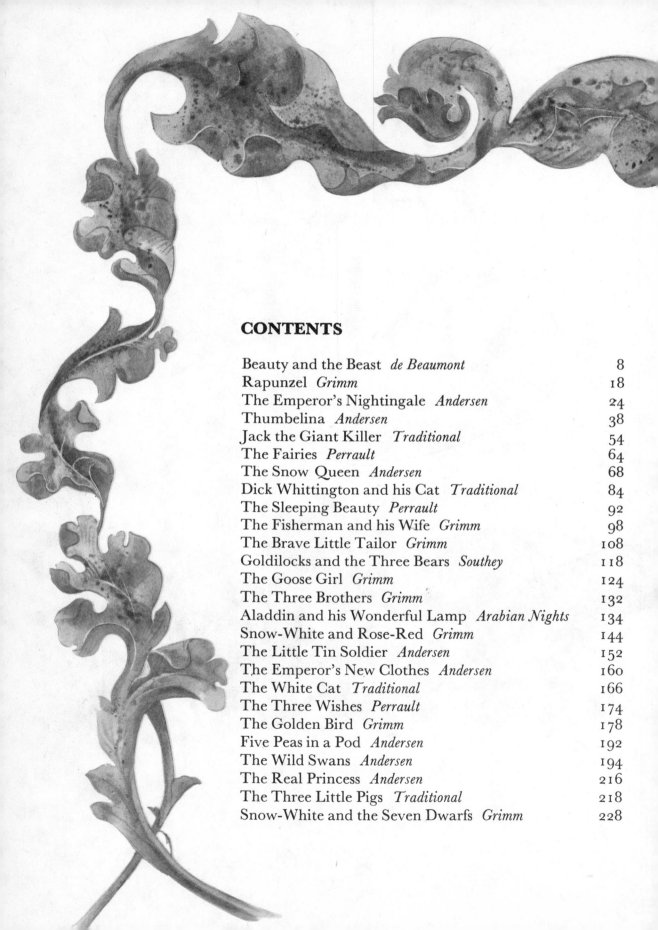

CONTENTS

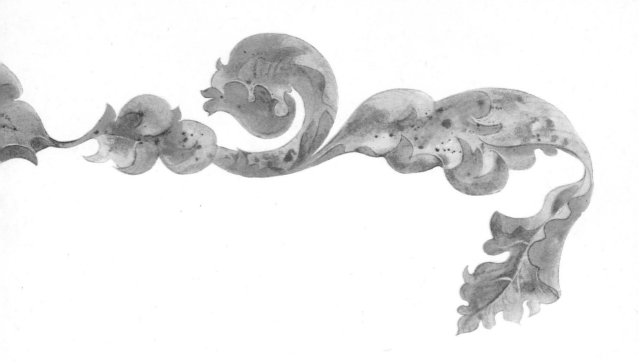

ILLUSTRATORS

Joan Beales

David Bryant

Eric Critchley

Elisabeth and Gerry Embleton

Ron Embleton

Gareth Floyd

Frank Francis

Porter-G

Ron Hanna

Lynette Hemmant

Peter Kesteven

J. E. Nieuwenhuis

Hilda Offen

K. J. Petts

Joanna Ross

Jenny Thorne

Hugh Urquhart

INTRODUCTION

One of the joys of owning a book like **My Giant Treasury of Fairy Tales** is that you can choose almost any fairy story you like to name and then find it here.

Believing as I do that fairy tales will always be among the world's best loved stories, it gave me enormous pleasure to gather together in one big book this collection of tales by such master story-tellers as Hans Andersen, the Brothers Grimm and Charles Perrault.

Many of us, long after we have grown up, still remember the fairy tales of our childhood days, and I began by retelling all my own favorites. But this was to be a giant book of fairy tales, so I included all the familiar stories as well as others which are perhaps not quite so well-known, but make exciting reading.

What a dull place our world would be without such stories! Hans Christian Andersen, the father of the true fairy tale, thought so. He believed that he was writing not only for small children but for grown-ups too, and he once said that he could sit in his own modest kitchen and his imagination would, in the twinkling of an eye, transform it into a sumptuous palace.

The beautiful pictures, drawn by a number of gifted artists, help you to share in the enchantment of the stories, and if you find yourself, at some stage, being carried through the night in a flying trunk, or dining with a white cat who is a lovely princess in disguise, don't be surprised!

Everything is possible when you settle down to read a proper fairy story!

J.C.

BEAUTY AND THE BEAST

There was once a rich merchant who had three pretty daughters. The merchant gave them all that money could buy, for he was very rich.

The name of his youngest daughter was Beauty. She was so kind and so gentle that everyone loved her, and she was the merchant's favourite child.

One day the merchant heard that all his ships had been lost at sea and that he was penniless. He sold his fine house and carriages to pay his debts, and when he had done this, he took his three daughters into the country to live.

'We must learn to be poor,' he told them sadly. 'We must live as peasants.'

The old man and his three daughters no longer wore fine clothes. Beauty looked beautiful, even in her ragged dress, but her sisters complained bitterly. They could not forget that they had once had gowns of silk and velvet to wear, and a carriage in which to ride. 'Our hands are white and smooth!' they cried. 'How can you expect us to work like peasants?'

Beauty did not complain. She grieved because her father was so upset. 'We must help him,' she told her sisters. 'We must learn to cook and sew and work in the fields.'

As soon as it was daylight, Beauty was up and busy. She

swept and dusted the cottage until it shone like a new pin. She made the beds and cooked the breakfast, and when all this was done she took a basket full of washing down to the stream and washed the sheets in the clear water, just as she had seen the country women do.

Down by the gurgling little stream Beauty made friends with the singing birds and with the little lamb that followed her wherever she went. Sometimes her two elder sisters would go with her, but they did not help her. Instead they would stand, hands on hips, jeering at her.

'There goes Beauty,' they would say, 'with her rough hands and tangled hair!'

Beauty was so kind and gentle that she did not answer her sisters. Instead, she worked harder than ever, hoping that they too would learn to work.

One day a messenger brought news that the merchant had the chance of saving some of his fortune.

'I must go on a journey,' the old man told his three daughters. 'Tomorrow I must go to the port where one of my ships lies at anchor. What presents shall I bring you back, my dear ones?'

'We want new dresses and shoes and bracelets!' cried his elder daughters eagerly.

But all Beauty asked for was a single red rose.

The merchant mounted his horse and rode away.

'I hope he remembers our presents,' cried Beauty's two

sisters, who were so greedy and vain that they could think only of themselves. 'How foolish you are, Beauty! What a stupid thing to ask for. A single red rose, indeed!'

Alas for the merchant's hopes! When he reached the port where he hoped to find one of his ships, he was told that he could not claim the merchandise aboard unless he went to law. The law suit dragged on for many days, and, at the end of it, the merchant found himself poorer than ever.

He set off for home with a heavy heart. What would he say to his daughters? How would he tell them that he had no gifts for them after all?

'Only Beauty will understand,' the merchant thought as his horse carried him over the miles.

As the day wore on, dark clouds gathered in the sky, the wind howled eerily through the trees, and thick, blinding snow began to fall. It wasn't long before the merchant realised he was hopelessly lost in a deep forest.

Weak from hunger and nearly frozen, the old man had almost given up hope of getting through the night alive when, suddenly, he saw through the trees light streaming from a window.

Urging his tired mount forward, the merchant found himself approaching a large castle. 'Surely some Prince has built himself this retreat in the forest,' the old man told himself. 'He will take pity on me and give me shelter for the night.'

But before seeking shelter for himself, the merchant made for the stables that were built in the courtyard. To his surprise and joy, there was everything his horse could want for comfort.

'You have served me well this night,' the merchant said as he threw a blanket over his horse's back. 'And now here is your reward, for there is enough fodder here to feed a dozen horses.' He left the stables and made for the castle.

So weary was the merchant that he did not ask himself why the castle doors stood wide open, or why there was no sign of servants. He stumbled down the long passages until he came upon a large bedroom furnished in a most splendid way. Wearily he flung himself on the bed and fell fast asleep.

As soon as it was daylight, however, the merchant set out to find the Prince. He searched the castle, and then wandered into the garden. He met no one, and the old man grew troubled and anxious.

When he was almost on the point of giving up his search, the sight of some beautiful red roses reminded him of Beauty. 'At least she shall have her present,' he thought to himself tenderly. And with that he plucked a single rose from a bush.

No sooner had he done so than there stood before him the most hideous creature imaginable. Trembling, the old man flung himself upon his knees before the Beast.

'Oh miserable, wretched man!' roared the Beast in a

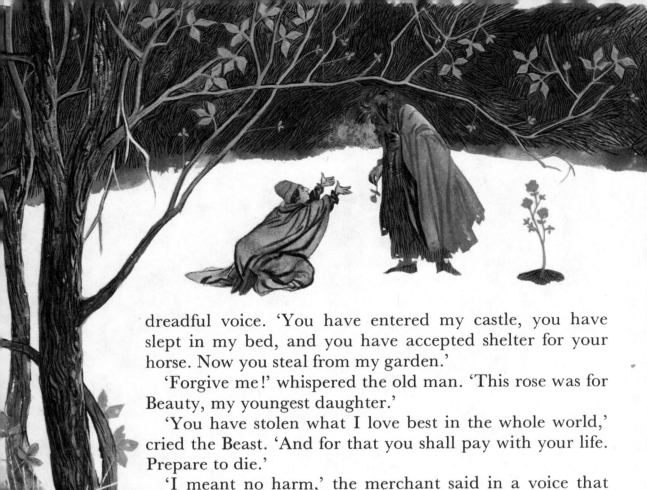

dreadful voice. 'You have entered my castle, you have slept in my bed, and you have accepted shelter for your horse. Now you steal from my garden.'

'Forgive me!' whispered the old man. 'This rose was for Beauty, my youngest daughter.'

'You have stolen what I love best in the whole world,' cried the Beast. 'And for that you shall pay with your life. Prepare to die.'

'I meant no harm,' the merchant said in a voice that quavered. 'I beg you to permit me to return home.'

'On one condition,' replied the Beast. 'You must promise to bring your daughter to me at the end of three months. Promise, and you are free to go.'

The poor old man was so terrified that he found himself agreeing. 'After all,' he thought, 'three months is a long time. Perhaps I will find some way to escape this promise.'

'Remember,' said the Beast, 'a promise is a promise and may not be broken. You are free to return home, but go first to the room where you passed the night. There you will find a box of gold. Take it. The gold pieces will serve to remind you that you have promised to bring your daughter, Beauty, here to me.'

The merchant found the gold and left the castle. His horse found its way out of the forest, and that same day the merchant arrived home.

For a time he could not speak, so deeply sunk in despair was he. But when his two elder daughters clamoured for their presents, he told them the whole dreadful story.

'Your rose has cost me dear,' he said, turning to Beauty. 'Alas, what have I done? What have I done!'

Beauty did her best to comfort her father. 'Three months —why, that is a long time,' she said.

But her father would not be comforted.

As the months passed, he began to say that he would go to the Beast and offer himself. 'I am old,' he told Beauty. 'My life is worth little compared to yours.'

Beauty would not hear of such a thing. 'I shall accompany you, father,' she vowed. 'We will face the Beast together.'

When the day of departure came at last, her two sisters did their best to look sad; they even rubbed their eyes with onion so that they appeared to shed tears. The truth, however, was that, being so jealous of Beauty, they were pleased to be rid of her.

It was almost dark when, at last, the father and daughter

reached the forest and came upon the castle. As before, the merchant stabled their horses in the courtyard; then, taking Beauty's hand, he led her into the castle.

They soon came upon a vast banqueting hall and saw there a table laid for two. Plates and goblets were all made of solid gold, and the food was fit for a king.

'Well, father, we might as well eat,' said Beauty, seating herself at the table. But the unhappy merchant could not swallow a morsel.

When supper was over, the Beast himself suddenly appeared before them, and Beauty shuddered at the sight of his terrifying appearance.

The Beast addressed her in a surprisingly gentle voice. 'You have come here of your own free will, I take it?' he asked her. And as Beauty nodded, he went on, 'Then you must be ready to say goodbye to your father in the morning.'

Father and daughter spent the night in each other's company. In the morning, with many tears, the merchant said goodbye to Beauty for the last time.

After she had watched him ride off, Beauty dried her eyes and wandered aimlessly through the castle.

To her surprise, she came upon a door with her name on it. Inside she found everything her heart could desire. The room was so beautiful with its white satin walls and delicately patterned carpet that, despite her grief, Beauty gave a little gasp of pleasure. But what pleased her most was the white bookcase full of books. When she pulled one out and opened it, there, in letters of gold, were the words, 'You are mistress of this castle; ask for anything you wish.'

The rest of the day passed more quickly than Beauty could have imagined and, when supper-time came, she found her place laid in the banqueting hall.

It was then that the Beast came to her for the second time, and Beauty could not help trembling at the sight of him.

'May I watch you eat?' he asked in the same gentle voice he had used before.

And Beauty answered, 'You are the master here.'

As Beauty began to eat, the monster said, 'Tell me, Beauty. Do you find me so very ugly?'

Beauty was silent. But her father had taught her always to speak the truth and at last she whispered, 'I do. But you do not frighten me as much as I thought you would.'

Each evening after that, the Beast came to her at supper-time, and brought her gifts. He was so kind and thoughtful that Beauty grew to look forward to his visits. If he were late she would run to meet him.

One night the Beast asked her in a low, humble voice, 'Beauty, will you marry me?'

'No, no, never!' cried Beauty, and she shrank away from him.

Soon after this, the Beast gave Beauty a magic mirror. In it she could see her old father lying ill in bed. 'I must go to him,' she told the Beast. 'Please let me return home for a little while.'

'Very well,' said the Beast. 'But you must promise to return to me at the end of eight days. If you do not, I shall die.'

'I promise,' cried Beauty. 'Yes, yes, I promise!'

'Then take this ring,' said the Beast, giving her a band of gold. 'Shut your eyes and wish upon it. Wish that you were home.'

Beauty did so, and when she opened her eyes she found herself at the cottage door. How pleased she was to be back; but her sisters were filled with envy at the sight of her dressed like a princess.

Beauty sat with her father each day, and he grew much stronger because she was there at his bedside.

This made the two sisters even more jealous.

'He loves her best,' one said to the other. 'And to think she lives in a real castle!'

'Let us keep her here,' said the other. 'We shall make her break her promise to return. Then the Beast will be angry and punish her. He might even put an end to her.'

'Our father will die if you go now,' the sisters told Beauty when the eight days were up. 'And we shall miss you so much ourselves that we shall be heartbroken. You must stay.'

Their false words of affection moved Beauty so much that she agreed to stay eight more days. One night, however, she dreamt that the Beast was dying. The dream was so vivid that, when she awoke in the morning, she touched her magic ring and wished herself back once more in the Beast's castle.

In the gardens she came upon the poor Beast under a tree. 'I am too late!' Beauty cried when she saw him stretched out on the grass as if he were dead. And she bent down and kissed him gently.

'Don't die, Beast,' she whispered, 'for I know now that I love you as you are.'

No sooner had Beauty uttered these words than the Beast was transformed into a tall and handsome Prince.

'You have broken the spell with your words of love,' cried the Prince joyfully. 'A wicked fairy cast her spell upon me, long years ago. It could be broken only by a girl who loved me as I am.'

Soon, to the delight of her father and the grudging approval of her sisters, Beauty and her Prince were married, and lived in the castle happily ever after.

RAPUNZEL

Long ago a young couple lived in a house that was close to the castle of an enchantress. From her top window the wife could look down into the witch's garden, which was always filled with beautiful flowers and herbs with strange-sounding names.

No one dared to go into this garden, least of all the husband and wife, for the evil nature of the old witch was very well-known. However, one day the wife fell ill. The only thing she asked for was a salad made from the roots of a purple flowering herb that grew in the witch's garden.

'I dare not go there,' her young husband told her. 'What if the witch should catch me?'

His wife became steadily worse, and at last her devoted husband scaled the high wall that surrounded the enchantress's garden and picked some of the herbs. Then he made a salad for his ailing wife.

After she had eaten it, his wife declared that already she felt much better, but that she would surely die if he could not bring her more of the life-giving herbs.

Hoping that his second raid on the witch's garden would again be successful, the husband agreed. But this time the witch was waiting for him.

'You dare to steal my precious plants!' she shrieked. 'For that I will lay a curse upon you both.'

'My wife is sick,' answered the poor man, white with fear. 'She will die if she does not have some of this purple herb that grows in your garden. Forgive me and let me go.'

But the enchantress held him fast with her eyes, and he was rooted to the spot. 'Only on one condition,' said she. 'When your wife has her first-born you must give it to me. I will care for the child as if it were my own.'

So anxious was he to be away that the husband agreed, and the witch permitted him to pluck an armful of the flower, which she called ramponzolo. 'Remember,' said she as he prepared to scale the high wall. 'Your first-born!'

After his wife had recovered, the husband told her of the witch's threat, and she exclaimed, 'What would an old witch want with a child? Let us forget it, husband, and be happy, for I have a feeling that we shall have a baby of our own before the year is out.'

Her forecast came true; a lovely baby daughter was born to them before the year was out. Alas, before the baby was one day old, the enchantress appeared; she scooped up the child in her arms and vanished.

The witch called the child Rapunzel, after the name of the herb, and, when she was twelve years old, shut her up in a high tower.

Even at twelve, Rapunzel was as beautiful as the sun, and her long hair, which was fine as spun silk, was of great length. The only human being she ever saw was the old enchantress, whom she addressed as Dame and learned to trust.

As there was neither door nor stairway inside the tower, whenever the witch came to visit Rapunzel, she cried:

Rapunzel, Rapunzel,
Let down your hair to me.

Rapunzel then ran to the window and let down her long hair; it swung like a golden rope and the witch grasped it and climbed upwards.

After several years it chanced one day that the Prince of a neighbouring kingdom came riding past the tower— from which came the most beautiful singing he had ever heard in his life. Overwhelmed by curiosity, he stayed within earshot of the tower until presently along came the enchantress.

Rapunzel, Rapunzel,
Let down your hair to me,

called out the witch, and down came the golden rope of hair, and up it climbed the witch until she reached the turret window and vanished inside.

The young Prince, who was tall and handsome, decided to try his fortune, and the next night, when it was dark, he stood underneath the turret window, and called out,

Rapunzel, Rapunzel,
Let down your hair to me.

At once the golden rope of hair swung down from the window, and, grasping it, the Prince climbed upwards. As soon as he was in the room facing Rapunzel he gasped aloud at her beauty, and the girl was equally attracted to such a handsome young man—the first she had ever seen. 'I cannot leave you here!' cried the Prince.

'And yet you must,' returned Rapunzel, 'for there is no way in or out of this tower except by my hair.'

'Then I will come to you each night after the witch has
made her visit,' said the Prince. 'And we can work out
a plan.'

But Rapunzel had already thought of one. 'Bring with
you a skein of silk,' she said. 'Do likewise with every visit
you make. I will weave a rope of silk, and when it is long
enough, it shall be my escape ladder! Then you must take
me on your horse far away from this place.'

Everything went well; the young Prince made his visit
to the tower each night, bringing with him a skein of
silk. When he had gone, Rapunzel set to work on her
silken ladder.

The witch, who made her visits to the tower in the
afternoons, suspected nothing until, one day, Rapunzel
blurted out, 'Tell me, good Dame, why do I take twice as
long to pull you up as I do my Prince? You must be much,
much heavier . . .'

At these words the enchantress flew into a dreadful
rage. 'Wicked girl!' she cried, and, taking her scissors, she
snipped off Rapunzel's long golden hair. Then she cast a

spell over Rapunzel so that she fell asleep; when she awoke she found herself in the middle of a desert.

The enchantress settled down to wait for the King's son, but first she fastened Rapunzel's long braids of golden hair to the window hooks.

> *Rapunzel, Rapunzel,*
> *Let down your hair to me,*

the Prince called out as usual when he came to the tower. And the witch threw down the golden braids. Up he climbed and came face to face with the spiteful, angry enchantress.

'Your little bird has flown,' she hissed at him. 'You will never see her again.'

In his shocked despair the young man hurled himself out of the window and landed, many feet below, on a bramble bush whose cruel thorns put out his eyes. Unable to return to his own kingdom, the unhappy Prince wandered through the countryside for many years. One day he came to the very desert where Rapunzel had made a home for herself.

On seeing him she ran to him and threw her arms round his neck while tears of love and pity flowed down her cheeks. The proud Prince bowed his head, and her tears splashed into his sightless eyes and made him see again.

Supporting each other they made their way out of the desert. The Prince took her to his father's palace where they married and lived for fifty years in great contentment.

THE EMPEROR'S NIGHTINGALE

Once upon a time the Emperor of China lived in a splendid palace that was believed to be the most beautiful in the whole world. The floors were made of crystal, the doors of solid gold, and the ornaments fashioned out of the most delicate china.

The grounds and the gardens were so large that it would have taken a thousand days and a thousand nights to walk round them once. Among the rare and beautiful plants, blue lakes shimmered in the sun. Beyond the lakes stretched a forest where the birds sang their songs undisturbed.

One of these birds was the pride of the Chinese people. It was a nightingale. There were, of course, other nightingales in the world, but this particular nightingale sang so beautifully that all who heard her song could never forget it.

Strangers who came to China to visit the imperial palace declared that the palace was indeed a marvellous sight; marvellous, too, they vowed, were the gardens surrounding the palace. But when they went into the forest and listened to the nightingale they could find no words to express their wonder and delight, but stood with their mouths wide open.

In their own country, those who had been to China sighed and became pale and sad, and their friends asked them, 'Why are you so sad?'

They answered, 'We want to hear the nightingale sing again—the nightingale in the imperial forest of China.'

A Japanese poet even wrote a poem that he dedicated to the bird with the golden throat. It went something like this:

'In China I have heard a great many wonderful things. But the most wonderful of all is the song of the nightingale in the forest. It is more beautiful than all the other wonders put together.'

This poem fell into the Emperor's hand, and after he had read it through from beginning to end he was very sad.

'Woe is me!' he cried. 'Strangers to my country tell me of this wonderful bird in my forest and yet I know nothing of it; nor have I heard its song.' Then he rang a tiny golden bell that was set with diamonds and most splendidly designed.

Immediately the servants came running from all sides and, behind them, all the courtiers and the ladies-in-waiting.

'Disloyal subjects!' thundered the Emperor. 'Look into your hearts and ask yourselves if you have been true to your Emperor.'

All the courtiers and the ladies-in-waiting, even the Prime Minister himself, stood motionless and downcast before their Lord and Master.

'Traitors!' cried the Emperor again. 'If you were faithful to me you would have told me that in my royal forest there is a nightingale with a voice so wonderful that those who hear it are charmed beyond description. The whole world is talking about it! If you do not bring me this bird before midnight, each one of you will suffer everlasting banishment from my royal courts.'

At these words, the Prime Minister and all the ladies-in-waiting fainted away. The Prime Minister was the first to recover his senses, and immediately he left the palace and went to the royal stables, for in the company of horses he often had his most brilliant moments.

Presently, as the Prime Minister sat there, his head in his hands, a maid from the imperial kitchens came along. When she saw him, she stopped and said, 'Why do you look so sad, kind sir? I happen to know...'

The Prime Minister lifted his head, and when he saw who it was, he muttered, 'Whatever you know can be of little use to me. Run away and don't trouble me.'

'But I can help you,' protested the kitchenmaid. 'Everyone in the palace knows what the Emperor has said. The fine ladies-in-waiting may not have heard of the nightingale, but I have! I even know where she has her nest, for each evening I see her as I take my mother the scraps from the kitchen, and often I have heard the nightingale's wonderful song as I pass underneath her tree.'

At these words the Prime Minister sprang to his feet.

'If what you say is true,' he cried, 'and you can lead me to this nightingale, I shall give you a position of great honour in the imperial kitchens. You may even be allowed to serve the Emperor himself with his nightly cup of hot chocolate.'

'Noble sir!' cried the girl. 'How good you are! I promise
you that my words are true. Come with me now and you
will see for yourself that I know where the nightingale lives.'

As they passed through the bronze gates that opened on
to the forest, a number of the nobles from the court joined
them, and as they entered the forest they made a great deal
of noise.

Above all the chatter there was suddenly heard, in the
distance, the sound of lowing, and the Prime Minister
raised his hand for silence.

'Can that be the voice of the nightingale?' he cried. But
the kitchenmaid only laughed.

'Certainly not, good sir,' she answered. 'That noise comes from a cow in one of the royal fields.'

'Can that be the voice of the nightingale?' cried the Prime Minister again, as a frog croaked by the pond.

'Certainly not, sir,' answered the little maid with another merry laugh. 'That noise comes from the frog over there by the pond. I beg you to be patient, for we shall soon come upon the nightingale.'

As the wind dropped and everything grew still, the most beautiful sound in the whole world was suddenly heard— the nightingale's song.

'Where is she?' the Prime Minister cried, straining his eyes. 'Surely that must be the nightingale, but I cannot see her.'

'There she is!' cried the kitchenmaid, and she pointed to a small brown bird who was perched on the branch of the tallest tree in the forest. 'Now I shall speak to her.'

And with that she stretched out her arms to the bird. 'Nightingale, nightingale!' she called softly. 'His Majesty, the Imperial Lord Emperor, wishes to see you. Will you come with me?'

'Of course,' said the bird, 'with the greatest of pleasure. I will come back with you to the palace.'

The witching hour of midnight was just about to strike as the Emperor entered the great royal chamber and sat himself down upon his throne.

Trembling, the Prime Minister bowed low before him, and then pointed to a golden perch by one of the tall windows. 'Lord of the Sun, Master of the Moon and Stars,' he whispered, 'the brown bird of the forest has come to sing to you.'

'I cannot sing here,' said the nightingale. 'I can only sing in the green forest, my true home. Besides, the light is too brilliant. My song comes to me when the forest is dim, and the sun has set below the horizon.'

Immediately on hearing this, the servants rushed to put out the lights and open the windows so that the sweet-scented air of the forest filled the room. In the deep silence that followed, the Prime Minister began to tremble. 'If the nightingale still refuses to sing,' he thought, 'we shall be most dreadfully punished.' He fixed his eyes on the nightingale, and then to his great joy the little bird opened her mouth and began to sing.

So beautiful was the song that it touched the hearts of all

who heard it and, most of all, the heart of the Emperor. Tears of joy began to roll down his cheeks.

When the nightingale had finished her song, the Emperor rose to his feet.

'Never in all my royal life have I been given so much pleasure,' he said to the nightingale. 'I wish to reward you.' And with that he commanded that his golden slippers should be given to the nightingale as a present. But the little brown bird refused the handsome gift, saying that the Emperor's tears were reward enough.

'If you will stay at my court,' the Emperor went on, 'you shall be given all that your heart desires.'

The nightingale agreed, and a special golden cage was made for her. But the Emperor was so afraid that she would, one day, wish to return to her forest home that he allowed her to go out only twice in the day and once in the night, and she was most carefully guarded. Silken threads were fastened to her legs and held by twelve footmen.

One day, the Japanese Emperor, who was a cousin to

the Emperor of China, heard of this wonderful nightingale, and he decided to send a present to his imperial relative.

It was a toy nightingale, made of solid gold and set with diamonds and other precious stones that glinted and sparkled in the sun. This clockwork nightingale, when it was wound up, sang a tune very like that of the real nightingale and, at the end of the song, the golden bird nodded its head. The Japanese Emperor had the fabulous mechanical nightingale placed in a box which bore just one word on the lid, NIGHTINGALE, but inside, he wrote in his spidery writing the words:

> *This is the most perfect nightingale in the world,*
> *and it comes to you from the Emperor of Japan!*

Alas, this gift, far from pleasing the Emperor of China, made him very angry because he saw it as an insult to his own living nightingale. And for a day and a half he talked about making war on Japan.

'You must not think of such a thing,' his Prime Minister told him. 'This toy nightingale is made of solid gold and is a thing of great beauty. Let us keep the gift and say no more about it.'

But the Emperor was not satisfied, and finally he called a Council meeting that lasted six hours. The Council decided that the wisest thing to do was to send a letter to the Emperor of Japan, and this is what it said:

'Our Sovereign Lord thanks you for your magnificent gift, but he would inform you that the living nightingale of China *is worth much more than the toy nightingale of Japan.*'

The last words were written in very small, spidery writing, but were easy to read through a magnifying glass.

'We shall have a competition,' the Emperor of China declared, when the letter was finally sent. 'Then we shall

decide which of the two nightingales sings the most sweetly.'

On the evening of the competition between the two birds all the courtiers and all the ladies-in-waiting were in the throne room, and outside, in the gardens, were many thousands of the Emperor's loyal subjects. When all was ready, the Prime Minister wound up the clockwork nightingale. As soon as it began to sing, the little nightingale of the forest joined in. But, unfortunately, they failed to sing in tune, and the noise was too horrible for words.

'Let them sing in turn,' commanded the Emperor.

The toy nightingale sang first, and so sweet was its song that the crowds clapped their hands and cheered loudly, especially when the golden nightingale bowed its jewelled head and moved its glittering tail up and down.

'Now, let my own living nightingale sing,' the Emperor ordered. But when the Prime Minister turned to look for her, the little nightingale had disappeared. In the excitement of hearing the clockwork bird sing, the footmen had forgotten to stand guard over her, and she had escaped through an open window.

'What does it matter?' everybody began to say. 'The little brown bird was ugly compared to this dazzling, golden creature. And her song was no sweeter. Let us hear the golden nightingale again; we could listen to it all night long.'

So, for the thirty-fourth time, the mechanical nightingale sang its song and, for the thirty-fourth time, everyone in the palace and the gardens vowed that the jewelled bird was by far the best. Even the choir-master, who should have known better, declared that the toy nightingale's song was the sweetest he had ever heard. Only the kitchenmaid, who now occupied a position of some importance in the royal kitchens, thought differently, but no one would listen to her.

The Emperor declared that henceforth the toy nightingale would lie on a silken cushion near his bed and that it be known as: *The Royal Singer of the Imperial Rest Hour.*

By the end of the year the little brown bird was quite forgotten. Rich and poor alike sent presents to the golden bird, and poets wrote verses about it—until, one night, something dreadful happened

As usual, the Emperor lay on his great bed with his eyes closed, waiting to hear the sweet song of his clockwork nightingale. Instead, all that came from the bird was a whirring and a squeaking, a rasping and a grinding, which set the Emperor's teeth on edge. He sat up in bed, staring at his precious bird in horror. Then, suddenly, with a final squeak, the bird's clockwork inside gave up completely, and there was silence.

The Emperor summoned the Court Watchmaker to come to him immediately.

'I will do my best, Your Majesty,' said the Watchmaker, 'to put the clockwork in order again, but I would ask that you do not permit this bird to sing more than once a year, for I can see its metal plates are almost worn out.'

When the news was noised abroad that the Emperor's golden bird could no longer sing each day, all the people wept and wrung their hands. The Prime Minister took it upon himself to visit the towns and villages so that he might comfort the people with long speeches in which he told them that nothing was wrong. The little bird could still sing.

This state of affairs went on for five years until, one day, the Emperor of China fell seriously ill. He was so ill that the people began to fear that he might die, and many of them came to the palace and stayed in the gardens all night long so that they might hear, from hour to hour, how their Emperor progressed. But the poor Emperor showed no sign of getting better, and sometimes he lay so still that those who were caring for him thought that he was already dead.

The Emperor was not dead, but he knew that death was very close, and in his dreams he lived again his past life; he remembered all the wicked things he had done, as well as all his good deeds. When the bad dreams came, the poor Emperor grew hot and fearful, and then he would suddenly open his eyes and call for music.

'The song of my golden nightingale,' he whispered to

those around him, 'this is what I desire above all else.' But the golden nightingale had already sung its song for the year, and none dared wind it up again.

When he was alone again, the poor Emperor fell into black despair, afraid to die and afraid to live. Then, suddenly, from the open window there came the sweet song that he longed so much to hear. It was the song of the nightingale of the forest who had come to comfort him.

As the brown bird finished her song, the Spirit of Death, who was waiting to claim the Emperor for his own, asked for one more song.

The little bird sang most cunningly of the soft-petalled roses in the gardens and the sweet-perfumed lilac and the rich green of the forest. And suddenly the Spirit of Death longed to see all these things so much that he flew out through the open window, forgetting all about the Emperor whom he had meant to take with him.

Immediately, the Emperor was almost well again, and he rose from his bed and, going to the window, kissed the head of the gentle nightingale. 'You have saved my life,' he said. 'How can I reward you?'

'The tears you shed,' answered the nightingale, 'when I first sang for you were the truest reward I have ever had. I shall stay with you now and sing you to sleep each night until you are quite recovered.'

Then the Emperor went back to bed, and the nightingale began her sweet song all over again. But before sleep came to him, the Emperor spoke once again. 'If you will stay with me always,' he said, 'in the morning my servants will take the toy nightingale to pieces and throw it away.'

'That I cannot do,' said the nightingale, 'for I could not be happy in this great palace. If you keep me from my forest home I shall only die of sadness; but whenever you want me, I shall be there to sing for you. I will sing you songs that will help you to rule over your people so that they will always be happy and contented. My songs will make you the wisest Emperor in the whole world. But promise me one thing.'

'I will promise you anything you ask,' said the Emperor. 'Tell me what you would have me do.'

'Only this,' said the bird. 'When you learn from my songs how to rule over your vast empire with justice and love, do not ever tell anyone that it is a nightingale's song that teaches you such things.'

The Emperor's eyes closed, and the nightingale sang to him until he was fast asleep.

Outside the royal bedchamber, the Prime Minister, the courtiers, and all the ladies-in-waiting had made up their minds that the Emperor was dead. But the next morning, to their astonishment, they found their Emperor was standing straight and proud by his window, his crown sitting firmly on his head. While they stood there staring, speechless with surprise, the Emperor turned to them and, a twinkle in his eyes, said, 'Good morning!'

THUMBELINA

Once upon a time there was a pretty young wife who wanted more than anything else in the world to have a little child. At last she made up her mind to go to an old witch, who was very clever and knew many spells. The woman did not waste any words when she found the witch.

'Will you help me to find a child?' she asked.

'Yes, I will help you,' said the old witch-woman. 'Take this barleycorn and plant it in a flower-pot. Then wait and see what happens.'

The woman was so grateful that she gave the witch a silver sixpence for the advice, and as soon as she arrived home she planted the barleycorn in a flower-pot.

Every day she went to the flower-pot to see if anything had happened. And at last, one day, she saw that a happy bud had formed. The bud was large and beautiful, and the woman thought it looked like a tulip. When she bent down to kiss the red and yellow petals, the bud burst open.

'So it *is* a tulip!' the woman exclaimed. 'A real flower!' And as she gazed down into the very heart of the flower, she saw that it enclosed a tiny child—a girl child. She was so small that she was exactly the size of the woman's thumb. Overcome with joy, the woman lifted the dainty little girl from her flower cradle.

'I will call you Thumbelina!' she cried. She set about looking for a cradle that would be small enough for her new little girl. When she found a walnut shell in the kitchen, she knew it would be just right.

'This will be your cradle,' she told Thumbelina as she polished the shell. 'And these violet leaves will serve as a mattress, and this sweet-smelling rose petal will be your blanket.'

One night, as Thumbelina lay asleep in her nut-shell cradle, a huge, ugly toad found its way into the cottage through a broken pane in the window. When he saw lovely little Thumbelina fast asleep, the toad exclaimed, 'Ah-ha! She will make a beautiful bride for my son!' And with that he picked up the shell and carried it out into the garden.

At the bottom of the garden there was a stream, and on the far bank there was swamp-bog. This was where the toads lived.

'Look what I have brought you, son!' the toad cried, but all the toad's son could say in reply was: 'Croak, croak, croak.'

Overcome by her dainty appearance, Father Toad and Son Toad decided to leave Thumbelina on a waterlily leaf while they made plans for the wedding.

Poor Thumbelina! She cried as if her heart would break, especially when the toads took away her nut-shell bed. She cried so much that the silver fishes in the stream came to comfort her.

'You are too dainty,' they told her, 'for that stupid toad. We are going to set you free.'

Then they began to nibble at the stem that anchored the waterlily leaf to the river bed. Soon, the leaf broke away and was carried off by the stream.

Thumbelina began to smile as she drifted along. The sun made everything look so beautiful that she was no longer afraid. She laughed aloud when a gaily coloured butterfly landed on the leaf beside her, and quickly she took off her belt and tied the butterfly to her waterlily boat so that it might sail more swiftly.

But alas for Thumbelina! Her adventures were not nearly at an end, for suddenly out of the sky swooped a huge cockchafer.

Greenish black in colour, it looked like a fat, ugly beetle as, with a whirr of its glossy wings, it settled on the leaf.

The cockchafer thought he had never seen anything as beautiful as Thumbelina, and he picked her up and flew off with her into a tree, while the lily leaf with its butterfly sail floated away.

Thumbelina was much too frightened to take in all the nice things the cockchafer began saying to her.

'I think you are very pretty. Quite the prettiest thing I have ever seen. You'll make me a charming wife, to be sure . . . all the relations must see you . . . how they will admire you and envy me . . . I'll just go and fetch them . . .'

And with that the cockchafer flew into the next branch, and was presently back with some of his aunts and uncles. They stared at Thumbelina. 'What a very odd little creature,' said one of the aunts at last. 'Only two legs, and no feelers!'

'Just look at her waist,' said another. 'And how thin and scraggy she is . . .'

The cockchafer was so put out at the rude remarks that he began to have grave doubts about Thumbelina. Finally he said, 'Perhaps I have made a mistake—a very foolish mistake.' And he picked her up. 'I'm sorry,' said he as he dropped her on a large daisy. 'You are not for me after all.' Then away he flew.

Thumbelina stayed in the forest all through the long, hot summer. Out of the blades of grass she fashioned a soft bed that she hung under a leaf; this would shelter her from both the rain and the hot sun. During the warm, sunny days of summer, Thumbelina was happy. Then the days grew shorter and the wind blew colder. She saw

the birds leave their homes and fly away to warm, sunny lands, and she watched the leaves turn to yellow and brown.

The snow came and the flakes seemed far bigger than herself. Poor Thumbelina! How she shivered in the icy wind. Her dress was in rags, and it was impossible now to find shelter under the leaves, for they had all withered away.

'I shall die out here in the forest,' Thumbelina whispered to herself, 'unless I find strength enough to leave this place.'

Close to the forest there was an empty field. It is true that the earth was frozen hard, but the short, brown stubble gave more shelter from the snow, and it was there that Thumbelina at last found her way. The very next day, she discovered a tiny hole hidden away under some straw. The hole was really the front door to a snug little house belonging to Miss Fieldmouse.

'You poor child,' cried Miss Fieldmouse when she came out to take a private look at the white world stretched in front of her. 'Come inside; you will find my kitchen wonderfully warm, I assure you.'

Gratefully, Thumbelina followed Miss Fieldmouse into the warm kitchen, which was stacked with grain.

'I have not eaten for such a long time,' she whispered. 'Could you spare me a little barleycorn, please?'

'Bless you!' cried Miss Fieldmouse, who had a very kind heart. 'There's more than enough for both of us. Of course I can! But why not stay here with me for the winter? You need not pay me anything for your board and lodging. All I ask is that you keep my kitchen free from dust, and in the long evenings tell me stories of the world outside.'

Thumbelina gladly accepted the shelter, and for a few days she was very happy, for Miss Fieldmouse was not hard to please.

'We are going to have a visitor,' she said to Thumbelina one morning. 'Actually, he is my neighbour. He comes every week to see me, and he is very rich. As soon as he heard about your fine stories, he wanted to meet you. I do declare, it's most likely he will want to marry you, and how lucky that would be for you. He doesn't see very well, but he is very kind and *very, very* rich.'

Miss Fieldmouse's wealthy neighbour was Mr. Mole. When Thumbelina saw him come into the kitchen, she knew that she could never marry him, though he was dressed in shimmering black velvet.

Very soon Mr. Mole began to boast of all his rich possessions and his great learning. But when Thumbelina talked of the sun and the beautiful flowers in the forest, he had nothing good to say about them. The truth was, he had never seen such things, as he spent all his days underground.

However, to please Miss Fieldmouse, Thumbelina sang some of her prettiest songs, and Mole was delighted. He even began to talk about marriage, although he did not go so far as to mention a date, for he was a cautious fellow. After all, he had only just met Thumbelina.

'I tell you what,' he said at last. 'You must come and visit me. Miss Fieldmouse will take you along the tunnel that I have dug between our two houses. But watch out for a dead bird that has been lying there ever since the first days of winter.'

The very next day, Miss Fieldmouse and Thumbelina set out along the passageway to visit Mr. Mole. Although Mr. Mole was extremely shortsighted he had good ears, and so he was able to set out to meet his visitors long before they reached the end of the dark tunnel. He came upon them just where the bird was lying, and Thumbelina saw that it was a swallow. Mr. Mole edged it to one side with his fat, sleek body.

'How thankful I am not to be a bird! We won't be bothered with his twitterings next year, that's certain. It is a great relief to know that my future children will be able to look after themselves in the winter.' And he gave Thumbelina a friendly pat on the shoulder.

Thumbelina could see the bird more clearly now, for, quite by accident, Mr. Mole had knocked a hole in the

roof of the tunnel when he moved the bird. Through this the sun was shining.

'You are quite right about being born a bird,' Miss Fieldmouse told her friend and neighbour. 'There is simply no joy in it. Here we both are, snug and warm, while up above the birds are cold and hungry.'

Thumbelina said nothing to this, but when Mr. Mole and Miss Fieldmouse turned their backs on her, she bent down over the swallow and gently kissed its head. 'Poor little bird!' she whispered. 'Perhaps it was you who filled my summer days in the forest with happiness as I listened to your song.'

Mr. Mole insisted on filling up the hole before going any farther. Then, when he was satisfied with his efforts, they continued on their way.

'How dark and stuffy it is here,' Thumbelina thought to herself when at last they were in the Mole's sitting-room, but she was too polite to say so; and at the end of the short visit, it was quite clear that Mr. Mole was very pleased with himself and his visitors.

That night, Thumbelina could not sleep. She tossed and turned in her tiny bed. Then, unable to bear it any longer, she got up and began weaving a beautiful rug out of the dry hay that was lying all over the floor. When it was finished, she pulled it along the passage until she came to the swallow. 'This will keep you warm,' she whispered, 'even if you never fly again.'

And as she went close to the bird she knew, suddenly, that the swallow was not dead after all, for she could hear the feeble beating of its heart. She remembered how Miss Fieldmouse had told her that if a swallow is left behind in the winter it will nearly always die.

'I will not let you die,' Thumbelina whispered. 'I will take care of you.' And she wrapped the rug of hay more closely round the stiff body. Quickly she sped back to the kitchen to fetch her mint-leaf blanket which would serve as a pillow for the swallow's head.

'I cannot stay with you now,' she told the bird, 'but I shall come back tomorrow night and every night through the long winter until I make you strong again . . .'

Thumbelina said nothing of her adventures to Miss Fieldmouse because she was afraid that she would stop her going out the next night. Instead, she worked harder than usual in the kitchen and dining-room, polishing and sweeping, and in the evening she told the lady mouse her best story so that she would go happily to bed.

This time, before Thumbelina sped down the passage, she put some water on a flower petal in case the swallow was able to drink.

To her great joy, she found the bird's eyes were open, and at the sight of her, the swallow said in a weak voice, 'Thank you for saving my life. I shall never forget you.

Soon, when I am stronger, I shall be able to fly away and find the sun once more.'

'Alas!' said Thumbelina after she had given her new friend a drink from the petal. 'It is snowing outside and bitterly cold. If you try to fly away now you will only die in the snow. You must stay here and grow strong. No one will harm you, for I shall keep our secret.'

Thumbelina's heart was so moved by the swallow's trust that not once, during the long winter, did she miss paying him a daily visit and slowly, but surely, he grew strong again. When Spring came, and the sun began to warm the ground, the swallow was ready to fly away.

'Come with me,' the swallow said, after Thumbelina had made a hole in the tunnel roof. 'If you sit on my wings, I will take you to the green forest and the sun will kiss your pretty hair.'

But Thumbelina shook her head. 'Miss Fieldmouse has been very good to me,' she said. 'I could not leave without saying goodbye to her; that would be too unkind.'

'Then you must say goodbye to me, Thumbelina,' said the swallow, and with that, he lifted his wings and flew up through the hole and into the blue sky.

Thumbelina watched him go, her eyes full of tears; she knew now that the whole earth was warm and rich. Outside the yellow corn had grown so tall that it seemed as if the mouse's home was buried under a golden forest.

Every day now, Mr. Mole came to see her until, at last, to the delight of Miss Fieldmouse, he asked her to be his wife.

'It is the best thing you can do,' Miss Fieldmouse said after he had gone. 'Moreover, it is my dearest wish.'

So Thumbelina agreed, and no sooner had she said 'yes' than Miss Fieldmouse made her sit down and begin sewing her trousseau.

'You must have plenty of linen, and several pretty dresses,' she told Thumbelina, 'or Mr. Mole will be disappointed in us.'

Mr. Mole said the wedding was to take place at the very end of the summer when it was cool and pleasant. So every morning and evening, Thumbelina went to the entrance of the little house to catch a glimpse of the blue sky and the bright sun which she knew she would not see again after her wedding day. When autumn came, Thumbelina had finished her trousseau, and the mouse told her, 'The wedding will be in four weeks' time. Everything is arranged.'

When Thumbelina heard this she could not keep back her tears.

'I cannot marry Mr. Mole,' she cried. 'I don't want to be buried under the earth for the rest of my life.'

'You foolish child,' snapped Miss Fieldmouse angrily. 'I shall bite you with my pointed teeth if you say such things. Anyone else would be proud to marry such a handsome husband who boasts a smart coat of rich, black velvet. As for the future, you will never be hungry again.'

On the day of the wedding, Miss Fieldmouse made poor Thumbelina put on her prettiest dress, and when Mr. Mole arrived, he told her that very soon now they would be going underground.

'You may take your last look at the sky, the trees and flowers, and the warm sun,' he told her kindly, 'as you seem to be fond of them.'

In deep distress, Thumbelina ran outside. As she stood there among the stubble—for by this time the corn had been harvested—she lifted her arms to the sun and then she kissed the tiny red flowers that clustered round her feet. 'Tell the swallow, if he ever comes back, how much I love him,' she whispered. 'Tell him that I shall never forget him.'

And at that very moment she heard a whirr of wings. It was her old friend, the swallow, setting out on his long journey to the land of the hot sun. As soon as the swallow saw Thumbelina, he swooped down with a cry of delight and sat at her feet.

'Today,' she told him, 'is my wedding day. I am to
marry that old and horrid mole whose home is under the
earth. I shall never see you again, or the sun, or the flowers,
or the green fields.' And as she talked tears streamed down
her face.

'Winter is coming,' said the swallow when he had listened
to her story. 'I cannot stay here, but why not come with
me? I will take you far away from Mr. Mole and his
miserable house. Climb on my back and fasten yourself
to my wings with your belt. I will take you over mountains
and far away to a land where it is always summer and the
flowers are always in bloom. You saved my life when I
was dying. Now I will save yours.'

'Yes, yes, I will come with you,' answered Thumbelina.
And with that she climbed on to the swallow's back, and

tied her belt to his strongest feathers. Away they went, over the forest, over the sea, and over the high, snow-capped mountains. And when she was cold, all Thumbelina had to do was to snuggle down between the warm feathers.

At last they came to a land where purple grapes grew on the hillside, where there were lemon and orange groves, and where the sweet scent from a thousand different flowers filled the air.

The swallow came to rest beside a deep blue lake. On the shores of this shimmering lake stood a castle of shining white marble.

'There among the eaves is my home,' the swallow told Thumbelina. 'But I could scarcely expect you to be happy in such a place. No, my nest is not for you. Instead, you must choose the flower you like best and I will place you among its petals.'

Thumbelina clapped her hands with joy as she gazed about. There were so many wonderful flowers to choose from. But, at last, she pointed to a large white flower whose sweet perfume filled the air.

'Dear swallow,' she cried, 'put me on that white flower; I know I shall be happy there.'

But when the swallow carried her to the flower, Thumbelina saw there was someone else there before her, someone who wore a golden crown on his head; he was no taller than herself and he had two tiny golden wings.

'I am sorry,' whispered Thumbelina. 'I really didn't know this was your flower.'

'You have chosen my palace,' the tiny man said. 'I am King of all the Flowers here.'

Thumbelina smiled. Never in all her life had she seen anyone she liked more. And the King smiled back. Never in all his life had he seen anyone as fair as Thumbelina. 'Tell me your name,' he said.

'Thumbelina.'

'I would like to give you a new name: I will call you *Maia,* a name that means "Queen of the Flowers". Will you accept this new name, Thumbelina, and be my Queen?'

What did Thumbelina say? Her eyes shone as she stretched out her hands to the King of the Flowers, and all her dark memories of toads, moles, and cockchafers were banished forever in her newfound happiness.

So Thumbelina and the King of the Flowers were married, and the swallow and all the King's subjects came to the wedding, which was so pretty that no words can describe it.

The swallow sang his most beautiful song as a wedding gift, and the King gave his new bride a pair of silver wings so that she could visit his subjects whenever she wished.

So Thumbelina found happiness at last. As for the swallow on his return journey he told Thumbelina's story to all who would listen to his beautiful song.

JACK THE GIANT KILLER

Once upon a time, when good King Arthur reigned over England, there lived a farmer. His farm in Cornwall was large, and the farmer was blessed in all he did. His cattle were fat and well-fed and his crops flourished.

Over and above this, however, the farmer was particularly blessed in his only son, Jack, for there was no more willing or quick-witted boy in the whole county.

One day Jack and his father were called to a meeting in the Town Hall. There Jack heard, though not for the first time, about the dreadful acts of the giant of Mount Cornwall.

'I do declare,' said the Town Clerk, 'that unless something is done about this giant the whole of Cornwall will be laid to waste. Furthermore, whoever kills this man-eating, cattle-devouring giant may take, for his own, all the great treasure he keeps in his cave.'

'With your consent, father,' whispered Jack, 'I think I would like to try my luck with this Cornish giant, for it won't be long before he seizes some of our cattle and sheep.'

'You are welcome to try,' said the farmer. 'But take care of yourself.'

'Leave it to me,' said Jack. 'So far I've been able to think my way round most problems. This giant should be easily overcome.'

The next day Jack set out for the Cornish Mount. He took with him a pick and shovel, and he slung a shepherd's horn round his neck. It was winter and soon dark, but Jack reached the Mount by nightfall.

Presently Jack heard a noise like the whistling of a hurricane from a cave halfway up the mountain, which told him that the giant was now fast asleep and snoring.

Jack set to work; with his pickaxe and shovel he dug a deep pit outside the giant's cave, and covered it over with straw and sticks. Then, as soon as it was light, he blew a shrill note on his horn.

Out rushed the giant, rubbing the sleep from his wicked eyes. As soon as he caught sight of Jack, he roared with the strength of ten lions, 'You impudent little monster! I'll crush you like a beetle and fry you for breakfast . . .'

Jack stood firm. The giant lumbered forward to grasp him and, of course, crashed down into the deep pit from which there was no escape.

Jack laughed as he looked down on the trapped giant. 'A little man can easily outwit a giant,' said he, 'if he has the brains . . .' And taking his pickaxe he brought it down on the evil giant's head and killed him.

Jack went into the cave, found the treasure, and took it home with him.

When news of the terrible giant's death was spread abroad, all the people in the towns and villages, who had previously gone in fear of their lives from the giant, came together and voted that Jack should be known as 'Jack the Giant Killer'. Then they gave Jack a silver sword and a belt with his title embroidered on it in letters of gold.

Jack settled down on the farm again, but some months later his father sent him on a journey to Wales to purchase some sheep. On the way Jack had to pass through a wood;

being tired, he lay down under a tree and fell asleep.

It so happened that the wood belonged to another giant, who lived in an enchanted castle in the valley beyond. The giant, out for a stroll, came upon Jack.

Jack's belt told the giant all he wanted to know, and he scooped up the boy in his hand and strode off with him.

Jack opened his eyes as they reached the enchanted castle. When he found himself the giant's prisoner, he shook with fright.

'You may well shake!' roared the giant. 'And don't ask me for mercy, my little Jack the Giant Killer. I'll give you a choice, though. You can be boiled or fried . . .'

Jack made no answer, and the giant took him up to a turret room in the castle, tossed him into a corner, and went off, locking the door behind him.

Left to himself, Jack watched from the window. Soon

he saw the giant leave the castle. As there was nothing else he could do, Jack kept guard at the window until he saw the giant, with a companion, come striding down the hill towards the castle gates.

'Well,' said Jack to himself, 'it is now or never!' And he took hold of two lengths of strong cord that were lying in a corner of the room. He made two nooses, and sat back to wait for the approaching giants.

As they came beneath his window, Jack dropped the nooses round their necks. The giants were taken by surprise, and in their struggles they bumped each other's heads with such force that they both dropped senseless to the ground.

Seizing his chance, brave little Jack slid down one of the ropes and, with his silver sword, cut off their heads. Then he ran into the castle and set free all the prisoners.

Refusing to take the gifts the freed men offered him, Jack continued on his way. By nightfall he was a long way from the nearest market town, and he made up his mind to ask for shelter at the first dwelling house he came to. The valley through which he was passing was a lonely one, and Jack was pleased to find a house with lighted windows.

No sooner had he knocked on the door than it was flung open by a monstrous two-headed giant, the very sight of whom made Jack quake at the knees.

'Come in, come in,' said the two-headed giant with a beguiling smile on each face as he looked down on Jack. 'Strangers are always welcome.' The giant said this, knowing quite well what he meant to do with Jack when he got him inside the house.

Jack went in and the giant showed him the room where he was to sleep. 'I hope you find the bed comfortable,' he said with a leer, 'and not too big.'

He went downstairs, and Jack could hear him pounding about in the kitchen—and singing. It was a strange song; Jack caught only a few words at a time, but they were enough to warn him that the giant meant to dash out his brains with a club.

'So *you* think,' said Jack to himself. 'And if the song is not true then no harm will be done. But I'll sleep the night under the bed instead of in it.'

Into the bed he put a log of wood that, in the dark, could be mistaken for a sleeping figure. Satisfied that he had taken every reasonable step to protect himself, Jack crept under the bed. He was just about to close his eyes when in came the giant.

The giant raised his club and crash! down it came on the log of wood. With an immensely evil chuckle, the giant stumped away, certain that he had made an end of Jack.

When Jack came downstairs the next morning, the giant was so shaken at the sight of him that he almost choked himself with his tea.

He recovered, however, and managed to ask if Jack had passed a comfortable night.

'Pretty well,' Jack answered lightly, 'though I had a feeling there was a rat in the room, for it gave me one or two taps with its tail.'

The giant turned pale at this but he said nothing. He put before Jack an enormous bowl of cold porridge.

'Let us see how you get through that,' said the giant.

While the giant was busy with his own porridge, Jack tipped his bowl into a big leather purse that he wore under his jacket. When the giant looked up, all Jack's porridge was gone.

'That was a tasty morsel,' said Jack. 'Now I shall show you a trick.' He took a knife from the table and through his coat slit open the concealed leather purse. Out poured all the cold porridge.

'Remarkable,' said the giant. 'If you can do it, so can I.' And he picked up a second knife with the intention of copying Jack and, of course, killed himself.

Jack continued on his way, purchased the sheep, and returned to the farm. But now he had a taste for adventure and he set out to rid Cornwall of every giant.

One of Jack's greatest admirers was a wizard who had once been the captive of the two-headed giant; he gave Jack three presents that would help him to conquer other giants. These were a handsome horse that could travel as swiftly as the wind, a sword of wonderful keenness, and a cloak that would make its wearer invisible.

Armed with such magnificent gifts, Jack felt he could not fail. He jumped on his horse and rode away in search

of giants. After some four days' travelling he entered a
dark spreading forest, where he came upon a colossal giant.
This giant had, only minutes before, taken captive a pair
of lovers, and was dragging them, by the hair, to his den.

Jack leapt from his horse, threw his invisible cloak
about him, and brought out his magic sword.

The giant was so enormously tall that Jack could not
reach his heart, so he cut off his legs; when the giant fell
roaring to the ground, Jack cut off his head.

The giant whom Jack had just killed had a brother
as fierce and evil as himself. After a short ride, Jack came
upon him at the edge of the forest.

Once again Jack flung himself from his horse, put on
his invisible cloak, and advanced towards the giant.
But he managed only to prick the huge giant with his

sword. And the giant, thinking that he had been stung by a wasp, took hold of his cudgel and began flaying the air in all directions. Jack skipped nimbly from side to side, pricking the giant at every opportunity, until presently the giant over-balanced, thus enabling Jack to kill him with his magic sword.

Well pleased with his day's work, Jack left the forest and continued on his way until he came to a tall, grey house at the foot of a high mountain.

He knocked at the door, and it was answered by a bent old man. 'I am Jack the Giant Killer,' said Jack. 'I have pledged myself to rid this county of giants.'

'Then you are very welcome here,' said the old man, 'for at the top of this mountain there lives a giant whose sole companion is a magician of great wickedness. Their latest dreadful deed was to seize the lovely daughter of my lord and master, the Duke, and change her into a deer.'

Jack did not wait to hear much more. After tethering his horse to the gatepost he set off up the mountainside. And when the giant's castle came in sight, he put on his invisible cloak.

Two snarling leopards guarded the entrance to the giant's castle, but Jack passed between them unnoticed. Inside the castle itself he found the giant and the magician having supper together; he could hear the pitiful shrieks of their prisoners in the dungeons.

Wasting no time, Jack leapt on to the table, drew his magic sword, and being totally invisible, had no difficulty in despatching both the giant and his evil companion. He soon freed the prisoners, many of whom had been changed into birds and beasts by the magician. Among them he found the Duke's lovely daughter who, like the other transformed prisoners, had returned to human form, for the death of the magician had broken all the magic spells.

This giant, Galligantus, turned out to have been the last of the giants of Cornwall. On learning this fact, Jack returned home to the farm. But the fame of his deeds reached the ears of King Arthur himself, and, that same year, the King summoned Jack to his court.

'What would you have,' asked the King, 'as a reward for your great deeds?'

Jack answered, 'I would like to meet again the Duke's lovely daughter.'

This was easily arranged. The young man and woman, who already liked each other, now fell completely in love, and were shortly afterwards married. King Arthur himself attended their wedding. As a further reward, Jack was given a fine house close to the farm, and there he lived with his gentle bride for many happy years.

THE FAIRIES

Once upon a time there lived an ill-tempered widow woman with two daughters. The younger daughter, Rose by name, was the prettiest, kindest girl you could hope to meet and as different from her sister, Griselle, as day is from night.

Truth to tell, Griselle was the image of her disagreeable mother, and the two got along very well together. They treated Rose worse than a servant, making her wash the floors, peel the potatoes, and walk half a mile to the well each day for water.

Rose accepted her lot without tears or sulks, and on summer days she would sing to herself as she trudged down to the well carrying the heavy pitcher.

One morning, when she reached the well, an old country woman with a bundle of sticks under her arm and a shawl round her thin shoulders asked Rose to give her a drink.

'Of course I will,' said Rose. 'Just let me draw some fresh water and you may have as long a drink as you want.'

The old woman was really a fairy. She had heard about Rose's sweet nature, but she wanted to test the girl for herself. After she had drunk the water, and Rose had asked if there was anything further she could do, the fairy said, 'You are a dear child, polite and gentle. I am going to give you a present. Flowers and jewels will fall from your lips whenever you speak.' Then she vanished.

Rose picked up her pitcher and hurried back to the cottage, but the meeting with the fairy had made her later than usual and her mother was waiting for her.

'Lazy good-for-nothing!' she screamed. 'Where have you been all this time? I'll teach you!'

'I am sorry,' said Rose. And then stopped to stare in amazement at the three flowers and the three rubies that had dropped from her lips.

Her mother stared too. 'What do I see?' she gasped. 'Flowers and rubies coming out of your mouth. You're bewitched, child!'

Then Rose began to tell of her meeting with the old woman at the well. As she spoke, diamonds and rubies showered down, covering the step and tumbling on to the grass. Her mother listened attentively and for the first time for years she did not scold or slap Rose. Instead she shouted for Griselle.

'What is it, mother?' asked Griselle in a sulky voice. 'I was just doing my hair.'

'I want you to hurry down to the well,' said her mother. 'Take this pitcher and fill it with water. When an old woman with a shawl round her shoulders asks you for a drink, be sure to oblige.'

'I don't see why I should,' said Griselle sulkily.

'You will, when I tell you,' said her mother, scarcely able to speak in her excitement. 'You will be given a present. Rubies and diamonds will drop from your mouth whenever you open it. Now hurry, hurry.'

But Griselle did not wish to be seen carrying a common pitcher. 'I'll take the silver flagon,' she said. 'Don't rush me, mother. I must do my hair properly and look my best.'

When at last Griselle was ready, she picked up the silver flagon and set off for the well. The sun was shining, the birds were singing, and the sky above Griselle's head was a soft blue, but Griselle paid no attention to the beauty around her. On her face was an ugly scowl. She hated walking, and besides her slippers were already pinching her feet because they were a size too small.

When she reached the well, she flung the silver flagon on to the grass and looked about her. There was no sign of an old woman with a shawl, and Griselle's scowl deepened. But presently, out of the forest, came a grand looking lady, richly robed.

This was the same fairy who had spoken to Rose but, of course, Griselle did not know this.

'Will you give me a drink?' the lady asked. 'I am very thirsty.'

'Why should I?' said Griselle rudely. 'You look rich enough to employ servants. Send for one of them. But don't expect me to act like one.' And she turned her back on the fairy.

'You are not very polite,' said the lady. 'And well deserve the gift which I now bestow on you. With every word you speak, toads and snakes will drop from your lips.' Then she vanished.

Griselle shrugged her shoulders, picked up the silver flagon, and set out for home. 'Just wait until I see that

sister of mine!' she thought to herself. 'And my mother—the pair of them have sent me on a wild goose chase, that's to be sure.'

As soon as she was in sight of the cottage her mother ran forward to greet her. 'Well?' she asked eagerly. 'Did you see her?'

'I did not,' Griselle began. Then she stopped, for three toads and three snakes had dropped out of her mouth.

Her mother gasped in horror, and Griselle fled screaming into the cottage, scattering toads and vipers as she went.

When the widow had recovered from the shock, she began to look for Rose so that she could punish her. But Rose was nowhere to be found. Knowing that she would be blamed for everything, she had fled into the forest.

As darkness began to fall, Rose found herself in a strange part of the forest, and she began to weep. Where could she go? What would happen to her?

The sound of her soft weeping caught the ear of the king's son who had been hunting in that part of the forest all day. When he came upon Rose and saw how pretty she was he almost fell in love with her there and then.

'I cannot leave you here alone in the forest,' said the Prince. 'Tell me who you are and where you live.'

But as soon as Rose began to speak, precious stones fell from her lips, and the Prince begged her to tell him the whole story.

As he listened, the Prince fell so deeply in love with Rose that he asked her to come back to the palace with him and be his wife.

So Rose and the Prince were married in great splendour, and they lived happily ever afterwards. As for Griselle, when news came of her sister's good fortune, she became so spiteful that even her mother could not put up with her—or with the toads and snakes that were all over the cottage. She drove her into the forest, and there Griselle lived, an outcast with only the creepy crawly things of the forest for company.

THE SNOW QUEEN

There was once upon a time a most wicked gnome whose greatest delight was to make people unhappy. He ruled over a company of imps as wicked as himself. One day to amuse them he made a mirror.

There was something very strange about this mirror. No beautiful or good object could be truly reflected in it. The loveliest meadow would look like a field of turnips, and the most beautiful rose would look like a poisonous weed. But when anything ugly or wicked was reflected in the mirror, it came out very clearly and grew to an extraordinary size.

The wicked gnome greatly enjoyed himself with this mirror, especially when good and honest people looked into it and saw themselves as monsters.

One day his servants, the imps, took the mirror into the heavens, thinking that they would poke fun at the angels with it. But at the sight of so much glory, the imps began to shake and tremble; the mirror slipped from their hands and broke into a thousand pieces.

This was the very worst thing that could have happened, for the splinters of glass fell down on the earth. They entered people's hearts and turned them to ice. This pleased the wicked gnome enormously and he laughed until his sides ached.

In one big city, which was so crowded scarcely any family had a garden, there lived two little children.

The parents of each were poor; each family lived in an attic joined to the other by a balcony. These two little children were not brother and sister, but they loved each other just as much as if they had been.

In front of each of their windows they made a pretty flower garden by filling a big box with earth, and there they grew tiny rose trees and mustard and cress.

The little boy's name was Kay and the little girl was called Gerda.

When the winter came and Kay and Gerda could not see each other through their windows because of the frost, they made peepholes by putting a warm penny on the frozen window panes.

One winter's night when Kay was getting ready to go to bed, he saw that the snowflakes outside were falling on

the flower-box. Suddenly one of the snowflakes began to grow and grow until it took the shape of a young girl.

Kay, as he watched, saw that she was taller than Gerda and that her beautiful white dress was covered in starry snowflakes. Kay knew that she was alive, this beautiful girl, even though she was made of snow and ice. When he called out to her she disappeared.

All through the long winter months Kay and Gerda often talked about this strange ice maiden, but they forgot her when the spring came and the roses began to bloom and the swallows began to fly again. One day Kay and Gerda were playing together beside their garden when suddenly Kay cried, 'Something has got in my eye. Something has pierced my heart! What can it be, Gerda?' Gerda looked at her friend with anxious eyes.

'I don't know,' she said, 'but perhaps it will go.'

She did not know and Kay did not know that it was a splinter from the terrible magic mirror. The glass had found its way into Kay's eyes and into his heart, making it hard and icy cold.

The world was different for Kay now. He looked crossly at his little friend and told her that she was stupid and ugly. He looked at the beautiful roses and cried, 'These roses are not lovely at all. They are all worm-eaten and horrid.' And he kicked the box and pulled out the roses by the roots and threw them on the ground.

'Kay!' Gerda exclaimed, 'what is wrong? What are you doing? I thought you cared for the roses.'

But Kay only gave her a push and then ran away back to his own attic. From that day onwards everything that was good and beautiful seemed nasty and spiteful to Kay because the splinters of glass in his eye and in his heart were doing their work. He teased his grandmother cruelly. He laughed and jeered at Gerda and refused to play with her. And he mocked all the old people. When winter came again Gerda was broken-hearted, for she knew now that nothing would change Kay back into the boy she had once known and loved so much.

'I am going to play in the market with the other boys,' Kay told her one day. 'You can't come. I am taking my sledge.'

Once in the great market square, Kay and his friends began making nuisances of themselves by tying their sledges to the carts so that they had free rides. When Kay noticed a great horse-drawn sleigh driven by someone whose face he could not see because of the thick white fur she wore, he fixed his own little sledge to the big sleigh.

'This is fun!' he shouted as the driver of the big sleigh whipped the white horse to a gallop.

Away they sped, round and round the square and then along the main street and through the gates of the city. The snow began to fall in big white flakes and Kay wanted to break free. But the driver would not listen to his cries, and the white horse galloped faster and faster until the city was left behind and they were flying over ditches and hedges at a tremendous speed. The snowflakes were so big that they looked like huge white hens.

'Stop! Stop!' Kay screamed in terror, and at last the big sleigh did stop. Kay saw that its driver was a tall and beautiful lady. She was made of snow and she sparkled and shimmered as she bent over him.

It was the Snow Queen herself!

'You must ride in my sleigh, under my furs,' she said in a gentle voice, and she kissed Kay on the forehead.

Kay thought he was going to die when he felt the sharp, cold kiss that was colder than ice, but in a moment his strength came back and he began to smile. The Snow Queen gave him a second kiss, and after that he forgot all about his friend, Gerda, and his parents and his grandmother. He wanted only to be with the beautiful Snow Queen.

'You will come with me,' she said, and at her words a blanket of snow fell thickly all about them.

'I must take my sledge,' he cried, and the Queen nodded.

'The sledge will follow,' she said.

Away they went as if into the very heart of the snowstorm, and the sleigh seemed to be carried into the air by the snowflakes, for now they were passing at great speed over woods and lakes and seas. Soon they rose into the sky

where there were no snow clouds and where the moon
seemed very near.

Kay felt no fear and soon fell asleep, wrapped in the
furs of the Snow Queen.

All through the dark winter, Gerda wept for Kay. Over
and over again she asked the boys who had played with
him in the market square what had happened, but not one
of them could tell her.

'We saw him tie his sledge to a great big sleigh,' they
said. 'There was a driver and a beautiful white horse.
The sleigh went so quickly—perhaps Kay fell off the
sleigh into the river and was drowned.'

Gerda sobbed loudly when she heard this, and no one
could comfort her. Even when the spring came and she went
out alone into the woods, she would say aloud, 'Kay is
dead. I shall never see him again.'

The swallows would answer, 'We don't think he is dead.
We think you will see him again.'

Her grandmother gave Gerda a beautiful pair of new red
shoes, thinking they would give her pleasure, but no sooner
had she put them on than she said to herself, 'I shall go

down to the river and ask it about Kay. If the river has taken my friend it will surely tell me.'

She kissed her old grandmother who was still asleep, and then set off all alone to make her way to the river that flowed close to the school.

'Is it true?' she asked the river when, at last, she stood by the banks. 'Have you taken my friend, Kay? Look at these pretty red leather shoes. I will give them to you if only you will give me back my friend.'

It seemed to Gerda that the river answered 'yes' in strange little rippling movements. So she took off her beautiful red shoes and threw them into the water. But the waves pushed them back on to the dry land again.

'You must accept them!' Gerda cried. And she climbed into a small boat that floated among the reeds. Once again she flung the shoes far into the river. But the boat was not moored and soon it started drifting away. Gerda was frightened and began to cry until, suddenly, she thought, 'The river is taking me to my friend. I must stay quietly in the boat.'

The boat drifted downstream for a long time until at last it came close to the bank where stood a strange-looking cottage. Its window panes were different colours, red, blue, and yellow, and by its door stood two wooden

soldiers who presented arms to the boats as they sailed past. Gerda began calling for help, and out of the cottage came an old woman. She walked with a crutch and she wore on her head a big straw hat trimmed with the most beautiful flowers.

'Poor child!' the old woman exclaimed. 'This great river will take you far across the world if I do not help you.' And with that she waded into the water and used her crutch to take hold of the boat and draw it towards the bank.

'Tell me who you are and where you are from,' she said as she lifted Gerda on to dry land. Gerda told her all that had happened.

The old woman listened carefully, and when Gerda asked her if she had seen her friend, Kay, she answered, 'No, he has not come this way, but I am sure he will before long. Come inside and stay with me a little while. I have lovely cherries for you to eat. We shall get on very well together because I have long been wanting a little girl like you.'

Once inside the cottage the old woman began to comb Gerda's long golden hair, and Gerda soon forgot all about her friend, Kay, and wished only to stay with this kind lady, for, as you may have guessed already, the comb was magic. The old woman was, in fact, a lonely old witch, and she soon grew to love Gerda.

She was so anxious to keep the little girl that she made all the rose trees in the garden disappear by touching them with her crutch, for she was afraid the roses might make Gerda remember Kay and her past life.

One day, when Gerda was left alone in the cottage, she found the old woman's big hat and began to play with it. As she counted the flowers she saw that among them was a rose, and at once she ran into the garden to look for more roses, but not a single one did she find.

She was so disappointed that she began to cry; her tears watered the ground and fell on one of the rose trees that lay buried under the brown earth. Immediately the rose tree came to life. As soon as Gerda saw the lovely red roses she remembered Kay and why she had left home.

'What made me stay here so long?' she asked the roses. 'I must find Kay. Do you think he is dead?'

'No,' they told her. 'We have just come back from the land of the dead and he is not there.'

Gerda began to smile at that. 'Thank you, dear roses,' she said. 'I must not stay here a moment longer.'

Away she ran to the end of the garden and into the big green wood. Perhaps the birds would tell her if they had seen Kay.

As Gerda skipped along she looked up into the trees, and presently she spied a raven that was staring down at her curiously.

'Have you seen my friend, Kay?' she asked the raven, and he croaked back, 'Yes, yes, I saw him in the Snow Queen's sleigh. They were in a great hurry.'

'Where was the Snow Queen taking him?' Gerda asked.

And the raven answered, 'No doubt they were going to Lapland where there is nothing but snow and ice. Why not ask the reindeer over there to tell you about it.'

'The raven speaks truly,' said the reindeer. 'There is always snow and ice in Lapland. It is a good land for us.'

'Do you know where it is?' Gerda asked next.

'Of course I do,' the reindeer said with shining eyes. 'I was born there, and I played there with my friends in the fields of snow.'

'I want to help this little girl,' the raven croaked. 'I want you to take the child to Lapland for me—but you must move quickly.'

'Jump on my back then,' the reindeer said to Gerda. 'I must do what my master, the raven, asks.'

No sooner was Gerda on his back than the reindeer shot away with the speed of an arrow. Away through the great forest he ran and over the swamps. Nothing, not even the highest rocks, could stop him in his course. On and on they went until at last they came to Lapland.

The reindeer at last came to rest in front of a hut where an old Lapp woman was making fish soup.

78

Gerda was far too cold to utter a single word, but the reindeer began at once to tell the old woman all that had happened to Gerda and how she was trying to find her friend, Kay.

'You poor child,' said the old Lapp woman, 'you have many hundreds of miles to travel before you find the Snow Queen. She lives in a country called Finmark. I have a young friend there, and I will send her a message on this piece of dry cod. Perhaps she will help you.'

When the old woman had written her message, Gerda smiled her thanks. Then the reindeer set off at a great pace. As they sped through the forests and woods, the northern lights tinged the sky with beautiful colours, but the reindeer did not slacken his pace until at last he came to Finmark.

He knew where to find the friend of the old Lapp woman, and went at once to her house, which was below the ground. The reindeer knocked on the chimney pot with his hoof and the Finn lady (who was a very young witch) appeared as if by magic.

Gerda gave her the dried cod on which was written the message, and after she had read it the Finn lady disappeared for a moment. The reindeer told Gerda that most likely she was putting the cod to boil in her pot, for she never wasted a thing.

'You are very wise and you know all the great secrets of the world,' the reindeer said to her when she appeared again. 'I know that you can tether all the winds with a

piece of your cotton. I know too that you can give the strength of ten men to anyone who drinks your special magic brew.'

The young witch smiled and nodded her head.

'You would like me to help your little friend here,' she said, 'so that she may learn the secret of how to defeat the wicked Snow Queen. I can tell you much about Kay,' she went on. 'He is happy, but it is only because he has a splinter of glass in his heart and a speck of glass in his eye. These splinters have changed him; he can no longer understand what is good. His heart is as cold as ice— and that is why the Snow Queen has such power over him.'

'Can you not help Gerda to break the spell?' the reindeer pleaded. 'Tell her how she may remove these splinters from the heart and eye of her little friend.'

The witch shook her head.

'The child already has much power,' she said. 'The animals of the woods and forests obey her without question. This is because her heart is pure. I cannot help her more. You must take her to the gate of the Snow Queen's garden, which is but two miles from here, and leave her. She alone can defeat the wickedness of the Snow Queen.'

The reindeer did as the witch said, but when he put Gerda down before the tall gates he wept, so heavy was his gentle heart at the thought of leaving her alone. And Gerda clung to him and kissed him as she said farewell.

When the reindeer had gone, Gerda looked at the great palace that rose beyond the gates. The walls of the palace were made of hard-packed snow that had been pierced for doors and windows. It sparkled in the sun, yet it looked cold and forbidding.

Here Gerda knew she would find Kay, and at once she set out down the long icy path that led to the palace entrance.

No sooner was she inside than she saw Kay. He was sitting alone in a corner and he was trying to make up a word with letters cut out of ice. The word was 'eternity', and the Snow Queen had told him that if he could make this word out of his letters she would give him a new pair of skates and set him free.

Gerda ran quickly towards him and flung her arms round his neck.

'Kay! Kay!' she cried. 'Darling Kay! I have found you at last.'

But the boy neither moved nor spoke, and Gerda began to weep bitterly as she saw how cold his eyes were. Her hot tears flowed so quickly, one after another, that they reached Kay's heart as she held him, and his icy heart melted so that the terrible splinter of glass was washed away.

Now, at last, the boy raised his head and looked at his friend of long ago. Gerda began to sing. It was the song she used to sing to him on the balcony beside their tiny garden. She sang it so beautifully and so sadly that all at once Kay burst into tears. As he wept, the splinter of glass was washed out of his eye. Now he could recognise his friend.

'Gerda! Gerda!' he whispered. 'Where have you been all this time, and what am I doing here? Oh, how cold it is! How empty everything feels.'

They clung to each other, laughing and crying at the same time, and then Kay saw his letters of ice were forming themselves into the word 'eternity'.

'Look Gerda!' he whispered. 'Now I am free. The Snow Queen has no power over me. She cannot go back on her promise.'

Hand in hand they ran out of the icy palace. Suddenly spring was in the air; tiny flowers were pushing their way through the snow; the sun shone. Beside a green bush, heavy with scarlet berries, there stood Gerda's loyal old friend, the reindeer, and beside him another, younger reindeer.

'Come, Kay,' Gerda said, 'these two dear friends will carry us safely home.'

Together they left the land of eternal cold, and the reindeer carried them safely over the mountains and through the forests and across great rivers until, one day, they heard the church bells ringing, and Gerda knew they were home.

The two friends ran quickly along the narrow cobbled streets until they came to the winding stairs that led to their attic homes. Kay went up one way and Gerda the other, but they met on the balcony just as they used to meet long, long ago.

'Look Kay,' Gerda cried, 'our flower garden is more beautiful than ever before. See how the tiny rose trees have grown.'

But Kay had eyes only for Gerda, his dearest, truest friend who had brought him safely home.

DICK WHITTINGTON AND HIS CAT

There was once a young orphan boy called Dick Whittington. He was so poor that his clothes were always in rags,
but he had a merry way and an eager smile.

When Dick had nothing better to do he went to the
village square to listen to the talk of the old men. What
wonderful tales these men told—and most of them were
about the greatest city in the world, London.

'Why,' they told Dick, 'London's very streets are paved
with gold. There is no place like London for marvels . . .
you will have to see it for yourself.'

Dick, as he grew older, could think of nothing but this
wonderful city whose streets were paved with gleaming
gold. Imagine his excitement when, one day, a good-hearted
waggoner told him, 'Yes, I'm taking the wagon to London.
You can walk beside the horse, if you like. But mind,
you must find your own shelter, and your own food and
drink.'

Dick was overjoyed. He wrapped his few treasures in
a large red square of cotton. Then he tied his bundle to a
stick and slung it over his shoulder.

It was a very long way to London, but Dick was so
happy that he didn't mind when his feet began to ache.

'Soon I shall be rich,' he told the waggoner whenever they stopped to give the old horse a rest. 'Do you know, London's streets are paved with gold!'

On and on they went until at last the waggoner said, 'Well, not far to go now!'

Dick was so excited when they got to London that he began to run.

Poor Dick! All his excitement came to nothing! He tired himself out looking for golden streets, and the next day he was so faint with hunger that he had to beg in the streets.

'Please, will you spare a penny?' Dick asked the passers-by. 'I am so hungry and I have no money, not even a halfpenny to buy a crust of bread.'

But there was no one who would take pity on Dick. Tired and weak from hunger, he came at last to the door of a rich merchant called Mr. Fitzwarren. Dick was so weary he sank down on the pavement outside.

'Be off with you!' shouted the cook when she discovered him. 'We don't want any beggars here.'

'No!' said Mr. Fitzwarren, who happened to come along. 'The poor lad looks ill. We must take him in and feed him. Then he can help you in the kitchen.'

The cook was a big woman with a sour face and a bad

temper. She did not want to give Dick any food. But the merchant and his pretty, fair-haired daughter, Alice, came into the kitchen to make sure Dick had something to eat.

'You must find some work for the boy,' the merchant told the scowling cook. 'I want him to be happy here.'

'So do I,' said the gentle Alice. 'Poor Dick! How awful it must be to have no mother and no father.'

The cook said nothing. She stood over Dick just as if he were her prisoner.

'I'll teach him a lesson,' she thought, 'just as soon as I have him to myself in the kitchen.'

That same day the cook set Dick to work. She gave him all the dirty, horrid jobs to do. He had to sweep the floors and stoke the boiler and scrape the potatoes. Every now and then she would pick up the wooden spoon and chase him round and round the kitchen.

Every night the cook made Dick sleep in the attic. It was covered with dust and thick cobwebs, and was the home of countless rats and mice.

One day Dick came across some children playing with a cat. 'Will you sell me your cat for a penny?' he asked the little girl. 'That's all the money I have.'

'Yes,' said the girl. 'Give me your penny and take my cat. Have you got mice for her to catch?'

'Hundreds!' said Dick as he took the cat in his arms.

'Then she will catch them all,' said the little girl, holding out her hand for the penny.

And that is exactly what the clever cat did!

No wonder Dick loved his cat; and he never forgot to give her a special tit-bit from his own small supper.

One day his master sent for Dick and said to him, 'Dick, I am despatching my ship to a faraway land to trade. Would you like to give me some of your savings for this venture? It should be a very profitable one.'

Dick shook his head. 'I have no savings, master,' he said. 'But take my cat. She is a good mouser.'

So, when the ship sailed away, Dick's cat sailed with it, and soon there were no mice left on board.

The merchant and his daughter liked and trusted Dick, but the cook did not; and it was she who made his life a misery. At last Dick could stand it no longer. He made up his mind to run away.

'London is no place for me,' he told himself as he wrapped

his few treasures in his red cotton handkerchief. 'I'll leave this very night.'

There was no one to bid Dick farewell as he left the house, and he felt lonely and sad as he trudged through the dark streets, past the warehouses and the tall grey houses, the market places, and then over one of the bridges that spanned the River Thames.

When he could not take another step for weariness, Dick sat down on a milestone and, shivering with the winter cold, closed his eyes.

Just as his head began to nod, far away in the distance he heard the sound of bells. Dick sprang to his feet; it was as if the bells were ringing out especially for him.

'Turn again, Whittington, Lord Mayor of London,' they seemed to be saying. And Dick clenched his fists and shouted as loud as he could into the darkness.

'Yes, yes, I will turn again, you great Bells of Bow!'

So Dick turned back and, when he reached the merchant's house, crept silently inside and up the stairs to his attic. The next morning he went down to the kitchen without saying a word about his adventure.

Dick carried on doing his best to please everybody— especially the bad-tempered cook. Sometimes at night, in his dark, dingy attic, he wished he had never parted with his clever cat, for now the rats and mice had it all their own way. Besides, he missed his cat for her own sake, and longed to see her again.

On the face of it, this seemed unlikely, for the merchant's ship had been caught in a storm and driven on to an island peopled by hostile natives. It was given up for lost. Little did Dick know that his cat was going to be the means of saving the lives of the sailors.

It happened like this.

Brown-skinned natives, brandishing spears, attacked the stranded crew. But before they could do the sailors any harm, the captain cried bravely, 'Take us to your king. We have rich presents for him.'

The native warriors obeyed, and their ruler received the ship's captain with some show of politeness, speaking in a broken English that was easy to understand.

'We see no reason to help you,' said the king. 'And as many of my people are cannibals, you will make good eating.'

As the king spoke, the captain was surprised to observe how freely the mice and rats were permitted to run over the rich dishes set out before the ruler.

'It strikes me,' said the captain, 'that you do well to be cannibals, for all the more usual food will soon be devoured by this plague of mice and rats you have here.'

'You speak truly, white man,' answered the king. 'The mice are everywhere. They plague my people to madness; but we can do nothing about them.

'Then I shall,' cried the captain, 'if you give me your

promise to float our good ship again and see us on our way.'

The king, taken by surprise, gave his solemn word to help the captain to refloat the ship if he, the captain, could rid the place of mice.

'Leave it to me,' said the ship's captain, and he asked one of his sailors to release the cat, which they had brought ashore in a basket. Delighted to be free, the cat got down to business straight away, and within two days there was not a mouse or rat to be seen.

In his gratitude the king took the captain to his vast treasure room and loaded him up with boxes of gold and silver pieces. Then some of his people helped the sailors to refloat the ship.

Within the week the captain and his crew were safely aboard their ship and sailing for home. When the ship docked the captain went to report to Dick's master.

'The orphan lad must have his cat back,' said the noble

captain, 'and a goodly share of the treasure besides. For it was his cat that brought us the luck and the fortune.'

So Dick stayed on in London, rich beyond his dreams. He used his fortune for the good of others, and, in time, he married the beautiful Alice and settled down happily.

As the years passed, the king of England himself, Henry by name, met Dick, and was so taken by him that he dubbed him a knight: Sir Richard Whittington! And as if that weren't enough, all the people of London asked that Dick should be their new lord mayor.

As the great Bells of Bow rang out in his honour, Dick's thoughts went back to the time when he had so nearly run away. How thankful he was now that he had turned back.

There is nothing in the history books to tell us what happened to Dick's cat, but you can be sure she had fish and rabbit every day of her life. In truth, there is nothing in the history books about the Dick of this story. But there is certainly something about a good and famous man called Sir Richard Whittington who, one day, became Lord Mayor of London.

THE SLEEPING BEAUTY

Once upon a time there lived a King and Queen who were very happy together. One thing, however, spoilt their happiness—they had no children.

Imagine their joy when, at long last, the Queen gave birth to a dear little baby daughter!

'We must have a wonderful christening party,' the Queen cried, 'and invite all the good fairies to be her godparents. Each of them will give our child a precious gift that will help her to grow up into a gracious and lovely lady.'

On the day of the christening, the good fairies were given special chairs of honour, and each had placed before her a present of a gold case that held a golden spoon and fork and knife, all decorated with diamonds. No wonder the fairy godmothers were delighted. Just as they sat down to a magnificent feast, however, the doors of the great banqueting hall were pushed open, and there stood an ugly old fairy who had not received an invitation to the party.

'Only twelve places laid!' she muttered spitefully. 'They have forgotten *me*!' And her eyes gleamed wickedly as, one by one, the fairies went up to the baby's cradle to bestow on the sleeping child their gifts.

'You will grow up to be the most beautiful Princess in the world,' said the first fairy.

'You will be the most intelligent,' said the second.

'There will be none to equal your grace and charity,' said the third.

'You will dance more beautifully than any other princess that ever lived,' said the fourth.

'And you will sing like a nightingale,' said the fifth.

'And play every instrument with great skill,' said the sixth.

As the fairies continued to come to the cradle, the youngest of their company, seeing the wicked look in the angry old fairy's eyes, hid behind the curtain so that she might be the last to give her gift.

When it came to the bad fairy's turn, the King and Queen waited anxiously to hear what she would say.

'You shall die,' the old witch shrieked, 'from the prick of a spindle!'

The guests fell silent at these terrible words.

The twelfth and youngest came forward. 'Take courage, Your Majesties,' she cried. 'Your daughter will not die. It is true I cannot save her from this terrible curse, but she

will not die; instead, I will make her fall into a deep sleep that will last a hundred years. A king's son shall wake her.'

The King and Queen would not be comforted until they had passed a law that said that all the spinning wheels in the land were to be destroyed. No person in their kingdom might use a spindle—on pain of death.

The years passed, and the Princess grew up into a beautiful, laughing girl, so gracious and gentle that she was loved by all.

One day the King and Queen left the palace to stay at their country house, and the young Princess, who remained behind, was free to roam where she willed. Up and down the stairs she ran one afternoon until she discovered, at the top of one of the highest towers, a tiny attic room where an old woman sat spinning. Shut up in her

tower, this old woman had never heard of the King's command, nor did she know that her lovely visitor was the King's daughter.

'Show me what you are doing,' cried the Princess. 'I have never seen anyone spin before.'

But no sooner had she taken hold of the spindle than the sharp needle pricked her finger, and she fell to the ground.

Terrified, the old woman left her tower, crying out in distress, 'Come quickly, quickly!'

Just at that very moment the returning King and Queen drove through the palace gates. How unhappy they were when they saw their lovely young daughter still and silent on the floor! The King, remembering the wicked fairy's curse, knew that nothing could be done to save her.

'Make ready the finest room in the castle!' he cried, 'and lay her on a gold and silver bed, for there she must sleep for a hundred years.'

When all this was done, the King sent word to the good fairy, who swooped down upon the palace in her chariot drawn by dragons of fire.

'This is what I shall do,' she said. 'I shall send everyone to sleep for a hundred years so that when the Princess awakes, this castle will be just as she remembers it.'

And so it was done. Everything the fairy touched with her magic wand became instantly fixed. The officers and guards, the stewards and the cooks, the pages and the footmen—they all fell fast asleep just where they were. The horses in the stables, the dogs in the yard, even the pigeons on the roof-tops, fell fast asleep. The fire in the hearth died down, and the meat that was roasting on the spit stopped turning.

Only the King and Queen, after they had kissed their daughter, left the castle that day. As they drove sadly away, a thick hedge of briars and thorns sprang up all around the castle walls.

A hundred years passed. The country was ruled by another King. One day the son of this King was out riding when he unexpectedly came upon a thick hedge of briars and tangled thorns that barred his way.

'What lies behind?' he asked a passing woodcutter.

'A legend says that a Princess of great beauty lies asleep in the castle beyond,' answered the woodcutter.

'A Princess!' cried the King's handsome son, his eyes sparkling with excitement. 'And a great beauty! Let me be the one to rouse her from her slumber . . .'

'Many have tried before you,' the old man warned him, 'but none has succeeded in cutting his way through to the castle.'

The gallant Prince drew his sword as he ran towards the enormous hedge, but, to his astonishment, the thorny bushes parted before him, and soon he found himself at the castle gates.

As he crossed the vast courtyard he saw how the dogs lay sleeping beside their bones, how the cats and pigeons seemed carved out of stone, how the horses in the stables stood motionless with eyes closed.

His astonishment grew as he entered the kitchen. Here was the chef, caught by sleep in the very act of tasting soup from his ladle; and there was a scullery maid with mop and bucket, still as a statue. He paused only for an instant before racing along the silent corridors. At last he came to the room where the sleeping Princess lay.

'Oh, how beautiful you are!' he whispered, and he bent down and gently kissed her.

At the touch of his lips, the Princess opened her eyes and held out her arms. 'You have been so long in coming,' she murmured.

The castle came to life as the two embraced. Dogs barked; cats miaowed; pigeons cooed; the chef finished tasting his soup; and the scullery maid went about her business with the mop.

What happiness there was that day inside the castle! Prince Charming married his Sleeping Beauty in the castle chapel—and he alone knew that her wedding gown was at least one hundred years out of fashion. But never a word did he say to spoil the wonderful moment.

THE FISHERMAN AND HIS WIFE

When the world was still young enough to be magical there lived a fisherman and his wife. They were so poor that the only home they could find was a pigsty.

The pigsty was near the sea, and every morning the poor fisherman went out in his little boat. He rarely caught anything, but one day he hooked a flounder.

To his astonishment, as he began heaving the fish into his boat, it said to him, 'Don't kill me! I am really a Prince under an evil spell that cannot be broken. In any case, I would not be to your taste, whether I were fried or boiled.'

'As if I would!' said the fisherman. 'It would be on my conscience for the rest of my life to kill a fish that talked.' So saying, he unhooked the flounder and let it drop back into the sea. He caught nothing else that day and at last returned home.

When he told his wife about his unusual catch, she was quite angry. 'An enchanted Prince, you say?' said she. 'Then why didn't you ask him for some gift? He was surely in a position to grant your wish.'

'I never thought of such a thing!' said her honest husband.

'The first thing you do when you begin fishing in the morning,' said Sybil, for that was her name, 'is to call him and ask him for a nice little hut. Anything would be better than this pigsty.'

The next morning the fisherman rowed his boat to the same spot, and in a nervous voice called out:

> Flounder, flounder, in the sea,
> Come, I pray thee, here to me.
> My good wife, Sybil, will have her way,
> No matter what I do or say.

The sea was so calm that the fisherman was able to stand up in his boat as he shouted. Presently the flounder appeared.

'What is it?' asked the flounder. 'What does your wife want?'

'She wants a little hut,' said the fisherman in a humble voice. 'She's tired of the pigsty we have at present. It's the best I can afford, but there you are.'

'She has it already,' said the flounder, and dived back into the depths of the sea.

When the fisherman rowed home, the pigsty had gone, and in its place stood a sweet little cottage with a garden

back and front, a red-brick porch, and lace curtains on the windows.

Once inside, he found his wife arranging the gaily coloured cushions.

'About time too!' she said. 'Now we've got a proper place of our own at last.'

'We're very fortunate,' said the fisherman. 'Why, we can stay here, contented and happy, for the rest of our lives.'

'We'll see about that,' said his wife, and she bustled about the bright new kitchen and got him something to eat.

Every morning the fisherman went out to fish as usual. And as usual he fished and he caught nothing, or very little. But this did not worry him unduly, for at the end of the day, he had his comfortable cottage waiting for him. His wife did not nag so much, and the fisherman began to enjoy life.

One night, however, on their way up to bed, his wife said to him, 'Husband, I have grown tired of this tiny cottage. What I would really like is a big stone castle. Tomorrow you must call the flounder and ask for one.'

'Sybil, Sybil, I cannot ask again,' protested the fisherman. 'We have everything we need.'

But his wife gave him no peace all through the night, and in the morning the fisherman promised to call the flounder. He rowed his little boat to the spot where he had first seen the fish, and he called:

> *Flounder, flounder, in the sea,*
> *Come, I pray thee, here to me.*
> *My good wife, Sybil, will have her way,*
> *No matter what I do or say.*

The sea was calm as before, but it looked grey under the clouds, and the fisherman shivered as the flounder once again shot up from the depths.

'What is it? What does she want now?' asked the flounder.

'I do apologise for this,' said the fisherman in a weak voice, 'but she wants to live in a big stone castle.'

'She has it already,' said the flounder, and dived back into the depths of the sea.

When the fisherman rowed home the cottage had gone and in its place stood a huge stone castle. His wife waved to him from one of the turret windows. 'Come quickly,' she called. 'See what I have got! It's splendid inside.'

The fisherman ran through the courtyard into the castle. The first vast room he came to was hung with rich tapestries; tables and chairs were of solid marble; and goblets of gold and silver stood along the shelves.

'We have a deer park as well as a castle,' his wife told him excitedly. 'And orchards besides. Clap your hands, husband, and summon the servants. There are many of them.'

Half-fearfully, the fisherman clapped his hands, and immediately a dozen serving-men and pages ran to do his bidding.

Living in such splendour quite changed his way of looking at things, and he grew used to being waited on and eating venison. 'We're very fortunate,' said he to his wife. 'Why, Sybil, we can stay here, contented and happy, for the rest of our lives.'

'We'll see about that,' said his wife as she gave her daily orders to the servants. 'We'll see about that.'

Her husband gave her a frightened look, but she said no more until one day, some three weeks later. 'Husband,' said she, 'I have grown tired of this cold grey castle. I would like to be King and live in a palace.'

'You must be mad to speak so,' said her husband. 'Why should you want to be King? Isn't this enough for you?'

'No,' said his wife. 'And what's more I order you to seek out the flounder this morning. After all, you gave him his life. He will do anything you ask.'

And she nagged him so loudly that the fisherman ran down to the beach just to get away from her.

He rowed his little boat until he came to the spot where thrice before he had seen the flounder. Then he called out:

> *Flounder, flounder, in the sea,*
> *Come, I pray thee, here to me.*
> *My good wife, Sybil, will have her way,*
> *No matter what I do or say.*

The sea was no longer calm, and the little boat rocked as

the flounder shot up from the depths. 'What is it? What does she want this time?' asked the flounder.

'I don't know how to ask,' whispered the poor fisherman, trembling in every limb. 'But she wants to be King.'

'She is King already,' said the flounder, and dived back into the boiling sea.

When the fisherman rowed home, the grey stone castle no longer towered before him. Instead, he found himself looking at a magnificent palace of white marble, surrounded by gardens of breathtaking beauty.

As he strode through the gardens, stately peacocks moved out of his way, and doves cooed above his head. Not knowing quite what to expect, he entered the palace and made his way along vast shining corridors.

He found his wife in the royal throne room, seated on a tall golden throne and with a crown, some two feet high, perched on her head. She was surrounded by courtiers and ladies-in-waiting, and her soldiers, dressed in scarlet and silver uniforms, had to clear a path for him.

'Well, husband,' she said. 'I am King.'

'So I can see,' said the fisherman, wetting his lips with his tongue.

For a week or maybe less, the fisherman and his King-wife lived royally on the choicest meats and slept on the softest beds, and the fisherman began to accept that Sybil was King and must be served as such.

'We are very fortunate,' he said one evening as they strolled through the gardens. 'Why, Sybil, we can stay as we are, contented and happy, for the rest of our lives.'

'We'll see about that,' said his wife, 'for now I want to be Emperor.'

'You must be out of your mind!' cried the fisherman, narrowly missing falling backwards into one of the fountains. 'Quite out of your mind!'

'You must row out to sea first thing in the morning,' went on his wife as if she had not heard, 'and ask the flounder. He cannot refuse.'

After a sleepless night spent in argument, the fisherman went down to the shore early the next morning. He got out his little boat and rowed to the spot where he had four times before seen the fish. Then he called out:

> *Flounder, flounder, in the sea,*
> *Come, I pray thee, here to me.*
> *My good wife, Sybil, will have her way,*
> *No matter what I do or say.*

This time the waves were so high that they were in danger of swamping the little boat, and the sea was black and angry as the flounder swam towards him.

'What is it now?' asked the flounder. 'What does she want next?'

The fisherman was so afraid that he could scarcely get the words out. But he managed to stammer, 'She wants to be Emperor.'

'She is that already,' said the flounder, and was at once swallowed up by a wave of immense size.

When the fisherman rowed back to the shore, he saw that the white marble palace was now inlaid with gold and alabaster, and that soldiers and sentinels stood guard with crossed swords at the gates.

Almost fainting from fear, the fisherman made his way through a maze of corridors until he came upon his wife seated on a golden throne. Her gown was ablaze with emeralds. On her head sat a crown, taller than the first, and in her hand was a sceptre sparkling with diamonds.

'So you are Emperor now,' said the fisherman, quaking at the knees.

'Yes, I am Emperor,' said his wife. 'But already I am weary of this earthly power. I look at the sun, and I cannot change its course. I see the moon, and have no power to make it wane. Husband, I would be all-powerful. I would have the sun and moon and stars bow down before me.'

'That is surely impossible,' whispered the fisherman, growing deathly pale. 'Let us be happy and content with what we have.'

'As Emperor I order you to speak to the flounder,' said his wife. 'He cannot refuse, for you once gave him back his life.'

The fisherman turned away. He left the palace and went down to the shore. He got out his little boat and rowed to the spot where he had last seen the flounder. Then he called out:

> *Flounder, flounder, in the sea,*
> *Come, I pray thee, here to me.*
> *My good wife, Sybil, will have her way,*
> *No matter what I do or say.*

Around him the sea boiled, black and furious; streaks of lightning cracked open the dark clouds; the wind howled like a pack of hungry wolves. The fisherman was more afraid than he had ever been in his whole life.

But, as before, the flounder appeared out of the boiling sea.

'What is it? What does she want now?' asked the flounder.

Scarcely able to speak, the fisherman whispered, 'She would have the sun, moon, and stars bow down before her.' He stopped, unable to go on.

'She is no more than she once was,' said the flounder. 'You will find her in the pigsty.'

When the fisherman rowed back to the shore, the marble palace had vanished, but there stood the pigsty, and by the gateway stood his wife.

THE BRAVE LITTLE TAILOR

There was once a little tailor who sat all day by his window stitching busily. He usually sat cross-legged on his table, for being extremely short he found this position the most comfortable.

One sunny afternoon the little tailor was tempted to stop work and try some of the jam that he had recently bought from a passing farmer's wife.

To his extreme annoyance, however, no sooner had he got out the loaf and begun to spread the sweet-smelling jam on a slice of bread than he was plagued by a swarm of flies.

'Take that! And that! And that!' he shouted angrily as he hit the flies with a piece of cloth.

To his satisfaction, when he looked down he found that he had killed no less than seven at one blow.

'Imagine,' said he to himself. 'Seven of them at one blow!' And in high delight he gave up stitching the waistcoat he had been working on and began to make himself a belt. When this was done, he stitched on it the words SEVEN AT ONE BLOW before fastening it round his middle.

'The world must know about this mighty deed,' he thought. 'I'll not waste a minute, but set out right away.'

And he took a piece of Dutch cheese out of the cupboard to help him on his way.

When he found himself on the road outside the town, he stopped for a moment to gain his breath, and to take hold of a small brown bird that was caught in a nearby thicket.

'You'll do for company,' said he, and he placed the bird carefully in his pocket. Whistling cheerfully, he set out to climb the road that led through the mountains into the world beyond.

At the top he was surprised to come upon a huge, clumsy-looking fellow, almost twenty times his size. The giant, for he was most certainly a giant, was staring down the mountainside at nothing in particular when the tailor greeted him.

'I wouldn't mind sharing my travels with a companion such as yourself,' said the tailor, eyeing the giant up and down. 'What do you say?'

'I say you're an impudent little fellow!' roared the giant,

'and for half a cudgel I'd do away with you here and now —that is to say, if I could be sure of striking such a twittering midget . . .'

'You don't say,' said the little tailor cheerfully. And with that he unbuttoned his jacket and showed the giant his belt.

'Seven at one blow!' the giant slowly read. Concluding that it was men the tailor had killed, he looked down on the little man with more respect.

'Well,' said the giant, who was by no means quick-thinking, 'I tell you what. We'll have a trial of strength, and see how you get on. If you do well, I'll take you home with me to meet my brothers.'

'Done!' said the little tailor.

The giant picked up a stone and squeezed it until water ran out.

'Now you do the same,' said he.

'Certainly,' said the tailor, and he pretended to pick up a stone and squeeze it hard. In fact, all he squeezed was his piece of soft cheese, which presently melted with the heat of his hand.

'Very good,' said the giant when he saw the liquid. 'Watch me now!' And he picked up a boulder and threw it so far and so high that it looked like a pebble when it fell back to earth. 'Now you do the same,' said he.

'Done,' said the little tailor. And turning away for a moment he took the small bird out of his pocket and cast it into the air. The bird, rejoicing in its freedom, soared high into the sky and was soon lost to sight.

'Anyone can throw a stone,' said the little man quietly. 'But the stone comes down to earth. My stone was thrown so far and so high into the sky that you won't see it land!'

'Very good,' said the giant, 'but let us see if you can lift a heavy weight. That will be a real test of strength.' And he went to a massive oak tree that had been felled by lightning. 'Now,' said he, 'I'll take the trunk.'

'And I'll take the branches, for they are by far the

heavier,' said the little man confidently. But when the giant turned and bent down to hoist the trunk on to his great shoulders, the tailor hopped in among the leaves.

Thus it was that the giant staggered along bearing the weight of the whole tree and the tailor besides.

When the giant could no longer stand the strain, he cried out, 'I'm going to drop my end.'

'Do that,' answered the little man, and he hopped out of the branches just before they crashed to the ground. 'Why,' he exclaimed, 'I could have carried my end quite a bit farther. After all, I have killed seven at one blow . . .'

'You had better come along with me and meet my two brothers,' said the giant when he had recovered his breath. 'They will be honoured to meet such a brave little fellow.' And with that, he led the tailor down the mountainside and into a huge cave where two enormous giants sat at their supper.

The little tailor smiled at them cheerfully, and when they had finished their meal—a whole roast of sheep each—the first giant showed him the bed where he could spend the night.

The tailor found the bed uncomfortably big, so later, as the snores of the three sleeping giants echoed round the cave, he slipped out of the bed and crept under the table, where he passed the night.

Early the next morning, while it was still dark, the giants awoke.

'We'll rid ourselves of that impudent little cricket,' said the first giant, 'before we set about the day's business.' And he took his cudgel and aimed a mighty blow at the bed, which would have certainly flattened the little tailor if he had been sleeping there.

Laughing loudly, the three giants set off for the forest in high spirits. The little tailor, however, was far from dead. He too was in high spirits when he awoke, and shortly he set off on his travels. As he passed through the forest he came upon the three giants and greeted them like old friends.

Terrified out of their wits at seeing the little man alive, the
giants let out a roar and took to their heels.

Greatly encouraged, the tailor went on his way until he
came to a walled city. Passing through the gateway, he
soon found himself in the palace courtyard.

Being tired after his long walk, and having no money,
the tailor sat down by the wall and fell fast asleep.

As he slept, some of the palace servants came upon him
and read the words on his belt: SEVEN AT ONE BLOW.

'We must let His Majesty know immediately,' they
whispered to each other. 'He must see to it that such a
brave warrior fights on our side.'

'Certainly I will see him,' said the King when he was
told. 'With such a man on our side, our enemies will be
too frightened even to fight.'

The little tailor promised the King that he would serve
him well, and the King gave him a fine house and a bag
of gold. But as time went on the soldiers in the King's army
grew jealous of the little man. 'We shall all leave,' said their
Colonel-in-chief, 'unless you rid us of him.'

'I cannot lose my entire army for the sake of a stranger,'
said the King. 'Leave it to me, and I will find a way.'

So he sent for the tailor. 'In view of your great deeds and your courage,' the King began when the little man stood before him, 'I have decided to give you a most important task. If you succeed, you will marry my lovely daughter and gain, besides, half my kingdom.'

'Just tell me what the deed is,' said the little tailor.

'In the forest there are two red-headed giants of terrible strength,' said the King. 'For years they have stolen our cattle and devoured our armies—that is to say, whenever an army could be persuaded to march against them! Rid me of these giants and you shall have your reward.'

'Done!' said the little tailor. And he set out the same day. When he reached the edge of the forest he ordered the

trembling soldiers, who had accompanied him so far, to stay where they were.

'I will do this deed alone,' said he, and ran forward. After two hours, the brave little man suddenly spied the two red-headed giants sound asleep under a tree. And their snores were like the roaring of a pride of lions.

After looking at them for a while, the tailor bent down and silently filled his pockets with stones and pebbles. This done, he nimbly climbed up the tree until he came to a branch that hung directly over the two red-heads beneath. Taking a handful of stones, the little man let them fall on one of the sleeping giants, who woke up and began grumbling at his companion. 'Why do you plague me?' he roared. And he shook the other giant until he too was awake.

'I don't know what you mean,' said the second giant sleepily. 'Leave me alone.'

The two giants settled down again, and the tailor went on with his plan. This time he showered the second giant with stones; it was now the second giant's turn to mutter and complain. Presently, when both giants slumbered again, the little tailor dropped a big sharp stone on each, and soon the two giants were at each other's throats.

On and on they battled, tearing up huge rocks and using them as cudgels with which to beat each other. Safe in his own tree, the little tailor watched until both giants fell motionless to the ground. No doubt about it, they were dead.

When the King heard the news, he was far from pleased, though he was undoubtedly thankful to be rid of the giants.

'There is still one other task I would have you perform,' said the King.

'What is it? asked the little tailor.

'In that same forest where you destroyed the two giants,' said the King, 'lives a unicorn. This beast has killed many of my huntsmen, and no man, so far, has been able to trap him. If you succeed you will have my daughter's hand in marriage and half my kingdom besides.'

'Done!' said the tailor cheerfully.

As soon as he found himself in the forest, the little man set out to follow the unicorn's tracks. When he came upon the beast, the tailor took care to stand in front of a tree: then he began taunting it.

With a roar, the unicorn lowered its single horn and lunged out at him. This was just what the tailor expected the unicorn to do. He stepped neatly to one side so that the unicorn's horn rammed itself into the tree.

It was a simple matter then for the little man to take the beast captive—after he had sawn off the terrible horn!

The King hid his surprise when the tailor presented him with the hornless unicorn. 'You have succeeded where others have failed,' said he. 'Do me one more favour, and the reward is yours.'

The tailor hid his disappointment. 'What is it?' he asked.

'In the same forest lives a wild boar,' said the King. 'This beast is so fierce that it has trampled on women and children. Capture it alive, and you shall marry the Princess without further delay.'

As before, the tailor entered the forest alone. When the wild boar spotted him, it lowered its terrible tusks and charged. But the little man was well prepared. He retreated to a small chapel behind him, leaving the door wide open. After him charged the boar. But the tailor flung himself out of an upstair's window, and then rushed round and slammed the door shut, thus trapping the wild animal.

This time the King could find no more excuses for delay. The next day, the tailor and the beautiful Princess were married amid scenes of great splendour.

All went well for the tailor until, one night, having eaten too well at supper, he began to dream. 'Only one more waistcoat to stitch,' murmured the tailor, tossing and turning. 'Stitch, stitch, stitch!'

On hearing these words and others like them, the Princess guessed immediately what they meant and rushed to tell the King. 'He is nothing but a common tailor,' she sobbed.

The King comforted her as best as he could. 'Leave your door open tonight,' he told her. 'As soon as the tailor sleeps, my soldiers will rush in and behead him.'

But a friendly attendant heard every word of this, and informed the tailor who had once done him a good turn. 'So that's it,' said the little man.

That night he only pretended sleep. As soon as he guessed the soldiers were outside, he muttered, 'Only one more waistcoat; stitch, stitch, stitch. Seven have I killed at one blow. Now I will kill you . . .'

When they heard these words, the soldiers were overcome with fear and took to their heels; nor were they ever seen again. As for the little tailor, he was shortly afterwards made King and, as none ever dared to contradict him, he had a long and peaceful reign.

GOLDILOCKS AND THE THREE BEARS

Once upon a time there were Three Bears. There was Father Bear, and there was Mother Bear, and there was Baby Bear. They all lived together in a dear little cottage, right in the middle of the woods.

It was a neat, tidy little cottage, with a neat, tidy little garden where the Three Bears liked to sit on sunny days.

Father Bear would take out his newspaper to find out what had been going on in the big, wide world. Mother Bear would take out her knitting, which she never seemed to finish. As for Baby Bear, well, he was too small really to think of anything else but playing. So he would roll on the soft, green grass and play with his bright ball.

From all this, you will see that the Three Bears were a happy, contented family, and not a bit growly, except perhaps when Father dropped his newspaper in the mud, or Mother dropped a stitch that ran all the way down to the bottom. They were also a very tidy family, and each of them had his own bowl, and his own chair, and his own bed.

Father Bear, being the biggest, had the biggest bowl, the biggest chair, and the biggest bed.

All Mother Bear's things were middle-sized because she was middle-sized herself. It's not difficult to guess who had the smallest. Baby Bear, of course! He had the smallest plate, and the smallest chair, and the smallest bed.

'I wish I needn't always be the baby,' he would often squeak. 'Even babies have to grow up.'

But whatever he said did not make any difference to Father Bear and Mother Bear, for they still called him 'Baby', and he still had to have the smallest of everything in the cottage—even the smallest porridge bowl. Baby Bear minded this most because he adored porridge.

Now, in a manner of speaking, bears are supposed to like honey best of all. But these Three Bears liked creamy porridge best of all.

Every morning Mother Bear got out her big pot and made the porridge. When it was ready she ladled it into the bowls, which were always washed up and rubbed dry after every meal.

Early one morning, the sun began to shine so brightly that it made the Three Bears want to rush out at once to enjoy it. But Mother Bear had already cooked the porridge and put it in the three bowls.

'The porridge is very hot,' said Mother Bear in her nice soft voice. 'I suppose we could go out.' And Father Bear said in his big gruff voice, 'Yes, let's do that.' Baby Bear said in his wee tiny voice, 'Yes, let's go out this very minute.' So off they went for a walk in the woods.

No sooner had they left their cottage than along came a little girl, with big blue eyes and yellow hair. Her name was Goldilocks.

'I wonder who lives in that darling little house?' Goldilocks asked herself as soon as she saw the cottage. She went right up to the door and started to turn the handle. 'Most people lock their doors when they go out. So I expect this door is locked too.'

But to her surprise, she found that the handle turned and the door swung open. So, with her blue eyes as big as saucers, Goldilocks peered inside. Just for one little moment she hesitated in the doorway. Should she? Or shouldn't she? Then in she went.

'What a nice tidy room,' said Goldilocks as she looked all about her. 'And there's the table all laid for breakfast. Oh, I do feel so hungry. It's such a long time since I had anything to eat.'

With that, Goldilocks skipped over to the table and picked up the biggest of the spoons.

'I might just have a taste,' she thought.

It wasn't a very nice way to behave, was it? You wouldn't do such a thing, would you? You wouldn't go into somebody else's kitchen and begin to taste all the food.

Goldilocks did just that, and she didn't stop to think that she was being really naughty. First she picked up one bowl, and then another, and her big blue eyes had a very hungry look in them as she began to sniff the lovely, porridgy smell.

The porridge in the very big bowl was far too hot, and Goldilocks made a little face. The porridge in the middle-sized bowl was far too cold and she made another face. But

the porridge in the teeny weeny bowl—why, that tasted exactly right, and Goldilocks smiled happily. She dipped in the spoon and began to eat.

After she had eaten all the porridge, Goldilocks thought it would be pleasant to sit down. First, she sat on the biggest chair, but it was far too big and far too hard, and she jumped up quickly.

Next, she went over to the middle-sized chair. 'This one is certainly better!' she exclaimed as she sat down on the second chair. 'But it is really rather too soft for me. What a very odd place this is with all its different-sized bowls, and all its different-sized chairs. I wonder what that teeny chair feels like to sit on. I must try.'

With that she went across to the teeny weeny chair, which was Baby Bear's very own chair, and sat herself down on it. But not for long, for all at once there was a horrid, creaking sound.

Up went Goldilock's feet into the air as the poor little chair began to break under her.

'It can't be helped,' said Goldilocks when she had picked herself up. 'Now where can I have a nice rest? I think I must just take a look upstairs.'

So away upstairs she went to the bedroom, and there, to her great delight, she saw three beds. There was a very big bed, and there was a middle-sized bed, and then there was a teeny weeny bed.

'I'll try them all,' Goldilocks told herself. 'I might as well.' With that she began to try the very largest bed, which was Father Bear's own bed.

But somehow or other the bed was not right. The pillows were too high, and it was all too big. Goldilocks wriggled and wriggled in it. 'It's far too high,' she said at last. 'I wonder what the next bed is like? I think I must just try it to find out.'

The middle-sized bed was certainly better. It wasn't so high and it wasn't so hard, but somehow it wasn't right either. So Goldilocks didn't stay very long in it, for the teeny weeny bed next to it looked a very much nicer bed after all. And it was, for it was not too high, and it was not too hard. In fact, it was exactly right, and the very next minute Goldilock's head was on the pillow, and her eyes were shut tight.

As Goldilocks slept, the Three Bears came home. They were so tired and so hungry that they went at once to the table to eat up their porridge.

'*Somebody*,' cried Father Bear in his big gruff voice, '*somebody has been tasting my porridge.*'

'*Somebody*,' said Mother Bear in her nice soft voice, '*somebody has been tasting my porridge too.*'

'*And somebody has been at my porridge and eaten it all up,*' squeaked Baby Bear in his wee tiny voice.

And Baby Bear held up his empty bowl to show that it was just as he said. Father Bear looked very angry, and Mother Bear looked very angry too. Baby Bear, however, looked angry and sad. After all, it was his porridge and his breakfast that had disappeared.

'Just come over here,' said Father Bear at last, in his big gruff voice, 'and take a look at my chair. *Somebody has been sitting in my chair.*'

'*Somebody has been sitting in my chair too,*' said Mother Bear in her nice soft voice.

Then Baby Bear in his wee tiny voice squeaked, '*Somebody has been sitting on my chair, and has broken it to pieces.*'

After that it was hardly surprising that the Three Bears began to wonder what they would find if they went upstairs.

'*Somebody has been lying in my bed,*' cried Father Bear in his big gruff voice as soon as they were inside the bedroom.

'*Somebody has been lying in my bed too,*' said Mother Bear in her nice soft voice.

Then it was Baby Bear's turn. 'Come with me and look,' said he, so all the Three Bears went over to his teeny weeny bed to have a look.

Of course, you know WHO was lying there. Goldilocks! Baby Bear's eyes grew big as he stared down at her.

'Somebody has been lying in my bed,' he squeaked in his wee tiny voice, 'and here she is! Here she is!'

The Three Bears knew ALL about everything then. They knew who had eaten the porridge and who had broken the chair and who had upset their beds.

But Goldilocks didn't know that THEY knew because she was still fast asleep, and she went on sleeping.

The Three Bears had very cross looks on their faces as they stood by the bed. They were really very good-hearted bears, but they felt, quite rightly, that they were staring down on a very naughty girl.

Who knows what they might have done if little Goldilocks had not opened her eyes. But she did! And my word, what a fright she got!

What did Goldilocks expect to see, I wonder? Certainly not Three Bears! Out of bed she jumped and away she ran, down the stairs and out of the house, as fast as she could go. After her chased the Three Bears. Perhaps they only wished to tell her that they would forgive her. But Goldilocks didn't wait to find out. She didn't even stop to wave. She just ran and ran, all the way home. And never, never, never did she go into these woods again.

THE GOOSE GIRL

There was once a fair Princess whose mother, an ageing Queen, desired that her daughter should marry the handsome Prince of a neighbouring kingdom.

Before she sent the Princess on her way, the Queen gave her a horse, Falada by name, which could talk, and a small white handkerchief on which were three drops of her own royal blood.

'Keep this handkerchief always,' said the Queen, who loved her only daughter. 'As long as you have it, you will come to no great harm.'

Then the Queen gave her daughter many fine gifts of silver and gold and a box of priceless jewels. 'These gifts are your dowry, child,' she said. 'And, so that you will have company on your journey, one of my serving maids will ride with you.'

Mother and daughter took a fond farewell of each other, and the Princess rode off on Falada, with the maid following behind on a nag of no great merit.

After they had ridden some miles, the gentle Princess asked her maid to dismount and bring her a drink of water from a nearby stream.

To her surprise, the girl tossed her head and refused to dismount. 'If you want a drink so much,' she said, 'you will have to get it yourself. I see no reason why I should serve you.'

The gentle Princess said nothing to these harsh words, but dismounted and went to the stream. As she bent over the clear water, the three drops of blood on her white handkerchief whispered, 'Woe is this; if your mother knew, it would break her heart.'

No words passed between the two girls for the next part of the journey until, once more, the Princess was overcome with thirst. When she spied a glint of water through the trees, she reined in her horse and turned to her serving-maid. 'Please dismount and fill my golden cup with water from that stream by the trees,' she requested.

'I do not choose to be your servant,' replied the girl haughtily. 'If you are thirsty, go to the stream yourself.'

The gentle Princess dismounted and went to the stream. As she bent over to drink, the three drops of blood on her small white handkerchief whispered, 'Woe is this; if your mother knew, it would break her heart.'

The Princess made no answer but, as she leant farther over to drink, the white handkerchief fell from her pocket into the water and sank out of sight.

Seeing what had happened, the serving-maid gave a loud triumphant laugh. 'Now you are completely in my power!' she cried. And she forced her royal mistress to exchange gowns with her. When this was done, the maid mounted Falada and ordered the Princess to ride her own brown nag. 'Unless you give me your solemn promise never to speak to any human being of what has taken place in these woods,' she said, 'I will kill you.'

Terrified, the Princess gave her solemn promise to keep silent, and the two continued on their journey. The next day they arrived at the palace, and the King's son was there to greet his future bride. By his side stood the King himself, a kindly old man with deep blue eyes that missed little.

When the false Princess saw the old King staring at them, she said haughtily, 'This beggar maid is of no importance. I met her some way back. She is fit only for some simple task.'

'In that case,' said the old King, 'she can help our young goose-boy, Conrad. Guarding geese is not very difficult work.'

As plans for the wedding went ahead, the false Princess had only one fear. She knew that Falada could speak, and she was afraid that the horse might, one day, find the chance to tell the true story.

'I have only one small favour to ask,' she said to the Prince, who was clearly taken by her bold, dark looks, 'see that my horse is destroyed today. He all but threw me on the way here, and is both dangerous and useless.'

The real Princess, when she heard Falada's fate, wept bitter tears. 'Do not bury the head of the horse,' she said to the knacker. 'Instead, under cover of darkness, nail the head to the city arch so that I may see it each time I pass underneath on my way to the fields.'

The knacker accepted the gold piece that the true Princess held out to him, and that night he nailed Falada's head to the archway. In the morning, the real Princess and the goose-boy passed, as usual, underneath the arch, driving their flock of geese before them. 'Ah, Falada,' said the Princess looking up, 'how unhappy I am!' And Falada answered:

> *Alas, young Queen, how ill you fare;*
> *If this your mother knew,*
> *Her heart would break in two.*

Conrad, the goose-boy, looked at his companion in astonishment, but she said nothing.

No sooner had they reached the field than the real Princess let down her long golden hair, which was as fine and beautiful as spun silk. Conrad could not take his eyes off the hair.

'Give me a strand,' he said at last. When the Princess refused, he would have roughly plucked a few of the golden hairs himself, had not the girl suddenly begun singing:

> *Blow, blow, gentle wind, I say;*
> *Blow Conrad's little hat away.*

To his great annoyance, Conrad found his hat lifted off his head and blown down the middle of the field. He gave chase, and while he raced up and down after it, the goose-girl quickly braided her long, shining hair and put it up.

'I will not tend the geese with such as you!' Conrad vowed in a temper. That night he went to the old King and told him everything.

'I must see and hear these strange things for myself,' said the King, and he ordered the goose-boy to behave the next morning in his customary way. When the pair passed through the great, dark gateway, the old King was there, in hiding. He saw the goose-girl glance up at the horse's head, and he heard her say, 'Ah, Falada, how unhappy I am!' And he heard the horse reply:

> *Alas, young Queen, how ill you fare;*
> *If this your mother knew,*
> *Her heart would break in two.*

At a safe distance he followed Conrad and the goose-girl to the meadow. He saw how the girl's hair, when she let

it down, was golden and as fine as spun silk. And when Conrad would have plucked a few strands, he heard her sing:

Blow, blow, gentle wind, I say;
Blow Conrad's little hat away.

And the boy was forced to leave her and chase after his hat.

That night the old King sent for the goose-girl. 'Why do you act so strangely?' he asked her.

'Alas, kind sir,' she cried, 'I dare not tell you, for I have given my solemn promise never to speak of what has befallen me to any human being.'

'Then keep your promise,' said the King. 'But your heart will break if you do not speak. Tell your sorrows to this old iron stove.'

The Princess crept inside the large stove, and the wily old King stood by the pipe so that her words came to him clearly.

'No one in the whole world can help me,' the Princess sobbed. 'Yet I am truly a Queen's daughter, a Princess by royal birth, who must stand aside and watch a cruel and treacherous serving-maid, robed in my own gowns, take my place. I cannot break my solemn word so I must remain forever a goose-girl.'

In the morning the Princess found a gown of shimmering satin laid out in place of her rags—by order of the old King, who now knew the truth. In this gown and with jewels sparkling in her golden hair, the Princess was more beautiful than the sun itself. Presently the aged King came to lead her to the great banqueting hall. She was so dazzling in her beauty that the false Princess did not know her.

'Be seated,' said the King, placing her next to his son. 'Now,' said he to the false Princess, who sat there smiling confidently, 'what would you do to a girl who betrayed her mistress and was ready to steal her mistress's husband?'

'Why, I would have her head cut off,' cried the false Princess, suspecting nothing. 'And,' she added for good measure, 'I would throw it to the dogs.'

'You have spoken well,' said the old King, and he ordered his soldiers to seize the false Princess and take her to the dungeons.

Then he turned to his son. 'This gentle girl, who sits at your side, is the bride to whom you are betrothed,' he announced.

The Prince's heart was filled with joy at these words, for never in his life had he seen anyone as beautiful as the real Princess, whom he had believed to be a goose-girl.

There was no need for the Princess to speak; her shining eyes told him all he wished to know. 'We shall marry tomorrow,' he cried eagerly. And so they did, and were happy together for the rest of their lives.

THE THREE BROTHERS

One day a father called his three sons together. 'I am an old man,' said he, 'with nothing to leave you except this house. I want each of you to go out into the world and learn a trade. On your return I shall decide which of you has learnt the best trade, and leave him the house.'

All three brothers had set their hearts on inheriting the house, and each made up his mind to become a master at his chosen trade. The eldest son decided to become a blacksmith, the second son thought he would become a barber, and the youngest said that he would be a fencing master.

The brothers took a fond farewell of their father and went out into the world to learn their trades. They were lucky to find skilled teachers. The eldest son was soon one of the best blacksmiths in the country and had the honour of shoeing the King's horses. The second son became a skilled barber and cut the hair of the greatest nobles in the land. The third son soon mastered the art of fencing and was the victor in every duel.

When the time came for the brothers to return home and show their father what they could do, each of them was certain that he would win the house.

Their father greeted them affectionately. Turning to his eldest son, he begged him to prove himself.

'Let us go into the road,' said the eldest son, who had become a blacksmith. 'My chance will come.'

No sooner were they standing by the roadside than a coach drawn by two prancing black horses came rumbling past. The blacksmith ran after the coach, took all four shoes off the hooves of one of the galloping horses, and replaced them with four new shoes.

'Remarkable!' exclaimed his father. 'Now let us see what my second son can do.' As he spoke, a hare came running towards them across the fields. The second son, who was the barber, worked up a lather in his basin and, as the hare dashed past, he soaped and shaved off its whiskers with the speed of lightning.

'You are truly a master at your trade,' said the old man. 'I cannot say which of you should have the house. But let us see what the youngest of my sons can do.'

At that moment rain began to fall. 'Do not seek shelter,' said the youngest son, who was the fencing master. 'My sword will keep you dry.' And with that he began to flay the air with his sword. So quickly did his sword flash that not a drop of rain touched them even though it began to fall in torrents.

The old man stared in amazement. Never in his life had he seen such sword play. 'This is the most remarkable deed of all,' he said at last. 'You have won the house.'

Shortly after this the old man died, but the three brothers had grown to love and respect each other so much that they stayed together, plying their trades. And so skilled were they, in their different ways, that they became very rich. They lived to be a great age, and when they died, each within a day of the other, they shared the same grave, for even in death they wished to be together.

ALADDIN AND HIS WONDERFUL LAMP

Once upon a time there was a little boy called Aladdin who lived in faraway China. Instead of working hard after his father died, Aladdin spent all his time playing in the street. That was where the tall stranger found him.

This stranger was really an African Magician with great powers, and although Aladdin did not know this he was frightened when the man took hold of him.

'Is it not true that you are the son of Mustapha, the tailor?' asked the stranger.

'Yes,' said Aladdin, 'but my father has died and there

is nobody at home to look after my mother except me. I'm afraid we are very poor.'

'Alas,' said the stranger, 'your father was my own dear brother. Take this gold to your mother and tell her I will come and see her.'

'Is this another of your stories?' his mother cried when Aladdin told her what had happened. But the very next day the Magician appeared at their house and brought with him more gold and many presents.

Soon Aladdin and his mother came to think of the Magician as their friend.

'After I have bought you new clothes,' said the Magician, 'I will take you to a beautiful place outside the city.'

So Aladdin and the Magician set out together. On the way, the Magician promised Aladdin that he should have a shop of his own and want for nothing.

On and on they walked until at last they entered a strange, lonely valley. Giant twisted trees barred their way, and Aladdin grew afraid.

'Uncle! Where are you taking me?' he whispered, but the Magician pushed him on.

'Now, boy,' said the Magician at last, 'rest here while I show you something of my magic powers. But first, gather some sticks, for I would make a fire.'

Aladdin did as he was told, and soon the wood began to smoke and crackle. Then the Magician threw some strong-smelling perfume into the flames and muttered some strange-sounding words.

Just as Aladdin had made up his mind to run away, there appeared at his feet a heavy block of stone. 'Lift it by the brass ring,' commanded the Magician, 'and repeat the names of your father and grandfather.'

Poor Aladdin! How he wished he were a thousand miles away, but he could only obey. When he saw the deep darkness that lay beneath the stone, he cried out in fear.

'Down you go,' said the Magician. 'Take this ring; it will keep you from all harm. Gather what treasures you will, but bring me back the little old lamp from inside the cave.'

Down, down Aladdin went until at last he came upon wonderful gardens where the trees were hung with shimmering jewelled fruits, red, green, and silver, and nearby were vast halls, all richly decorated.

'Why, there's an emperor's fortune here!' Aladdin gasped as he filled his pockets with the brilliant fruit.

How old and dusty the lamp seemed when at last he found it. He hid it inside the folds of his silken tunic. Then he began his climb to the top.

'The lamp—give me the lamp!' cried the Magician when Aladdin came in sight.

'Help me up first, and then I will give you the lamp,' said Aladdin.

'No, no, the lamp! Give me the lamp,' snarled the Magician.

And when Aladdin still refused, the Magician, with a cry of rage, crashed down the stone blocking the entrance to the cave.

Two whole days passed. Aladdin was nearly fainting away from lack of food until, by chance, he rubbed the ring that the Magician had given him. Suddenly there stood before him a genie of immense size.

'I am your slave, the slave of the ring!' he said.

'The slave of the ring!' Aladdin repeated in disbelief. 'Then I command you to take me from this place.'

In a flash, Aladdin found himself outside the cavern. He was free! With a shout of joy, he began to run, and he kept on running until at last he came to his own street. 'Mother! Mother!' he cried as he saw her waiting by the door. 'Dry your tears; your son has come back to you.'

Once inside, Aladdin emptied his pockets and showed his mother all the wonderful, shining jewels in the shapes of fruit. Last of all he brought out the old, dusty lamp.

How they talked, these two, all night long!

'There is nothing in the house to eat, my son,' said his

mother when morning came, 'but perhaps today I will be lucky and sell my weaving.'

'Let us try selling the old lamp,' said Aladdin.

'Very well,' said his mother, 'but first I will clean it, for then it will fetch a better price.'

But lo and behold, with the very first rub from her duster, there appeared before them a gigantic genie!

'I am the slave of the lamp,' said the genie, 'and yours to command.' He was so enormously tall and strong, this genie, that Aladdin and his mother felt like dwarfs as they gazed up at him. 'Bring us something to eat,' said Aladdin, in a brave voice.

Never in all his life had Aladdin set eyes on such a feast. Why, the gold plate alone was worth an emperor's ransom, and then there was the food—the choicest fruits, and the deliciously flavoured dishes of rice, meat-balls, and fish.

'Come now, Mother, eat,' said Aladdin when the genie had disappeared. 'Don't look so frightened. Our good fortune is assured from this time on.'

But Aladdin's mother would not be comforted. 'Son, I beg you get rid of the lamp in case it is the work of evil spirits,' she wailed.

At this, Aladdin only laughed, saying, 'Don't worry, Mother. Here is enough food for a week or more and, when that is gone, I will sell the gold plates in the market.'

And this is just what he did. With the money, Aladdin not only bought rich food but also spent some on himself; and was forever buying a new robe or sash to wear when he went to the market or played with his friends.

So life went on for five years or more, until Aladdin was grown up enough to think about marriage and making a home for himself and a wife.

It chanced that, one day, Aladdin caught a glimpse of the Emperor's daughter as she was borne through the street in her sedan. Never before in his life had Aladdin gazed upon anyone so lovely. At once he vowed he would make her his bride.

'Mother!' cried Aladdin as soon as he got home, 'I have seen the only girl in the world I wish to marry. She is the Emperor's daughter.'

'You must be out of your mind,' answered his mother. 'You—marry the Princess!'

'Wait and see,' said Aladdin. 'I want you to put on your best kimono and go up to the palace with some of these magic fruits. Tell the Emperor that they are a gift from your son.'

Trembling with fear, Aladdin's mother obeyed, and at the sight of so many precious stones the guards admitted her into the Emperor's presence.

'My son has sent you a small gift,' said Aladdin's mother, dropping to her knees and offering the casket of jewels. The Emperor's eyes lit up greedily, for he had never seen such priceless beauty.

'Your Emperor accepts the gift,' said His Imperial
Majesty.

And Aladdin's mother answered, 'My son begs leave to
marry your daughter . . .'

If the Emperor had not been so taken with the jewels
he would have had her beheaded on the spot. Instead, he
hesitated, and his chief minister whispered, 'Ask for forty
gold basins to be filled to the brim with precious stones such
as these.'

On her return home, Aladdin's mother said, 'The
Emperor took the jewels; now he asks for forty gold basins

filled to the brim with precious stones. Be sensible, my son, and give up this hopeless quest.'

'That I will never do,' said Aladdin, and he got out his lamp and rubbed it. In a matter of minutes a vast procession of slaves, bearing golden basins on their heads, was on its way to the Emperor's palace.

'So rich a man is worthy of my daughter,' declared the Emperor when he saw the vast treasure. And he summoned his ministers to proclaim the wedding.

So Aladdin and the Emperor's daughter were married amid scenes of great splendour.

It seemed that Aladdin's happiness was complete. His Princess was the most beautiful girl in the whole of China; his palace, thanks to the slave of the lamp, was bigger and grander even than the Emperor's; he had the swiftest horses to ride, and an army of servants to command.

In time, Aladdin became loved and respected by the people for his charity to the poor, and he was frequently summoned to attend Councils of State.

One day while Aladdin was away, a bent old beggar with a tray of bright new lamps came to the palace.

'Just listen to him!' cried the Princess to her ladies-in-waiting. 'Here is an old man who has taken leave of his senses, for he is calling out "new lamps for old". I shall give him this dusty old lamp that my husband keeps in his room, and receive a brand new lamp in exchange.'

The old lamp seller was really the wicked Magician in disguise. News of Aladdin's riches had come to him in Africa, and he had set out immediately for China, determined to possess the magic lamp.

Once the lamp was in the Magician's hands, he wasted no time in calling up the genie. 'Take this palace and all inside it to Africa,' he ordered. The genie bowed low, and immediately Aladdin's palace and his Princess were transported to Africa.

Aladdin had little time for despair when he returned and found out what had happened, for he was set upon by

the Emperor's soldiers, who then made him their prisoner.

'Miserable wretch!' screamed the Emperor when Aladdin stood before him. 'What have you done with my child?'

'Give me forty days to find my beloved wife and my palace,' Aladdin said. 'Then punish me by death if you must.'

And so well did he plead that the Emperor let him go.

For four days and four nights Aladdin wandered throughout the province, searching in vain for his Princess. When he had almost given up hope he clasped his hands together in a gesture of despair, and lo and behold, the genie of the ring appeared before him.

'The ring—the ring!' Aladdin shouted. 'I had forgotten the ring, and I was wearing it all the time. I must have accidentally rubbed it.'

'Master, what do you command?' asked the genie.

'Good friend,' said Aladdin, 'restore to me my Princess and my palace.'

'That I cannot do,' said the genie, 'for only the slave of the lamp can do that.'

'Then take me to them,' cried Aladdin. No sooner had he said this than he found himself gazing upon his own palace set amid golden desert sands and waving palm trees.

As he stared at it, he saw his own dear Princess at the window; in less time than it takes to tell, they were in each other's arms.

When the Princess was able to speak, she said, 'I know now how foolish I was to give your lamp away. The Magician takes it with him everywhere.'

'Then we must find some way to get it back,' said Aladdin. 'Tell me, how does he treat you?'

'Like a slave,' she answered tearfully. 'I would not be able to talk to you now, dear husband, if he were at home. But he returns tonight; if he sees you he will kill us both.'

'Like a slave, did you say?' said Aladdin thoughtfully. 'Then tonight, when he returns, you must play your part well. Take this sleeping powder and drop it in his glass of wine before you serve him with it.'

The Princess showed Aladdin a place where he could safely hide inside the palace, and very shortly afterwards the Magician arrived.

That night the Magician was in a merry mood. It pleased him to treat the noble Princess as a slave, and soon he was telling her to pour out his wine. After the first sip or

two of the drugged wine, the Magician fell into a deep sleep.

On seeing this, Aladdin stole from his hiding-place and, drawing his sword, cut off the wicked Magician's head, which was perhaps the wisest thing to do.

Aladdin took the lamp, which he discovered in the Magician's robes, and rubbed it with all his might.

'I am yours to obey,' said the genie of the lamp, appearing before Aladdin.

'Then take us back to China,' ordered Aladdin. 'Let everything be as before.'

Thus it came about that Aladdin and his Princess were able to settle down once again in their fine palace. And there they lived in peace and contentment for the rest of their lives.

As for the wonderful lamp, in Aladdin's time it sat on a red velvet cushion in a glass case guarded by two soldiers. But who knows what happened to it after that? Who has it now, I wonder?

SNOW-WHITE AND ROSE-RED

Once upon a time there was a poor widow who had two daughters named after the two rose trees that stood in her little garden. One of the trees bore a white rose and the other a red.

Snow-White and Rose-Red were just as good as they were pretty and, moreover, they loved one another so well that they were never apart. They kept themselves busy helping their mother, who was growing old and frail.

In the summer they brought their baskets home laden with berries. But when winter came and the snow fell in big, soft flakes, their mother would not let them venture far into the forest.

'Bolt the door,' she would say, 'and pull up your chairs round the fire.'

Then she would put on her glasses and read aloud to her two daughters as they knitted. At their feet their pet lamb would lie peacefully sleeping, and, above their heads, their tame white dove would listen with cocked head.

On one such night, when all was warm and peaceful inside the cottage, there suddenly came a loud knocking at the door.

'Go quickly, Snow-White,' said her mother, 'and see who is there. It may be some poor stranger who is looking for shelter for the night.'

But when Snow-White went to the door and drew the bolt, there was no stranger at the door, but a huge, fat bear who thrust his head forward with the words, 'Let me in, I beg you, for I am half frozen, and your fire looks most welcome.'

'Certainly, let him in, Snow-White,' called her mother. 'The poor beast needs the comfort of our fire.'

But the bear still stood there in the doorway.

'Would you kindly sweep the snow from my back?' he asked. And both Snow-White and her sister did so, gently and carefully. Then the bear, looking pleased and grateful, approached the fire and stretched himself out on the mat.

'You may stay here as long as you wish,' the girls' mother told him, 'and come again whenever you have need of warmth.'

At dawn the bear left the cottage and padded away over the deep snow. That same evening, however, he returned, and Snow-White and Rose-Red played with him and made much of him. After that, the bear made it a habit to visit the cottage as soon as darkness fell.

When spring came and the birds in the trees were singing their welcoming songs, the bear said to Snow-White, 'I must leave you now until the autumn.'

'Where will you go?' Snow-White asked.

'Deep into the forest,' the bear told her, 'where my treasure lies hidden. In the winter, when the ground is hard and frozen over, my treasure is safe. But in the spring there is a wicked dwarf who tries to steal it.'

Snow-White and Rose-Red were sad to see the bear go, for they had come to look upon him as a friend.

'Go into the forest and bring me some dry sticks,' their mother said one morning. 'You will enjoy the forest now that it is green again, and perhaps it will help you to forget the bear.'

As the two children wandered along the moss-covered paths, they suddenly saw in front of them a fallen tree trunk, and the oddest little creature imaginable beside it.

'It's a dwarf,' Snow-White whispered, taking her sister's hand. 'And look, the end of his long white beard is caught in a cleft of the tree.'

'He seems very angry,' Rose-Red whispered back. 'He's jumping about like a cricket.'

The little man, when he saw them, began to scream, 'Why do you stand there like two statues? Why don't you help?'

'How did it happen?' Snow-White asked.

The little man shouted, 'You are just as stupid as you are curious. Never mind how it happened. Just stop staring and help me.'

At this, Snow-White and Rose-Red took hold of the manikin's coat and pulled. No matter how hard they tugged, however, they could not free him. The little man moaned and raged at them in turn.

'Please be patient,' Snow-White said at last. 'I have an idea.'

Taking out a small pair of scissors from her pocket, she snipped off the point of his beard.

The dwarf was free, but he had lost four inches from his beautiful white beard and, instead of being grateful, he scowled fiercely. Gathering up a sack of gold that had been hidden by the long grass, he went on his way without even a 'thank-you'.

The next day Snow-White and Rose-Red went down to the pond behind the cottage. 'Look at that giant grass-hopper leaping about at the very edge of the water!' Snow-White suddenly exclaimed.

'It's that dwarf again!' Rose-Red cried. 'And he has been fishing, for his white beard is all tangled up in his line.'

'And there's a big fish on the end of the line,' smiled Snow-White. 'If he doesn't take care, the fish will pull him into the water.'

This was all too true, for now the dwarf was hanging on to some tall reeds in an effort to save himself. Snow-White tried, in vain, to free the beautiful white beard from the fishing line. Then Rose-Red took out her scissors, and snip, snip, off came another four inches of the dwarf's fine, white beard.

'Fools! Idiots! You have spoilt my appearance!' screamed the dwarf in a terrible rage. And with that, he picked up a sack of pearls that had been hidden in the bushes, and disappeared behind a big stone.

That same day Snow-White and Rose-Red were passing through the forest on their way to the village to do some shopping for their mother.

'I wonder why that eagle is flying round and round,' Snow-White said as the big brown bird swooped over their heads.

'He must be after something,' said Rose-Red. Then they saw with horror that the eagle was attacking their irritable old friend, the dwarf, who was trapped under a stone.

'Help me! Help me!' the little man screamed when he saw them, for by this time the eagle had taken firm hold of his jerkin.

The two sisters rushed forward and grasped the little man firmly by the arms. The big bird did not easily give up, however, and the struggle went on and on until finally, with a harsh cry, the eagle flew off without its prey.

No sooner had the dwarf recovered from his fright than he began to shout, 'Fools, idiots, look at my jacket! You have torn the sleeves out of it. Why couldn't you be more careful?' And then, without a word of thanks, he threw a sack of diamonds, which had been hidden behind a rock, over his shoulder and disappeared into a nearby cave.

The sun was shining in the blue sky as Snow-White and Rose-Red made their way back through the green forest. How surprised they were to come suddenly upon the dwarf again.

Thinking that he was all alone, he had spread out on the ground all the precious, sparkling stones from his sack. As they both stood there, wide-eyed at the wonderful sight, the dwarf looked up and saw them. 'Why do you stand there staring?' he snapped. 'Haven't you anything better to do? Be off with you!'

He made such a noise with his screaming and shouting that he failed to see the big brown bear—until it was too late.

'Spare me! Spare me, Lord Bear!' squeaked the dwarf as the bear picked him up in his broad paw and held him fast. 'Take all my treasures, even these precious stones; only spare my life. What does a bear want with a miserable creature like myself? Why not take these children here? They will make a tasty dinner.'

But the bear, without even bothering to reply, threw the little dwarf on the ground with a deadly blow.

Snow-White and Rose-Red clung to each other, eyes shut tight. They did not recognise the bear as their old friend of the winter until he turned to them, saying in a gentle voice, 'You are quite safe, Snow-White and Rose-Red. Open your eyes. Have you forgotten your friend of the long winter nights?'

When they opened their eyes they saw, not a bear, but a tall, handsome young man robed in a cloak of gold.

'This wicked dwarf bewitched me,' the young man told them. 'And after stealing many of my treasures condemned me to wander the forest in the shape of a bear. Only by his death am I delivered and able to recover my fortune.'

All three excitedly hurried back to the cottage, where

the young man told Snow-White's mother that he was truly a King's son. 'For many months,' he said, 'I have loved Snow-White with all my heart.'

Snow-White and the Prince were married. Rose-Red married his brother, whom she met at the palace. And there they all lived happily for many years.

Their widowed mother made her home in the palace too. From her window she could see the two rose trees, one red and one white, that she had brought with her. To her joy they flowered even more beautifully in the royal gardens than they had done beside the cottage.

THE LITTLE TIN SOLDIER

Once upon a time there was a little boy who was given the most wonderful present for his birthday. This was a box of tin soldiers. There were no less than twenty-five soldiers in the box, and they were all brothers. They had been made, you see, from the same old large tin spoon.

'What a marvellous present!' cried the boy as he took the soldiers out of their box. 'How fine they look!'

Then, as he set out his tin soldiers, the boy saw that one of the soldiers had only one leg.

'But he can stand as firmly as the others,' said he, 'so I will leave him here beside the castle.'

The castle was made of cardboard; in front of it was a shining lake with swans on it and a row of neat green trees. What matter that the lake was really a mirror and the swans were wax! It was a pretty scene.

In the eyes of the one-legged tin soldier, however, the prettiest thing of all was the dancing girl who stood, balanced on one leg, at the castle gates. She was also cut out of cardboard, but her dress was of a most wonderful softness, and there was a shining golden star at her waist.

'How beautiful she is,' sighed the tin soldier. 'She is just the wife for me.'

Then he thought that perhaps she, too, had lost a leg, for he did not know that, being a dancer, she could balance on one foot. And he grew even more fond of her.

'I cannot ask her to be my wife,' the tin soldier said to himself. 'She lives in a castle; I have only a box. But perhaps I can get to know her.'

And with that he took up a position behind a funny old tobacco jar and a snuff box. From where he stood, stiff and straight, he had a very good view of the dancing lady.

When it was time for bed, his brothers were put back in the box, but the little tin soldier was not visible, and so he was left behind on the table.

Now that the house was silent, the toys began to enjoy themselves. The jack-in-the-box sprang up and down, the nutcrackers jigged all round the castle, and the conjurer did tricks and made sly remarks about the other toys.

In fact, the only two who did not move from their positions were the dancing lady and the little tin soldier.

'Tin soldier! Tin soldier,' cried the saucy conjurer, 'why don't you keep your eyes to yourself?'

In the morning the boy found the tin soldier still standing stiff and straight, and he put him up on the window ledge.

Suddenly, without warning, the window flew open, and down fell the tin soldier, head first.

Down, down, down he dropped, spinning round and round as he fell.

The boy rushed downstairs and out into the street to search for the tin soldier; he did not want to lose one of the set.

The little tin soldier could have called out, 'Here I am!' But he did not. 'Soldiers in uniform never cry out,' he thought, and he stayed very still and quiet.

At last the boy went indoors again, sad because he had only twenty-four tin soldiers left to play with.

'How big and lonely the world is out here,' the tin soldier said to himself after the boy had gone. 'How tiny I must be.'

Though he was afraid he did not show it. Nor did he move. Then it began to rain, and soon his smart red and blue uniform was shinier than ever with the splashes of rain.

As soon as the rain stopped, along came two ragged little boys. They spotted the tin soldier at once.

'Look!' cried one. 'There's a tin soldier. Let's give him a sail.'

And they made a paper boat out of an old sheet of newspaper and put the soldier in it.

The brave tin soldier did not blink an eye, but he wondered to himself what would happen next as the boat sped along. And he wished—yes, he wished with all his heart—that the lovely dancing girl might be beside him. For then, he felt, he would mind nothing at all.

The boat tossed from side to side as it rushed along. Then it started going round and round in circles before it finally shot into a long, dark tunnel of water.

This made the soldier feel quite seasick, but he still stood stiff and straight. And he kept both eyes to the front, in the manner of all good soldiers.

The water tunnel was a drain that ran under the road. It happened to be the home of several fierce water-rats.

As soon as they spied the little soldier in his paper boat they wanted to know about him.

'Stop there! Stop!' they ordered harshly.

'We want to see your passport! Show us your passport!' the biggest of the water-rats demanded.

'But I have no passport,' said the tin soldier, and how glad he was when the current carried him out of reach of their long, sharp teeth.

The dark water swept him along, faster and faster.

'My goodness me . . .!' the little tin soldier thought to himself. 'Whatever is going to happen next?'

He saw ahead of him a patch of light. There was a loud, rushing noise, and the boat was whirled into the deep waters of the canal.

The brave soldier held himself as straight as he could, but his boat was sinking underneath him. Soon he was up to his chin-strap in water.

'Never again shall I see my sweet lady of the castle,' he told himself when the boat began to fall apart. 'Nothing can save me now!' he cried as he saw the gaping mouth of a huge fish waiting to receive him.

Oh, but how black it was inside that fish! And how airless it was! But never for a moment did the brave soldier try to make life more comfortable. He held himself as stiff as though he had been on guard duty.

After a few moments the fish began leaping this way and that, thrashing the water with its tail, for it was caught on a hook. Soon it lost its strength to fight any more.

'Ah!' cried the old fisherman as he began to pull strongly on his line. 'I've caught a fish of some size here. This is going to please the wife.'

'I'll take it to the market right away,' said his wife at the sight of the fish. 'It will fetch a good price.'

And now here comes the oddest part of the story of the little tin soldier. The fish was bought by the cook who worked in the little boy's house. As soon as she began cutting up the fish she struck something hard inside.

'Come quickly,' she called to the little boy. 'Here is a very strange thing!' And she pulled out the one-legged tin soldier.

'It's mine! It's mine!' cried the little boy joyfully. He began to clap his hands with delight at having found his tin soldier again.

The boy put his long-lost soldier on the shelf above the fire so that he would dry quickly. And from there the soldier saw all his old friends. How his heart thudded when his eyes fell upon the pretty dancing girl!

'She is just as beautiful as I remember her,' he told himself as he stared down at her. 'Why, it is just as though I had never been away.' And he fixed his eyes upon her in a loving gaze.

Stiff and straight stood the soldier. His heart beat all the faster when he saw that the dancing lady was looking at him.

'She remembers! She remembers!' he told himself. And he felt proud, in a humble kind of way, that he had been through so many adventures.

He thought of his twenty-four brothers in their box and he was thankful he was not shut away in the box with them.

The next day some school-friends came to see the little boy, and one of them took hold of the brave little tin soldier and threw him into the fire. Nobody knew why.

Shortly afterwards the door blew open and the draught lifted the pretty dancing lady right off her feet. It tossed her into the golden flames—straight into the arms of the brave, faithful tin soldier, who was slowly melting. And they burned together, in a blaze of golden light.

In the morning the little boy looked at the empty grate where, last night, the big fire had been.

Sadly he picked up a lump of tin in the shape of a heart. It was all that was left of his tin soldier. And then he saw beside it a golden star, blackened with ash. It was all that was left of his pretty dancing lady.

What do you think he did then? Why, he buried them together in the garden, amid the flowers.

THE EMPEROR'S NEW CLOTHES

Once upon a time there lived an Emperor who loved clothes so much that he spent all his money on them. In fact, he could think of nothing else all day long.

His palace stood in the heart of a busy city, and men from many countries came to visit him.

One day two strangers arrived who quickly learned about the Emperor and his fondness for new clothes. These two men were neither good nor honest, and they saw a way in which they could deceive the Emperor and gain great wealth for themselves.

They called themselves master weavers, saying that they had the power to weave the most beautiful material in the world. They talked about the colour and the pattern of this wonderful material, adding that if anyone who gazed upon it was by nature a fool, he would not see it.

Very soon the Emperor came to hear of the two weavers, and he said, 'I must have a robe made of this extraordinary material. It will surely be the finest in the whole of the country. And it will also enable me to tell in a flash which of my ministers are fools.'

The Emperor sent a message to the two rogues to come to the palace and take his measurements so that they could begin weaving at once.

The two false weavers immediately demanded a large

sum of money which the Emperor paid. They set up their looms in a room in the palace, and pretended to spin. But not a single thread did they put on their bobbins.

After a time the Emperor, who could think of nothing else but the magnificent new robes being woven for him, decided that he must find out how far the weavers had progressed.

'I shall send one of my most trusted ministers,' he said to himself, for he did not like openly to admit that the magical power of this splendid material rather frightened him.

When his oldest and most honest minister stood before him, the Emperor said, 'All your life you have served me with great intelligence and wisdom. You will be able to judge how wonderful this cloth is when you see it. Go now to the weavers and then report back to me.'

But when the wise old minister entered the room where the two imposters sat before their looms, his eyes opened wide with astonishment, for it seemed to him the looms were empty.

'Good gracious me! I can't see a thing!' he said to himself, and he rubbed his eyes and went up to the loom.

'That's right,' said one of the weavers. 'Take a good look and judge for yourself the true magnificence of these wonderful colours and the beauty of the pattern.'

The old man rubbed his eyes for a second time. He saw nothing, nothing at all, for the very good reason that there was nothing to see! 'Well now,' he thought, 'I have been carrying out my duties for the last twenty years with wisdom and skill, but can it be that I am a fool after all? No! No! I shall never dare tell the Emperor that I cannot see this wonderful material.'

As he stood there, one of the rogues asked, 'Well, what do you think of it?' And the minister replied in a friendly approving voice, 'It seems very handsome to me. Indeed, the pattern is magnificent and the colours most delicate. I shall tell the Emperor that I am well satisfied with your progress.'

After the old minister had gone, the rogues sent a message that they required more gold to buy silk, and

this was sent the next day; but all the money went into their own pockets.

The following week, the Emperor sent another of his faithful ministers of state to enquire how the weaving was getting on.

'Is this not the most wonderful material?' exclaimed one of the rascals as the minister gazed down on the looms. 'You have arrived in time to watch a length being completed.'

'I'm sure I'm not a stupid man,' the second minister was thinking while they talked. 'And yet I cannot see this material. If I tell him this, the Emperor will take me for a fool and I shall end up by losing my position.'

And so he too praised the cloth, and when he returned to the Emperor he told him that it was beautiful beyond description.

The time came when the Emperor, longing for his new robe, could not keep away from the two weavers. And so, accompanied by his courtiers, and with his trusted minister at his side, he went to the room that had been given over to the spinners.

'Truly,' cried the old minister, staring at the looms, 'never in my life have I seen cloth like this . . .'

The Emperor blinked. He did not rub his eyes, because Emperors never rub their eyes. But the fact is, he saw nothing! Nothing at all! 'Am I a fool?' he asked himself. 'For if I am, I have no right to be Emperor. I could not bear the disgrace of losing my throne.' And so, like the others, he began to exclaim, 'This material is indeed magnificent! You will find that I am not slow to reward you for your great skill.'

As the Emperor finished speaking the members of his court in attendance joined him with a chorus of praise.

The Emperor announced that he would wear his new robes in the great public procession that was to take place in a few days' time.

The night before the procession the two imposters

pretended that they were now ready to take the cloth off the looms. This done, they made cutting movements in the air with a huge pair of scissors. Then they sat down crosslegged, as tailors do, and began to sew with a needle that had no thread in it.

When they stood before the Emperor the next morning, they raised their arms as if they were holding up a garment. 'We have your robes here, Imperial Highness,' they said. 'They are as light as cobwebs. Will you try on your fine new clothes so that we may satisfy ourselves that they fit perfectly?'

The Emperor undressed, and the two rogues pretended to hand him one garment after the other. As he stood before the long mirror, the Emperor turned this way and that. His mind was confused; he felt deeply uneasy, for it seemed to him that he had nothing on at all. But he said aloud, 'Very becoming! The richness of this material is amazing . . .'

'I am ready now,' he said to the master of ceremonies, who came to tell him the procession was formed. And the master of ceremonies praised the Emperor's new clothes in a voice so loud that it made the Emperor feel much better.

Slowly and proudly he walked down the royal stairway and into the courtyard. As a fanfare of trumpets sounded he took his place at the head of the long procession— under a canopy bearing the imperial coat of arms in silver and gold.

'How splendid our Emperor looks in his new clothes!' the crowd shouted.

And with an imperial wave of his imperial hand the Emperor saluted his cheering subjects. With every step he grew more confident until, suddenly, a child's shrill voice was heard above the cheers.

'Look Mummy! Our Emperor has no clothes on!'

'The boy is right,' some of the crowd began to whisper, and the whisper grew to a roar that soon reached the Emperor's ears.

Perhaps, in his heart of hearts, the Emperor had known the truth all along, but men act foolishly out of vanity and pride. Now there was nothing he could do, but being an Emperor he walked on with stately steps.

THE WHITE CAT

There was once a King whose three sons were all splendidly brave. The King loved them well enough but had no wish to give up his kingdom to them before he was ready. He therefore decided to give them a test that would send them out into the world.

'I want you, within a year, to find me a little dog,' he told them when they stood before him. 'And I declare that whoever finds me the best-looking and most attractive dog will inherit my kingdom on my death.'

The three brave Princes were surprised at their father's wish but they did not show their feelings. They left the castle, and the two elder brothers set out for a distant country, hoping to find a dog that would be pleasing to their father.

The youngest Prince, however, as soon as he had left the capital, began buying dogs. He bought spaniels and greyhounds, lapdogs and bulldogs, until he had so many dogs that he was forced to give them away as he went along the road.

'There is nothing special about any of these dogs,' the young Prince told himself. 'I will start again.' And he gave away the last of his dogs, a spaniel.

The Prince was now far from home. When the sun set

he took a path that led him into a deep forest. As rain began to fall he saw ahead of him a most wonderful castle whose light came from the thousands of jewels that studded its walls.

As the Prince pushed open the castle's golden gates he was conscious of twelve hands that took hold of him gently and pushed him forward. The hands led him into a room so magnificent and so richly furnished that the Prince could only gasp with astonishment. And presently the same hands took away his wet and travel-stained jerkin and dressed him in a robe of finest brocade.

In this room was a table laid for two with gold knives and forks. In a little while a number of cats entered the room, each one carrying a musical instrument. They took their positions and began to scrape the violin and guitar strings with their claws. The Prince had scarcely recovered from this astonishing sight when the most beautiful white cat he had ever seen entered the room and came towards him.

'My handsome Prince,' she said in a soft purring voice that went straight to the young man's heart, 'I welcome

you to my castle. I would like you to stay here as my guest for a long time.'

The White Cat took her place beside the Prince, and a meal was served that consisted of pigeons and mice. The Prince ate the pigeons and the white cat ate the mice. Afterwards the Prince was given wine to drink so that he would forget his past.

For a whole year the young Prince and the white cat lived together in the castle.

On summer days the White Cat gave the Prince a wooden horse to ride. It galloped without tiring through the forest. For his amusement, the cat orchestra played their strange music each evening.

The twelve hands waited upon him as if they were his slaves, combing his long black curls and serving him in every way.

When the year was up the young Prince suddenly remembered his quest and was distressed and downcast. 'I know why you are sad,' said the White Cat in her gentle voice. 'In a few days' time your two brothers will be presenting themselves to your father, the King. Each will have a dog. You too can have a dog. Take this acorn. It contains a dog more attractive than you can imagine.'

'Dear Princess Cat,' cried the young man, 'do not mock me! How can this acorn contain a dog?'

'Put the acorn to your ear,' said the cat.

The Prince did as she requested, and it seemed to him that he heard a whispered bark, which thrilled him. Placing the acorn in his pocket, he mounted the wooden horse, which the White Cat promised would take him safely to his father's palace, and galloped away.

When the three sons presented themselves before the King, the King looked at his youngest and said, 'You have no dog. I take it that you have failed in your quest to find one.'

'That is not so!' exclaimed the youth. And he brought the acorn out of his pocket. He opened it and the King saw,

lying on a tiny leaf-bed, the smallest dog imaginable. The King and the court were silent in their amazement as the little dog, whose long-haired coat was the colours of the rainbow, jumped from the acorn and ran freely about the floor.

The eldest son had a lapdog and the second had a greyhound, but neither of the dogs could compare with this marvellous acorn-dog. And both brothers admitted as much.

The King, however, could not accept the fact that his kingdom must pass to the youngest son, and so he said, 'I have one more quest for you to undertake. You must each find a girl and bring her here in a year's time. Whoever finds the most beautiful maiden shall marry her and inherit my kingdom.'

The youngest son went back to the White Cat and told her what he had to do. 'I will help you,' she said. 'Stay here with me, and we shall make merry until the end of the year.'

The months passed quickly until, at last, the time came when the Prince was obliged to return to his father's palace. 'I will help you,' said the White Cat, 'to take back the most beautiful Princess in the world. You must cut off my head and my tail and cast them into this fire.'

Horrified, the young Prince refused over and over again to do such a dreadful thing to his beloved white cat. But the white cat begged him so earnestly to obey her that at last he drew his sword and cut off her head and her tail and cast them into the fire.

At once there stood before him the most beautiful girl he had ever seen in his life. And all around him the cats had become fair maidens.

'I was born a Princess,' the White Cat told him, 'but my mother, the Queen, fell into the power of some evil dwarfs. To save me, one of the fairies of our court turned me into

a white cat, and all the maidens who attended my mother were likewise changed into cats.'

As the lovely Princess talked on, the Prince, who had already been half in love with the white cat, now fell completely in love with the Princess.

'I will take you back with me to my father's kingdom,' cried the Prince at last. 'My father will not be able to deny your beauty.'

Hand in hand they left the castle where, in the courtyard, stood a glittering coach drawn by six prancing white horses whose hooves were studded with precious stones.

When the King's castle came in sight, the Princess drew the curtains and changed herself once more into the white cat. Then she entered a box, inlaid with mother-of-pearl and rubies.

'Present me thus to your father, the King,' said the Princess before the Prince closed the lid.

The King received his three sons with affection. 'Your maidens are indeed beautiful,' he said, gazing at the two young girls who stood beside his elder sons. 'It will be difficult to choose between them.'

'I too have brought you something,' said the youngest Prince. 'A soft little white cat with velvet paws.' Amid the amused smiles of the lords and ladies of the court he placed the bejewelled box open at his father's feet.

Suddenly there was a flash of light so brilliant that the King's eyes were dazzled, and out of the box stepped the young Princess, a crown of white roses in her long golden hair.

'My dear,' said the King when he had recovered his wits, 'you are brighter than the sun. I must give my kingdom to my youngest son.'

With a deep curtsey the young Princess replied, 'Not so, Your Majesty. For my father has six kingdoms over which he rules. When I marry your son, they shall all be his.'

So it was settled. The King's elder sons married the maidens they had found on their travels, and the King gave each of them half his kingdom. The youngest son married his beautiful Princess, and they went off together after a festive wedding the like of which had never before been seen.

As for the King, he retired to the country in company with his tiny acorn-dog, and what with taking it for walks and caring for his small estate he lived to a ripe old age.

THE THREE WISHES

There was once upon a time a hard-working woodcutter who was quite desperately poor. Moreover, he had a wife with a nagging tongue that went clickety-clack.

At last the woodcutter, in his unhappiness, wished that he were dead, for it seemed to him that not a single dream of his had ever come true. Now it happened that his deep despair reached the ears of the great God of Thunder, whose name was Jupiter.

That same day, just as the woodcutter was about to fell one of the forest trees, Jupiter appeared before him. The woodcutter, in his fright, dropped to his knees and begged for mercy.

'I have not come to punish you,' said the Thunder God. 'I have come to grant you three wishes. As your happiness depends on them, think carefully before you make them.'

'Indeed I will,' whispered the woodcutter. Whereupon Jupiter vanished.

Trembling with excitement, the woodcutter ran home to his wife. Before she had time to reproach him for leaving work, the woodcutter told her his wonderful news.

'Think of it, wife!' he cried. 'Three wishes! Why, we can be rich! You'll wear diamonds and rubies in your hair!'

'Hold fast, John,' said his wife when at last she understood. 'We must not make these wishes rashly. We must take time to think about them.'

'You are right, of course,' said the woodcutter. 'Bring out our last flagon of wine and let us have a drink.'

'And you make up the fire, husband,' said his wife, and she smiled at him. 'It will be like our courting days.'

So husband and wife, for the first time in many a long year, settled themselves comfortably before the fire.

'Ah,' said John as he sipped the wine, 'this is very pleasant. I wish we had some sausages to go with the wine...'

Hardly were the words out of his mouth than a long string of sausages came into the room, snake-like from the corner of the chimney. The woodcutter's wife, who had the sharper wits of the two, saw at once what had happened.

'Fool, donkey, imbecile!' she screamed. 'You have wasted one of our three wishes. You talked about diamonds and rubies, but you wished for sausages...'

'Not so fast, wife,' said John, scratching his head. 'It was the wine, surely. It dulled my brain, I do declare. Well, don't go on so. We have two of the wishes left...'

But his wife, almost beside herself with rage, did go on. She sat there in the chair facing him and screamed at him, 'Donkey, donkey! You have the brains of a donkey...'

The poor woodcutter, feeling sorry enough for himself as it was, could scarcely be expected to put up with his wife's harsh words for long. He grew red in the face, his eyes blazed, and he finally shouted, 'Hold your tongue, woman! Will nothing stop your nagging? I wish that one of these sausages was stuck to the end of your nose. Then maybe you wouldn't open your mouth so wide.'

Alas, no sooner had the woodcutter made this second wish than it was instantly granted. The first sausage in the link fixed itself to the end of his wife's nose.

The poor woman was beside herself; never a beauty at any time, the sausage dangling from her nose made her look both ridiculous and ugly, and tears began to roll down her cheeks.

'Well,' said John at last. 'Here's a pretty kettle of fish. It's up to you, wife. What do you want? Will you have the rubies and diamonds and stay as you are? Or do I make my third and last wish to remove that sausage?'

'I cannot go through life like this,' sobbed his wife. 'Make your third wish, husband, and rid me of this horrible sausage.'

'Very well,' said John, and he made his wish.

So the woodcutter never did become rich. For the rest of his days he remained a woodcutter, and a poor one at that. As for his wife, her tongue went clickety-clack in much the same way as it had always done. But now she was grateful to her husband for just one thing—that he had not left her with a fat sausage fixed to the end of her nose.

THE GOLDEN BIRD

Long ago, when the world was young, there lived a King who had a golden apple tree. This tree stood in the gardens behind the palace and was the King's most treasured possession.

As soon as the tree bore fruit, its golden apples were counted and their number reported back to the King. One morning, however, servants came to the King with the dreadful news that one of the precious apples was missing.

'A watch must be kept!' cried the King, greatly upset.

'And I shall be the one to keep it,' insisted the eldest of his three sons.

So that night, the eldest son went into the garden, but as twelve o'clock struck he yawned and closed his eyes, being unable to keep awake.

In the morning another golden apple was missing, and the King's eldest son had to confess that he had fallen asleep.

'Let me guard the tree tonight,' said the second son. 'I shall not fail to keep awake.' But the same fate overcame the second son. When twelve o'clock struck he yawned, closed his eyes, and fell fast asleep.

In the morning another golden apple was gone.

The youngest of the King's three sons then stepped forward and asked if he might be allowed to watch.

The King thought little of his youngest son, for he was, by nature, rather slow and gentle. 'You won't do any better than your brothers,' said the King harshly.

But the young prince pleaded so hard that at length the King gave his consent. And the following night the third son went into the garden. Twelve o'clock struck and the young prince was still awake. Presently, to his surprise, he saw a golden bird swoop on to the tree and take one of the golden apples in its beak. The young man shot at the bird with his bow and arrow. The arrow struck the bird as it flew off, and one of its golden feathers fell at the young man's feet.

When the King saw the golden feather he called a meeting of his council, at which it was agreed that the single golden feather was worth half his kingdom. 'In that case,' declared the King, 'I will not rest content until I have the bird itself.'

'And I will be the one to find it and bring it back to you,' said the eldest son, who thought a great deal of himself and his cleverness.

He set out that same day, and after walking some miles

came to a dark wood. The only living creature he saw was a fox, and immediately he raised his gun.

'Don't shoot!' cried the fox. 'I know you and I know what you seek. If you spare my life I shall tell you how to find the golden bird. Pass through this wood and you will come to a village. There you will see two inns— one brightly lit and noisy with merrymaking, the other small and dim. Choose the latter in which to spend the night . . .'

The King's eldest son laughed scornfully at this piece

of advice; he raised his gun and pulled the trigger. But the fox, with tail outstretched, dived into the bushes and vanished.

By nightfall the eldest son had reached the village. He saw the two inns and, without hesitation, entered the one that was brightly lit. There was so much merry talk and pleasant company that the King's eldest son forgot all about his search for the golden bird and decided to stay there as long as his money lasted.

The King waited in vain for news of his eldest son, and after some weeks sent out his second son to find the golden bird. At the edge of the dark wood, the second son also came upon the fox and would have shot him on sight if the animal had not spoken.

'I know you and I know what you seek,' cried the fox. And then he gave him exactly the same piece of advice as he had given his brother. But the second son was not in the habit of accepting advice; certainly not from a fox.

When he reached the two inns, his brother called to him from the window of the bright, noisy inn, and, without a moment's thought, he plunged inside. There he spent the night in merrymaking, and in the morning he too had forgotten all about the golden bird.

Several months passed before the King gave up hope of ever seeing his two sons again. 'Let me go and find the golden bird,' pleaded the youngest son, but the King had so little faith in him that he refused. However, the lad gave him no peace, and at last he let him go.

The fox was there by the edge of the wood when the youngest son appeared. 'Spare my life,' said the fox. 'I know you and I know what you seek . . .'

The youngest son laughed merrily. 'Why,' said he, 'I wouldn't shoot you even if I had a gun to do it with . . .'

'Then listen to me,' said the beast. 'And I will tell you how to find the golden bird. When you come to the village you will see two inns—one brightly lit and noisy with merrymaking, the other small and shabby with darkened windows. Choose the shabby one in which to spend the night . . .'

'I will do just that!' said the young man smiling. 'And thank you for your good advice.'

'I'll do more for you than give you good advice,' said the fox. 'Seat yourself on my tail and I'll take you to the village myself.'

Scarcely had the young man obeyed than the fox flew like the wind, over tuffet and stone, until they reached the village.

'I'll leave you now,' said the animal. 'Remember what I said.'

'I will,' answered the young man, and, without even glancing at the brightly lit inn, he entered the small shabby inn and there spent a quiet night.

Early the next morning he set out again and presently came upon the fox. 'I will help you again,' said the beast. 'This road will take you straight to the castle. This is the castle where the golden bird is kept. You must pass the regiment of soldiers that guards the castle. Go through all the rooms until you come to the last. There you will find the golden bird in a wooden cage. Pay no attention to the golden cage that hangs beside it . . . if you do, matters will not go well for you. Now remember . . .' Then the fox stretched out his tail. 'Seat yourself on my tail and I'll take you within sight of the castle . . .'

Away they went like the wind, over tuffet and stone, until the castle came in sight. The young man thanked the fox and went up to the castle where he passed swiftly through the regiment of sleeping soldiers.

Inside the castle he quickly found the room where the golden bird was kept. It was all just as the fox had said it would be. But, as the young man lifted down the wooden cage that held the bird, his eyes fell upon the empty golden cage.

'What a splendid cage!' he said to himself. 'It is a pity to leave it behind. Besides, the golden bird is too beautiful for this old wooden cage.' And with that he opened the front door of the wooden cage and grasped the bird. At the touch of his hand, the golden bird gave out a loud shrill whistle that roused the whole castle.

Soldiers came running from every direction; they fell upon the young prince and took him prisoner. In the morning he was brought before the King of that country, whose court of judges pronounced on him the sentence of death.

'So it shall be,' said the King, 'unless you can bring me the golden horse that runs faster than the wind. Do this, and not only will you gain your freedom, but I will give you the golden bird in exchange for the golden horse.'

The young man accepted the challenge, but he sighed deeply as he set off down the road. He had gone some distance when whom should he see by the roadside but his old friend, the fox!

'Your misfortune was your own doing,' said the fox, 'but I will help you just the same.' And he stretched out his tail. 'Seat yourself on my tail and I will take you to the castle where the golden horse is kept.'

Gratefully, the King's son seated himself on the tail, and away they went like the wind, over tuffet and stone, until the castle came in sight.

'The grooms will be asleep in front of the stable that holds the golden horse,' said the fox. 'You can lead the golden horse past them without fear of disturbing them. In the stable you will see two saddles, one of ordinary brown leather, the other of gold. Saddle the horse with the leather one. Do not touch the gold saddle or matters will not go well with you.'

Just as the beast had foretold, the prince passed by the sleeping grooms into the stable where the golden horse

stood. But when he saw the two saddles, the young man
thought, 'Such a magnificent animal should have a
magnificent saddle. I'll saddle him with this golden one.'

No sooner had he done so than the horse gave out such
a loud neigh that the grooms came rushing into the stable.
They took hold of the King's son and threw him in prison.

The Lord of the castle passed a sentence of death on
the young man in the morning—'Unless,' said he, 'you
can bring me back the beautiful Princess who lives in
the golden castle a hundred leagues from here . . . If you
do this, I shall not only give you your life but the golden
horse as well.'

To his relief, the young man had travelled but a few
miles when he came upon the fox. 'You do not deserve
my help,' said the animal crossly. 'But I cannot leave you
to your fate. Seat yourself on my tail and I will take you
within sight of the golden castle where the beautiful
Princess lives.'

Away they went like the wind, over tuffet and stone,
until the golden castle came in sight.

'Wait until it is dark,' said the fox. 'When the castle sleeps the beautiful Princess will leave her room and walk in the garden. Take her in your arms and kiss her. She will go with you then. But first she will plead with you to let her bid her parents farewell. You must refuse her this favour—otherwise matters will not go well with you.'

Just as the creature had foretold, the young man found the Princess in the garden. He held her and kissed her and she went with him quietly. But as they reached the gates she began to weep softly, saying, 'Spare me just one moment

186

to kiss my parents farewell.' The young Prince shook his head, but the beautiful Princess continued to plead, falling at his feet.

'Very well,' said he at last. 'I can see no harm in it.'

No sooner had the Princess bent over her father than the King awoke, and his shouts roused the whole castle. The young man was then taken prisoner and cast into a deep dungeon. In the morning the King sent for him, saying, 'Today you must die—unless you can level the tall hill that blocks the view from my bedroom window. You have eight days. If you succeed you will gain your life and my daughter's hand in marriage.' Now the King said this because, in his heart, he knew that he had given the young man a hopeless task.

And hopeless it seemed to the Prince as, with spade and shovel, he attacked the hill. On the seventh day, the hill was as tall as it had been on the first day. Throwing down his spade, he buried his head in his hands. When he looked up, there was his old friend, the fox, beside him.

'I don't know why I bother about you,' said the fox. 'Your present misfortune is all your own fault, but I cannot see you die. Go to sleep now, and I will take care of this hill myself.'

In the morning, when the Prince awoke, the hill was no more! Shouting for joy, he rushed into the King's presence with the glad news. Having given his word, the King had no choice but to hand over his daughter, the beautiful Princess, to the young man.

Together they left the golden castle and presently came upon the fox sitting by the roadside. 'So far so good,' said the creature. 'Now I will tell you how to obtain the golden horse and still keep the beautiful Princess. When you come to the castle of the golden horse, the Lord of the castle will gladly give you the horse in exchange for the Princess.'

'That is so,' said the Prince. 'But I do not wish to leave my future bride behind.'

'No need,' said the fox, a trifle impatiently. 'Shake hands all round as soon as you have mounted the golden horse. But shake the hand of the Princess last of all. As soon as you take hold of her hand, pull her up into the saddle beside you and gallop away. There is no horse in the world as fleet of foot as the golden horse.'

This time the young man did exactly what he had been told, and the plan succeeded beyond his dreams. When they were safely out of reach of the castle, the fox came out of the bushes by the roadside and the Prince drew rein.

'Now,' said the fox, 'I will tell you how to get the golden bird. Leave the Princess in my care and ride on to the castle of the golden bird. They will gladly bring out the bird and give it to you in exchange for the golden horse. As soon as you have the cage in your hands, gallop away. There is no horse in the world able to catch you up.'

All worked out according to plan. The King's youngest son gained possession of the golden bird and returned to the fox and his Princess.

'Now,' said the fox, 'I will claim my reward. When you reach the wood, kill me with your hunting knife, and then cut off my head and feet.'

The Prince shrank away from the fox in horror. 'That I could never bring myself to do,' he cried in dismay.

'Very well,' said the fox sadly. 'But one further word of advice. Whatever you do, be sure never to sit on the edge of a well.' And with that he vanished into the woods.

The Prince with his treasures set out for home. When he came to the village of the inns, he learned that two wicked men were due to be hanged that very day, and recognised them as his two brothers. 'I will buy their freedom,' said the Prince, and the bargain was struck.

His two elder brothers pretended to be grateful, and their younger brother gladly consented to eat with them once they were in the woods.

'Sit down on the edge of this well,' said the eldest, 'while we prepare the meal.' No sooner had he done so

than the second brother pushed him backwards into the well.

In high delight the wicked brothers took possession of the beautiful Princess, the golden horse, and the golden bird, and made their way back to their father's palace.

The King loaded his two sons with honours and scarcely seemed able to recall that he had ever had a third son. His only fear was for his treasures, for the golden horse would not eat, the golden bird would not sing, and the beautiful Princess wept all day long.

Meanwhile the King's third son was not dead. Having fallen on soft moss, he suffered no injury at all, but the well was so deep that he could not climb out. After many attempts, he was just about to give himself up as lost when his trusted old friend, the fox, joined him in the well. 'You forgot my advice,' said he, 'and you do not deserve my help. But I cannot see you perish. Take hold of my tail and I will pull you up.'

When the King's youngest son was safely out of the well, the fox said, 'Now listen to me carefully. If your brothers find out that you live, they will kill you. You must disguise yourself as a beggar and enter the palace.'

This the young man did, and no sooner was he within the palace walls than the golden horse began to eat, the golden bird began to sing, and the beautiful Princess left off her weeping and went to the King. 'I am happy again,' she told him, 'because somewhere inside this palace my true love waits for me.' Then she told the whole story.

The King sent for all the people inside his palace, and when the Princess saw the tall young man in beggar's rags, she fell upon his neck and kissed him.

The King recognised his youngest son, and he ordered the execution of the two wicked brothers. The other son shortly afterwards married the beautiful Princess, and all was happiness inside the palace.

One day, some time after the wedding, the Prince found himself in the wood where he had first come upon the fox.

And to his joy—there was the animal again.

'Is there a favour I can grant you?' asked the Prince.

'There is,' said the fox. 'Kill me now and cut off my head and feet. It is the only favour I ask.'

The Prince hesitated for a long time, but at last he did as he was asked. Scarcely had he done so than the fox changed into a man.

'Your beautiful Princess is my own dear sister,' said he. 'I thought never to see her again—not in my human form, for when I tried to protect her from a wicked sorcerer I was changed into a fox.'

'Come and live with us in the palace,' cried the Prince. 'Everything I have is yours . . .'

And so it was arranged, and matters went very well for the King's son for as long as he lived.

FIVE PEAS IN A POD

There were once five peas in a pod. They looked the same and they thought the same, each one telling the other that the whole world was green.

To begin with, the pod seemed quite big enough to hold them, but in the summer sunshine the peas began to grow, and the pod was soon uncomfortably small for them. Furthermore, they were no longer green but yellow, which upset them quite a bit.

'We really must consider what is going to happen to us next,' said the fattest of the peas.

'Something will—soon,' said the smallest pea.

And something did! That same day a little boy took the pod in his hand and pressed it open. Pop! The five peas rolled out into his hand.

'Good!' cried the little boy. 'Now I have five round peas for my new peashooter.' And he aimed the first of his peas at the sun.

The second pea followed his brother, but the third and fourth peas ended up in the gutter. To his dismay, the fifth pea found himself in a crack in the wood beneath an attic window.

By this window was a bed, and in it lay a little girl who was so ill that her poor mother feared she would die.

Every day the mother went out to work to earn a little money. And all through the hot summer and the cold winter the girl lay in bed, too weak to get up. Her mother was in despair. 'If only she had something to live for,' she would say.

After the cold winter came the first warm days of spring, and suddenly there was something that caught the child's interest. 'It's green,' she told her mother, 'and it's right under my window.'

'Why, it's a tiny pea-plant,' said her mother in surprise when she went to look.

'Now I have a pea-garden all to myself,' whispered the daughter, and for the first time for a whole year her eyes were bright as she tried to sit up.

'Let me move your bed closer to the window,' said her mother. 'You must be able to watch your little garden grow.'

And when this was done, the mother tied the slender plant to a stick so that it could stretch upwards to the sun.

'How pretty it is,' cried the little girl. 'What fun it is to watch. I am sure it will grow and grow...'

In the warm sunshine of the summer months that followed, the little pea-plant, from the last of the peas in the pod, continued to climb upwards. Then, one glorious day, it burst into flower.

'Look, Mother!' cried the little girl when her mother returned from work that day. 'My pea-plant has got a lovely pink flower.' And in her pleasure and excitement the little girl got out of bed. 'How well I feel!' she cried again. 'I feel that I have grown strong just watching my little pea-plant grow strong.'

Tears of joy and gratitude filled the mother's eyes as she watched her little girl walk, all by herself, to the window and gently kiss the pea-plant's pink petals.

The little pea-plant's heart swelled with pride. 'Two of my brothers went to the sun,' he said to himself, 'and two grew fat rolling in the gutter. But none of them made a sick child well again.'

THE WILD SWANS

You won't know this land where the widowed King and his eleven sons and one daughter, Elisa, lived. But the swallows do, because they fly there each winter.

The eleven Princes were royal indeed! When they went to school they each carried a silver sword and wore a shining star decoration on their velvet tunics. In the classroom they wrote with diamond pencils on slates of gold, and they could recite long pieces of poetry by heart in a most wonderful way.

As for little Princess Elisa, she had a crystal stool to sit on and glorious picture books and jewelled toys that were worth a king's ransom.

No wonder they were happy, but alas, their happiness did not go on forever. The King, who had been both father and mother to them for as long as they could remember, decided to marry again, and he chose for his second wife a woman who had no love for his children.

On the wedding day there was a great feast in the castle. But the new Queen would not permit her step-children to eat any of the good things prepared. Instead, she had them served with weak tea and sand, declaring that they could just pretend they were enjoying themselves.

And very soon after that she said that the young Princess Elisa must leave the palace.

'Let the peasants in the country bring her up,' she said. 'I want none of her here.'

Then it was the turn of the eleven Princes. Using all her dreadful powers, the evil Queen set about persuading the King that his sons were not worth troubling about, and in time he came to believe that this was true.

When the right moment came, the Queen called them together and cried, 'Go out into the world and manage for yourselves. Fly away like great voiceless birds.'

But the wicked Queen could not harm the brothers as much as she would have liked, for at her words they changed into eleven beautiful wild swans and, with a strange cry, rose above the palace and flew away over the forest.

And what of Princess Elisa? Alone in a miserable cottage and watched over by an old peasant woman, Elisa had nothing to play with except a green leaf. Sometimes she would look through the hole she had made in it, and the sun would dazzle her so that she imagined it was the shining eyes of her lost brothers. The sun's warm caress on her cheeks would make her think it was her brothers' kisses.

But by now her swan brothers were far away, their strong wings taking them right across the world. They stopped only when they reached a vast dark forest that stretched as far as the sea.

Elisa grew more and more lovely with the passing years. The wind stirred the pretty rose hedge in front of the cottage and whispered to it, 'Is there anything more lovely in the whole world than you?' The rose hedge would answer, 'Little Elisa!'

On Sundays, as the old peasant woman sat outside turning the pages of her prayer book, the wind would flutter the pages and whisper, 'Is there anything more holy than you?'

The prayer book would reply, 'Little Elisa!'

The rose hedge and the prayer book told the truth, for Elisa was just as good as she was beautiful.

Far away in the palace, the wicked Queen suddenly had the desire to see Elisa, and so she commanded her presence at the castle.

Elisa was fifteen at this time, and so lovely that the Queen, when she saw her, would have changed her there and then into a wild swan and sent her away. This she dared not do, for the King was expecting to see his only daughter.

Instead, she hid her jealous rage. 'You shall see your father, the King, tomorrow,' she told Elisa in honey-sweet tones.

Long before Elisa was awake, the Queen hurried to her bathroom, which had walls of the finest marble and a bath the colour of the sea. Into this bathroom she took three toads and, dropping a kiss on each of them, said to the first, 'When Elisa comes to bathe, jump on her head so that she may become as stupid as you are.'

And to the second she said, 'Cling to her forehead so that she may become as ugly as you; then her father, the King, will not know who she is.'

And to the third she whispered, 'Secrete yourself in her heart so that she may become mean and spiteful and hateful to herself.'

She threw the three toads into the clear bath water, which instantly changed to a dull green, and waited for the Princess to appear.

Elisa did not seem to notice the toads as she stepped into the bath, but, as she left the water, her stepmother saw three red poppies floating on the surface. Her wicked plot had failed; Elisa's goodness had overcome the evil toads.

The Queen, in a fiendish rage, grasped hold of Elisa and began to rub her with walnut juice that stained her skin quite black. She spread an evil-smelling ointment all over the girl's face and tangled her hair, so that none, not even her own father, would know her. 'Now go to your father!' she screamed, and pushed her into the royal chamber.

The King was horrified when Elisa stood before him. 'This cannot be my daughter,' he cried. 'Send her away!'

Only the old watchdog at the gate and the swallows in the trees saw Elisa leave the palace. They knew her, but who would believe what they had to say?

Sobbing bitterly, Elisa stumbled on her way. Across fields and marshes, through woods and valleys she went, until at last she reached the heart of a dark deep forest. When she could walk no farther, she lay down on the soft green moss.

All was silent about her; the air was softly sweet, and the glow-worms were tiny twinkling stars in the moss and grass. Elisa closed her eyes, and soon she was sound asleep. As she slept she began to dream. She saw her brothers; they were writing with their diamond pencils on golden slates. Elisa showed them her books, which were worth the price of half her father's kingdom.

In the morning when she awoke, Elisa remembered her dream and was no longer afraid. 'I must find my brothers,' she told herself. 'They will protect me . . .' And she set off once again. As she walked along, the birds sang to her from the treetops, and the warm sun comforted her.

Presently Elisa came to a lake that was so smooth it was like a mirror. As she gazed into its clear waters, Elisa caught sight of her own reflection and gave a frightened cry. Surely this black ugly face could not be hers! Quickly she dipped her hands into the water and rubbed her cheeks clean of the walnut stain. Then she pulled off her ragged dress and plunged into the lake.

After her bathe, Elisa was more lovely than ever before. She dressed and carefully braided her long shining hair before setting out once again through the forest.

As she wandered on, the sky grew overcast, and soon the sun disappeared. How dark and lonely it was! Elisa ate some berries and drank from a small stream, and then she lay down on the grass and closed her eyes. As she slept, it seemed to her that a beautiful lady came to her. Without

speaking, the lady gazed down on her with gentle eyes, and Elisa stretched out her arms to her.

When she awoke, the young Princess remembered her dream, and with fresh hope in her heart set off once more. She had only gone a little way when she saw coming towards her an old woman carrying a basket of fruit. 'Take this apple, child,' said the old woman as she came up to her. 'You look tired and hungry.'

Elisa accepted the apple gratefully. Then she said, 'Tell me, old woman, have you seen eleven young Princes on horseback riding through this forest?'

'No,' replied the old woman, 'but I have seen eleven wild swans with golden crowns on their heads swimming on the lake. I saw them yesterday. Come, I will show you where this lake is. It is not far from here.'

And she took Elisa's hand and led her to a gently sloping hill at the bottom of which flowed a silver stream. The banks were heavy with trees whose branches drooped over the water, casting long thin shadows.

'Follow the stream, child,' the old woman said, 'and you will come to the lake.'

Elisa thanked the old woman, and walked along beside the winding stream. Soon she heard the sound of falling water, and then saw how the stream cascaded into a lake of immense size. So wide and deep it was that she gasped in amazement at the sight of it.

'This must be the sea,' she told herself at last, and yet there was no sign of a ship or sail.

As she stood there on the shore, Elisa saw how the water had fashioned pebbles out of the differently coloured stones, making them round and smooth, and she marvelled at the strength of the sea and at its patience.

And as she watched, the gentle waves lapped about her feet, and the pebbles rolled gently back and forward, and suddenly the Princess understood that the sea was trying to teach her a lesson.

'These little stones,' she told herself, 'are being polished and shaped by the patience of the sea and by their willingness to obey the touch of its ever-moving waves. I, too, must be patient and willing to go on, for now my heart tells me that this vast sea will one day carry me to my brothers.'

She saw at her feet, among the brown slippery seaweed, eleven white swans' feathers. The water on them glistened like tears as Elisa gathered them up and gazed at them.

The sea was her friend now; it had given her a present. As she stood there, the sky darkened and grew heavy with cloud, but the waves still danced, foam-flecked.

'Tell me about my brothers!' Elisa asked them.

But they did not answer her.

Just as the sun was setting, Elisa saw eleven wild swans with golden crowns on their heads flying across the sky. They flew one behind the other so that they looked like a broad white ribbon above the sea.

'They must not see me,' she told herself. 'I must find somewhere to hide.' And she left the shore and ran quickly uphill so that she might hide behind a bush.

As Elisa watched, she saw the swans glide gently to earth, and then as the sun finally dipped behind the horizon, she gave a glad cry.

The swans were no longer swans, but her own dear long-lost brothers!

Joyfully she ran down the hill, flinging herself into

their arms, and joyfully her brothers welcomed her, laughing and crying by turns in their sudden happiness.

'How much you have grown!'

'How pretty you are!'

'What lovely hair!'

Each one of them had something kind to say about their sister. Then they told their stories, and Elisa learnt how her cruel stepmother had changed her brothers into birds.

'We fly,' the eldest told her, 'as long as the sun shines in the sky. But when it sets our feathers drop off and we become our true selves again. That is why we must always seek some lonely shore as sunset approaches.'

'This place is not our home,' the youngest brother said. 'We live in a land far more beautiful than this beyond the sea, but the way to it is long and dangerous.'

'There is a single rock that rises starkly out of the sea,' said the second brother, 'and on this we must rest as soon as the sun sets; otherwise we should fall out of the sky in our human shape and be drowned.'

'Yes, that is so,' said the third brother, 'and there is scarcely room for all of us on this rock. When the sea is rough the waves sweep over it and over us—yet it is there

we must pass the night, no matter how wild, as humans.'

Elisa listened, her eyes round with pity and understanding.

'When do you take this great journey across the sea?' she asked.

'We must wait for the two longest days,' her eldest brother told her, 'for we may only return to our own land once a year for eleven days. That is why we are with you now.'

'What a joy it is for us!' cried the youngest brother, 'to glimpse again the castle where once we were children together And to see the church, where our own dear mother is buried, and to watch the wild horses run free in the meadows as we did when we were boys. All this we have already seen as we flew high over the land of our father, the King.'

'And now you have found me!' Elisa exclaimed. 'But surely it will soon be time for you to return.'

'That is so,' they told her.

'Then you must take me back with you, dear brothers. I want to be with you wherever you are. Take me to this strange land, I beg you.'

'That we cannot do,' said the eldest brother sadly. 'You cannot fly and we have no boat or ship at our command. Remember that when the sun rises, we change into swans again.'

'Oh! If only I could free you from the wicked curse that holds you,' Elisa said sadly.

But though they talked far into the night, they could think of no way to break the wicked Queen's power over them.

At last they lay down to rest, and Elisa held her youngest brother's hand until sleep came.

When she awoke, it was to the sound of great wings beating the air above her. The sun had risen and her brothers, changed once more into swans, were flying away—all except one, the youngest, who had chosen to spend his last day with his beautiful sister.

Tenderly Elisa stroked his white wings, and softly they whispered together as the hours passed. When night fell, once again the air was filled with the sound of beating wings, and the ten brothers returned. Then, with the setting of the sun, they became young men, tall and handsome and clad in princely robes.

'We have talked among ourselves,' the eldest brother told her. 'We are agreed that we cannot leave you here, Elisa, but are you brave enough to trust your life to us?'

'Yes, yes,' Elisa cried. 'I will go with you to the end of the world. I will brave every danger if only you will take me with you.'

'Very well,' said the second brother, 'this is what we shall do. We shall weave a net tonight. It will be strong and supple, made from the bark of the willows and the stems of the reeds. In this way we shall carry you with us over the mighty ocean.'

'Yes, yes,' agreed Elisa, her eyes shining. 'I know I shall be safe.'

There was no sleep for the brothers that night. Instead, they worked hard, weaving a net that would hold their beloved sister as they flew over the forests and the sea.

It was finished just before the sun's first rays warmed the sea, and they had only time to place their sister in the net before they were swans again. Then four of the brothers took the corners of the net in their beaks and carried it between them as they flew high into the clouds. Their little sister felt so safe and happy that very soon she fell fast asleep. And while she slept her youngest brother, with tender care, flew above her so that his wings acted as shade from the hot sun.

When Elisa opened her eyes, the swans were already far out to sea. For a moment she thought she was dreaming. Then, as she looked upwards into the blue sky and far downwards to the shimmering sea, she knew that this was no dream. Beside her in the net was the fruit that her youngest brother had thoughtfully provided for her to eat when she was hungry.

Elisa smiled her thanks, and then fear clutched at her heart, for the sun was suddenly blotted out by a black thundery cloud.

'I am holding you back!' Elisa cried in distress. 'But for me you could have flown twice as far. The sun will set and you will find no land on which to rest. Then you will all fall into the sea and be drowned.'

But the brothers flew on steadily. Beneath them, the wind whipped the waves into great white horses, and thunder rocked the heavens. Elisa clung desperately to her net as one flash of lightning followed the next. She was so frightened now that she could not hold back her tears. But she was afraid, not for herself, but for her brothers.

On and on they flew, sometimes dropping so low out of the sky that they seemed to be skimming the very surface of the boiling sea. At other times they soared upwards into the clouds, out of reach of the hungry waves.

Elisa shut her eyes, ashamed of her tears, and when next she looked she saw something that made her heart leap for joy. It was a rock, no bigger than a brown seal, rising out of the water.

Down, down, down the swans swooped. The sun had all but disappeared when at last they landed there. Elisa stepped out of the net and, as she did so, her brothers changed once more into royal Princes. The rock was so small that they were forced to link arms to prevent themselves from being washed into the sea.

Now the sky was a flaming red as the storm reached the height of its fury and the waves, mountain high, beat upon the rock.

'Do not be afraid, little sister,' the eldest brother said. 'So long as we love each other truly and cling closely together, we shall come to no harm.'

The night passed. With the coming of dawn the storm-waves grew calm, and when the sun came out the brothers changed once again into swans and flew high into the heavens, carrying Elisa in her cradle of reeds and willow bark.

They had been flying for some time when Elisa saw before her a most beautiful country that seemed to float in the air. It was a land of shining glaciers and steep rocks and in the middle towered a huge castle. Beyond this castle were forests of waving palm trees and fields of brilliant flowers, some as big as cartwheels.

'Can this be the country where my brothers are taking me?' Elisa asked herself.

'This land and castle belong to the Fairy Morgana,' one of her brothers told her. 'No human being has ever set foot in the fairy's castle.'

Even while Elisa gazed, the forest and the castle suddenly vanished and, in their place, stood twenty magnificent churches, all exactly alike, with high towers and pointed windows.

Elisa thought she could hear the sweet sound of organ music, but it was only the singing of the waves, and as she gazed, the churches disappeared, to be replaced by ten fine sailing ships.

Seconds later, they too had gone, and Elisa saw only a thick grey mist. She said nothing about all this to her brothers, for, far below, she saw blue mountains where towns and castles nestled. Down, down, down the swans dropped until they came to rest on a rock that stood before a cave.

'Here we shall stay,' the youngest brother said as he led her into the cave. 'Sleep well, little sister. May your dreams be happy.'

'If only I could dream of a way to save you from this wicked curse,' Elisa sighed. 'Then indeed my dreams would be happy.'

When sleep came, Elisa did have a dream. In her dream she was carried through the sky, far away from the cave, to the castle of the Fairy Morgana. There, on the threshhold, the fairy herself came to meet her.

Elisa recognised her at once. She was the same kindly old woman who had given her the apple in the forest, and told her of the wild swans with golden crowns on their heads. Yet the shining creature who stood before her was the most beautiful person she had ever seen.

The fairy held out a nettle to Elisa, saying, in a low sweet voice, 'Elisa, I can help you to free your brothers, but if you are to succeed you will need courage and determination. Look well at this nettle. By the cave where you rest there are many such nettles growing at its entrance, but these nettles have no power to help you. You must search out the nettles that grow over the graves in the cemetery. When you gather them you will find that they blister and burn your skin, but this pain you must endure. When you have gathered sufficient, crush them beneath your feet. The crushed nettles will become green flax from which you must spin eleven long-sleeved tunics. When you throw these tunics over your eleven swan brothers, the wicked spell that binds them will break.'

Elisa smiled with happiness at these words, and the fairy went on, 'Remember that many nettles will be needed. And be warned. No matter how long it takes, you must not utter a single word while you spin the tunics for your brothers. If you utter a single word, it will pierce their hearts and they will die. Their lives are in your hands from the moment you pluck the first nettle.'

As she spoke, the fairy touched Elisa's hand with the nettle and the girl woke up suddenly, thinking she had been scorched by flames. She rose then and ran to the opening of the cave where she saw nettles that reminded

her of her dream. She did not grasp them, however, but
set out for the cemetery where, growing above the graves,
was bed after bed of nettles.

How her hands were blistered and red as, one by one,
she pulled up the nettles and crushed them with her
bare feet. Sometimes the pain was so great that Elisa
wanted to cry, but she did not stop until her brothers
came upon her.

'Elisa! Elisa!' the eldest brother cried. 'What are you
doing? Look at your hands!'

When the youngest brother saw that his little sister
would not speak he began weeping bitter tears.

That night Elisa did not sleep. She went again to the
cemetery, and as she worked the heap of green flax grew
bigger and bigger. For many nights and days Elisa gathered
the stinging nettles until she had enough flax to weave
at least some of the tunics.

While she was spinning in her cave one morning, there
was a sudden blare of a hunting horn. Elisa trembled at
the sound of it, and at the fierce barking of the hounds
that told her the hunt was drawing near. She shrank back
into the shadows as one of the pack came bounding out
of the thicket and into the cave. Minutes later, it was
followed by other dogs, and then by the huntsmen, whose
leader was the King of the country himself.

Never had Elisa looked more beautiful as the King
stood before her.

'Why are you here?' he asked her in a kind voice. But
Elisa could give him no answer, for the lives of her brothers
depended on her silence.

'You are too beautiful to stay here alone,' the King
went on. 'If you are as good as you are beautiful I will
give you half my kingdom and a golden crown to wear
upon that pretty head. You must come back with me now.'
And he took Elisa's hand and led her to his horse.

The day was almost spent before the King drew rein,
and Elisa saw, stretching before her, a wonderful city

of white stone, and in its midst a great castle towering into the sky.

When they reached the castle, the King summoned his serving women and gave Elisa into their care.

'Take her to the royal wardrobe room,' the King ordered, 'and robe her in the softest silks. Put pearls in her hair, and see that she has gloves to cover these poor scratched hands of hers.'

Elisa spoke no words as she allowed herself to be led away, but her eyes filled with tears of despair.

The serving women exclaimed at her good fortune as they dressed her in a rich gown of blue silk and gave her soft white gloves to wear. They placed large glistening pearls in her long hair, and silver slippers on her feet. 'How pretty you look now,' they told her. 'Wait until the King sees you.'

The King showed his pleasure in Elisa's changed

appearance by saying, 'I vow you are the most gracious and beautiful lady in the whole of my kingdom. I will take you for my Queen, for I have lost my heart to you.'

Still Elisa uttered no word, and the King said gently, 'Go to your room now; you will find there the bundle of green flax with which you were busying yourself when first I came upon you in the cave, and the tunics that you did not wish to leave behind.'

Moved by the King's thoughtfulness, Elisa smiled for the first time, but once alone in her room she burst into frantic weeping.

The next day, bells rang throughout the white walled city, and the King and the silent Elisa were married.

Elisa was now Queen, and though she dared not speak, her beautiful eyes told her husband that already she loved him. Despite her new happiness, however, she did not forget her eleven brothers or the wicked spell that held them fast.

Night after night she would steal away to the room that the King laughingly called her 'little cave'. Once there, she would set to work on the tunics until the flax that she had brought with her from the cave was finished.

'I must go to the cemetery for more nettles,' Elisa told herself, 'for I have made only six of the tunics.'

The next night, as the castle slept, Elisa sped silently down the long corridors and out into the scented gardens that glowed silver in the moonlight. When she reached the dark forest she plunged in fearlessly, and presently came to the cemetery. There, to her horror, she saw a dreadful witch with long hooked nose and thin curving fingers seated on one of the gravestones.

For a moment Elisa almost lost courage. But with a silent prayer she turned her back on the witch and bent down to pluck the nettles. They stung and blistered her hands, but Elisa paid no attention to the pain. The witch watched her but spoke no words, and thankfully Elisa ran from the cemetery with her precious bundle.

It so happened that one of the King's powerful ministers saw Elisa enter the castle, and, being jealous of the King's love for her, he set out to do her mischief. 'I tell you, Your Majesty,' said he as soon as he met the King the next morning, 'I saw your wife return secretly to the castle. Only witches walk abroad at night. Ask her why she spins?'

Elisa was silent when her husband came to her with his question, and the King grew more and more suspicious of his gentle wife. When, once again, Elisa had to go to the cemetery, he followed her and saw for himself the ugly witch on the gravestone. 'So she *does* keep company with witches,' he said to himself in deep sadness, and heartbroken he returned to the castle.

'She must be burned at the stake,' the minister urged the next morning. 'We cannot have a witch among us.'

'My people shall be her judges,' the King cried. 'Have her brought forth!'

The King's soldiers dragged poor Elisa from her little room and threw her into a dark prison cell where the wind whistled through the barred windows. She had time only to take with her the heap of flax and the bundle of nettles that she had gathered the night before.

When the soldiers had left her, Elisa took up her work and commenced on the last of the tunics. Towards evening she saw, through the barred windows, a swan's wing. At the sight of it, Elisa began to sob with happiness; the next day she would be burned at the stake as a witch, but now that her brothers had found her, she would see them once again before she died.

One hour before daybreak the brothers, in human form, presented themselves to the castle and asked to see the King.

'That is not possible,' the guards told them. 'His Majesty sleeps, and none of us would dare to wake him.'

But the brothers persisted, refusing to go away, and so much noise did they make that the King himself woke up and came out to the castle gateway to find out what all the noise was about. Alas! The sun rose at the very moment he appeared, and all the King saw were eleven wild swans flying high above his head.

When the time came for Elisa to be brought forth by the soldiers, a great crowd had gathered in the square. They wanted to see the witch being burned at the stake, but the poor King could scarcely bear to look upon his Queen.

Elisa's cheeks were very pale and her lovely long hair covered her face as the King's men piled on the great logs of wood. But Elisa did not see them, for her eyes were on her work, and the crowd laughed and jeered as they saw that she was weaving green flax into a tunic.

One of the other servants ran from the castle and flung at her feet the ten tunics she had already spun. 'Let these burn with her!' he cried. No sooner had he spoken than eleven wild swans swooped down out of the sky. They made a circle round Elisa, flapping their great wings, and at the sight of them the crowd fell back in terror. Before anyone could stop her, Elisa had taken the tunics and flung them, one by one, over the swans.

Immediately the swans changed into eleven handsome

Princes, though the youngest had still a wing instead of an arm, for Elisa had not yet finished the last tunic.

'Now I can speak!' Elisa cried. 'These are my brothers who have been under a wicked spell. I am no witch.'

'It must be true,' the soldiers whispered to each other. 'See how the logs on the fire are changing into roses.' As they murmured among themselves the air was filled with the scent of a thousand roses and the square became a wonderful garden of sweetly perfumed flowers.

'The King! The King! Here comes the King!' the people shouted as the King ran towards his Queen.

'Let all the bells ring out their joyous news!' the King exclaimed, beside himself with happiness. 'Elisa is my true Queen. She will stay forever by my side.'

Then, one by one, the eleven brothers vowed obedience to the King who had taken their sister for his Queen. And Elisa, as she stood by her husband's side, was more beautiful than all the roses at her feet.

THE REAL PRINCESS

Once upon a time a charming young Prince made up his mind to marry.

'The girl I shall wed,' he told his mother the Queen, 'must be a real Princess.' And he left the palace to search the world over for her.

The Prince journeyed many thousands of miles; he met hundreds upon hundreds of pretty girls, many of whom claimed to be real Princesses. But somehow or other he could never be certain, and, at last, he returned home, quite worn out with his travels and very downhearted.

One night, as he sat alone by the window, there was a sudden violent storm of wind and rain, and, in the midst of it all, the Prince heard a loud knocking.

'A young girl claiming to be a Princess begs shelter from the storm,' his servant told him. 'Shall we admit her?'

'Do so at once,' said the Prince, and he sent word of their uninvited guest to his mother.

The old Queen went to see to the girl herself. 'Take off these wet clothes,' she said in a kindly way. 'Poor child, you are soaked to the skin. I will have the servants lay out a fresh gown for you and prepare a room, for you cannot face the storm again.'

'I ask only for shelter,' said the girl. 'Tomorrow morning I shall be gone.' She spoke with an air of importance.

The Queen, who had doubted the girl's story, began, almost in spite of herself, to consider whether this bedraggled creature could possibly be a real Princess after all. 'Well, we shall soon see,' she said to herself.

While the girl was being attended to by one of the servants, the Queen went in secret to the room that was being prepared for her. She placed a single pea on the bedstead and laid twenty mattresses, one on top of the other, over the pea. And not content with this, she placed twenty feather-beds, one on top of the other, over the mattresses.

When the girl had eaten, the Queen showed her the bed on which she was to spend the night, 'I will come to you in the morning,' said she, 'and see how you have slept.'

Early the next morning, the Queen went into the girl's room.

'I trust you had a comfortable night,' she said.

'I'm afraid not,' replied the Princess, 'I tossed and turned the whole night long and sleep would not come. Something small and hard must have found its way into the bed, for I am black and blue all over.'

The old Queen smiled and rushed off to tell her son. 'She *must* be a real Princess,' said she, 'for only a real Princess would have such a tender skin.'

'Indeed yes!' cried the charming young Prince in great delight. 'I'll ask her to marry me this very day.'

So the handsome Prince and the real Princess were married, and the tiny pea was carefully placed on a red velvet cushion in the royal museum so that its story would never be forgotten.

THE THREE LITTLE PIGS

Once upon a time there were three little pigs. They danced and jigged the whole day long, and led a merry life.

One day old mother sow said to them, 'It's high time that you went out into the world to seek your fortunes.'

The little pigs were very pleased when they heard this.

'We shall set out this very day,' they said. And away they went, dancing and skipping.

Presently, as they danced along the road, one pig said to the other, 'We must build a house.'

'We must build three houses,' said the third pig, who was by far the cleverest.

'Yes, let's build three houses,' said his two brothers. 'That way we shall each have a house of our very own.'

As they talked and planned, along came a man with a bundle of straw.

The first little pig took off his cap very politely when he saw the man. 'Please Mister Man,' he said, 'will you give me some of your straw to build a house with?'

'I will,' said the man. 'Here you are.'

Soon the first pig set to work. He began building his

house at once. And he ran up and down with his bundles of straw.

The house grew and grew. Soon there was only the roof to put on, and the window to make, and the door to fix.

At last the straw house was ready, and the first little pig was so happy that he ran in and out of the front door ten times without stopping.

Then he shut the door.

'What a clever pig I am,' he said to himself as he walked round and round his new home. 'I hope my two brothers are as clever as I am.'

He swept and he dusted.

He scrubbed and he polished.

And when he was quite tired out with so much work, he sat down for a rest.

Now the little pig did not know about Wolf, for no one had told him. But there *was* a wolf, and Wolf lived in the woods close by.

Wolf was a big strong ugly fellow with a long nose—so it wasn't surprising that his long nose soon told him that a pig was somewhere near.

He soon found the little straw house, and his long nose soon told him that a fat pink pig was inside it. But by now, of course, the little pig had shut the door of his house and was much too tired to think of going outside.

Just when it was growing dark, Wolf went up to the house. He knocked on the door. 'Little pig, little pig, let me come in,' said Wolf in a soft voice.

But the first little pig was too clever to do that. He had seen the old wolf from his window. So the little pig said, 'No, no, by the hair of my chinny chin chin.'

Then Wolf said, 'I'll huff and I'll puff and I'll blow your house in.' And he huffed and he puffed and he *did* blow the little pig's house in. Of course, the house didn't just fall down all at once. It took quite a long time.

First, some bits of straw blew away.

Then more straw blew away. ·

The roof came off, and the door fell in.

And still that old wolf huffed and puffed.

He huffed and puffed so hard that when at last *all* the house fell in, he had no breath left.

And all this time the first little pig was in a terrible fright. This way and that he ran in an effort to save his house of straw which was tumbling about his two pink ears.

But it's no use clutching at straws, for straws just blow away, as the little pig found out. And so at last, with a loud squeal, the little pig jumped over the last bit of straw and scampered away down the road as fast as his small fat legs would take him.

The old wolf had no puff left to chase the little pig, for he had huffed it all away.

The first little pig ran down the middle of the road, and by the time Wolf had got back some of his puff, the pig had got away.

Meantime, the second little pig had met a man with a bundle of grass and reeds.

The second little pig took off his cap very politely when

he saw the man. 'Please Mister Man,' he said, 'will you give me some of your grass and reeds to build a house?'

'I will,' said the man. 'Here you are.'

So the second little pig set to work. He began building his house just where he was.

The house grew and grew.

Soon there was only the roof to put on, and the window to make. It was a fine house, and the little pig was very proud and happy. He went in and out and round about, singing and whistling as he went.

Just then the first little pig came scampering up, and when he saw his two brothers he pretended that nothing was wrong.

'I think I'll come and live in your house,' said the first little pig to the second little pig. 'I see it has a nice strong front door.'

'Oh no you don't!' said the second little pig, and he went inside and banged his door shut.

'And you can't come with me,' said the third little pig. 'I want to build my house all by myself.' And off he went down the long road.

The first little pig made up his mind to spend all his days having fun.

'I will play in the woods,' he said to himself. 'All I have to do is to keep out of Wolf's way.'

The next day Wolf himself came along the road, and the first thing he saw was the little grass house. His long nose told him clearly that a pig was inside.

'Little pig, little pig, let me come in,' said Wolf in a soft voice, as he knocked on the door.

But the second little pig was too clever to do that. He had seen Wolf from his window, so he said, 'No, no, by the hair of my chinny chin chin.'

Then Wolf said, 'I'll huff and I'll puff and I'll blow your house in.'

And he huffed and he puffed and he *did* blow the little pig's house in.

But it took much longer, for the second little pig had built his house with grass *and* reeds, which made it stronger than a house of straw.

Besides, the old wolf was pretty hungry, and this made him feel weak. He didn't have much puff!

When Wolf found he could not huff and puff away the house at once, he tried huffing and puffing under the door, and the little pig was blown about like a leaf in the wind.

Then the walls fell in, and the pig found himself hurtling through the air. He landed right way up, and this gave him a chance to escape.

Off he ran, down the middle of the long road, as fast as his small fat legs could take him, and by the time the wolf had got some of his puff back, the second little pig was out of sight.

Wolf chased after him. But soon he had to sit down for a rest, and presently he fell asleep.

Meantime, the third little pig had met a man with a load of bricks. The third little pig took off his cap very politely when he saw the man. 'Please Mister Man,' he said, 'give me some of your bricks to build a house.'

'I will,' said the man. 'Here you are.'

So the third little pig set to work. He began to build his house just where he was—which was quite a long way down that long, long road.

He worked hard and he built with great care. He mixed cement and used it to fit his bricks neatly together. He hammered away at his roof, and then put tiles on it to keep out the rain. Last of all, he made a tall strong chimney so that he could have a nice warm fire to sit by.

The third little pig took a long time to build his house of bricks.

His arms ached from pushing his barrow.

He was hungry and thirsty working in the hot sun.

Climbing the ladder to fix the roof made him feel dizzy. But not for one minute did the third little pig give himself a rest.

'My house will be the best and strongest house that was ever built by a pig,' he told himself as he worked on.

And to keep up his spirits, he whistled a merry tune while he worked. And his house grew and grew. And the more it grew, the louder he whistled.

At last his house was ready. The third little pig went inside. He shut his big strong door and he settled down.

He had no sooner picked up his *Piglet Weekly* than there was a knock on the door. It was Wolf.

'Little pig, little pig, let me come in,' said Wolf in a soft voice.

'No, no, by the hair of my chinny chin chin,' said the little pig, and he went on reading.

'Then I'll huff and I'll puff and I'll blow your house in,' said Wolf.

And he *did* huff, and he *did* puff, but that house would *not* blow in. At last, after huffing and puffing and puffing and huffing until he had no puff left, the wolf thought of another plan to get at the third little pig.

'Little pig, little pig,' said the wolf. 'I know where there is a fine field of turnips.'

'Indeed!' said the little pig, who was very fond of turnips.

'Yes,' said the wolf. 'And if you will meet me at six in the morning I will take you there.'

But the little pig got up at five the next morning. He found the turnips for himself and brought the best ones back. Then he shut and bolted his door and sat back to wait for Wolf.

Wolf came along at six o'clock.

'Little pig, little pig,' he called through the keyhole. 'Here I am to take you to that fine field of turnips I told you about. Are you ready?'

When the pig heard this, he put his big stew pot on the fire and built up the flames. Then he sat back and waited. Presently he heard Wolf scrabble on to the roof, and then— there he was coming down the chimney, tail first!

Well, you can guess what happened next. That wicked wolf went tail first into the stew pot.

It was lucky for him that the pot was not quite big enough to hold him, for truth to tell the third little pig had set his heart on wolf stew for dinner.

Instead, Wolf got a very scorched tail and such a fright
that he leapt clean out of the window.

The little pig let him go.

'Goodbye, Wolf,' he called after him, 'for keeps!'

And the little pig was quite right, for the wolf was so
scared he just kept running until he was miles and miles
away from the pig and his stew pan.

And that's not the end of the story, either.

When the third little pig's two silly brothers saw Wolf
running away, they came out of their hiding-places.

'I built my house of straw,' said the first little pig. 'And
the wolf huffed and puffed and blew it down.'

'And I built my house of grass and reeds,' said the
second little pig. 'And the wolf huffed and puffed and
blew it down.'

'And I built my house of bricks,' said their clever brother.
'And there it is—still standing. You had best come and
stay with me.' And so they did—and all three lived happily
ever after.

SNOW-WHITE AND THE SEVEN DWARFS

Once upon a time a Queen sat sewing by her window. Outside, the snow fell gently down. As she sewed she pricked her finger, and three drops of her blood stained the white carpet of snow on the window ledge.

'How I wish I had a little girl whose skin is as white as snow, whose lips are as red as blood, and whose hair is as black as the ebony of my window frame,' she said to herself.

Some time later, the Queen did have a baby girl, and her skin was as white as snow, her lips were as red as blood, and her hair was as black as the window's ebony frame.

The Queen called her Snow-White, but long before Snow-White was grown up, the Queen died and the King married again. This time he chose for his wife someone who was beautiful, but also proud and jealous. Moreover, being half a witch, the new Queen had a magic mirror into which she looked every day.

> *Magic mirror on the wall,*
> *Who is the fairest of us all?*

she would ask it. And the mirror would answer:

> *Thou art the fairest of them all.*

228

But Snow-White was growing up and, with each passing day, becoming more beautiful. One morning, when the Queen asked the mirror to tell her that she was the fairest of all the women in the kingdom, the mirror answered:

> *Oh, Lady Queen, thou still art fair,*
> *But none to Snow-White can compare!*

From that moment, the Queen hated Snow-White and longed to be rid of her.

'Take the child deep into the forest,' she told one of her huntsmen at last, 'and kill her. And so that I may know that you have obeyed my commands, bring me back her heart.'

The huntsman did as he was told, but when the moment came to kill Snow-White he could not bring himself to do it. She was so lovely, and she wept so piteously.

'I will leave you here,' he said, putting away his knife. 'Do not return to the palace, but hide yourself away in the forest.' The kind-hearted huntsman killed a wild animal on the way home, and cut out its heart so that he could deceive the wicked Queen.

Left alone in the forest, Snow-White did not know which way to turn. As it grew dark she began to run, stumbling

over the stones and tearing her dress on the brambles, until suddenly she came upon a pretty little cottage.

'Perhaps there will be someone inside to help me,' she thought as she knocked at the door. When there was no answer, she opened it gently and went inside.

There was a long table in the middle of the room, and on it were seven tiny cups and seven tiny saucers, and along the wall stood seven tiny beds.

'I do feel tired,' Snow-White said to herself, and without more ado, she lay down on one of the beds and fell fast asleep.

The cottage was really the home of the Seven Dwarfs, who were away in the mountains working in the gold and diamond mines. As night fell, they made their way homewards, each one swinging his lighted lantern and thinking of his supper.

How surprised they were when they found Snow-White asleep on one of their beds.

'She is so lovely,' they whispered as they looked at her. 'We must let her sleep until the morning.'

The next morning, the Seven Dwarfs waited round the bed until Snow-White opened her eyes.

'Who are you? Where am I?' she asked in a frightened voice. And quickly and kindly the Seven Dwarfs told her who they were and that this cottage was their home.

'Now you tell us who you are,' they said, 'and what brought you here.'

So Snow-White told them her story, and the Dwarfs immediately invited her to stay with them.

'You can look after the house,' they told her, 'and cook for us and mend our clothes. We need someone like you. Do please stay.'

'I will be pleased to stay with you,' said Snow-White, clapping her hands. 'And I will do my best to take care of you all.'

But sometimes Snow-White was lonely after she had waved goodbye to the Dwarfs, who sang a song and carried their tools on their shoulders as they marched off to the mines.

Meantime, far away in the royal palace, the wicked Queen was quite certain that Snow-White was dead.

> *Magic mirror on the wall,*
> *Who is the fairest of us all?*

she asked hopefully. But the mirror answered:

> *Oh, Lady Queen, thou still art fair,*
> *But none to Snow-White can compare.*
> *Deep within the forest glen*
> *She stays with seven little men.*

The Queen went purple with rage. The mirror, she knew, could only speak the truth, so the huntsman had lied to her. Never again would she put her trust in servants. No, she, the Queen, would kill Snow-White, but first she must set about disguising herself.

She rubbed her face with earth to make it brown, and she dressed herself in an old pedlar-woman's clothes so that Snow-White, when she saw her, would not know her.

Before setting out, she filled her big basket with pretty bows and belts and bright blue ribbons.

She walked a long way through the forest until she came to the cottage of the Seven Dwarfs where, at the window, Snow-White sat mending the Dwarfs' socks.

'Good-day to you, little one,' the Queen called out in a cracked old voice. 'I have laces and ribbons in my basket to show you. Come out and choose one for yourself.'

'I must not open the door,' cried Snow-White as she leaned out of the window, her eyes shining at the sight of all the lovely ribbons. 'You see, my Dwarfs are away working in the mountains, and I have promised them not to leave the cottage.'

'It will take only a minute,' said the old pedlar-woman in a wheedling voice. 'Just one moment to try on these pretty laces.'

Snow-White, thinking to herself that such an old lady could do her no harm, left the window and ran to the door.

The wicked Queen pulled the laces so tightly around Snow-White that the girl could not breathe and fell to the ground. Chuckling to herself, the Queen hurried away, certain that Snow-White would not recover.

That night, when the Dwarfs came back from the mountains, they wept bitterly at the sight of their beloved Snow-White lying still, perhaps lifeless, on the floor.

'Quick,' said one, 'cut these laces; we may still save her.'

The Dwarfs were so relieved when Snow-White began to breathe again. They laid her gently on the bed.

'That old pedlar-woman was really your wicked step-

mother,' they told her as soon as she was well again. 'You must be more careful than ever to keep the door tightly shut.'

Meantime, the Queen had returned to the palace.

> *Magic mirror on the wall,*
> *Who is the fairest of us all?*

she asked. And the mirror told her:

> *Oh, Lady Queen, thou still art fair,*
> *But none to Snow-White can compare.*
> *She stays yet with her little men*
> *Deep within the forest glen.*

At this, the Queen fell into a dark and bitter rage, and vowed to destroy Snow-White in some other way.

Disguising herself once more, she filled her basket with combs and pretty things for the dressing table, but on one of the combs she spread her most deadly poison. Then she set out for the cottage of the Seven Dwarfs.

'I have fine and pretty things to sell,' she cried as she knocked at the door. 'And I have a comb here that is the most beautiful in the world.'

At first Snow-White would not come to the door, but from her window she could see how the comb sparkled in the sun as if it were studded with jewels, and she began to want it so much that she could no longer hold herself back. As she opened the door, the wicked Queen smiled cunningly.

'Here is a comb fit for a princess,' she mumbled. 'Let me show you how to comb that lovely black hair of yours.'

But scarcely had she run the comb through the girl's long black locks than Snow-White fell to the ground, the comb still tangled in her hair. 'Ah, this time I have really killed her,' muttered the Queen. 'She won't trouble me again!'

It so happened that on this day the Dwarfs decided to surprise Snow-White by coming home early. When they found her stretched on the ground as if she were dead, they knew that the wicked step-mother had once again paid her a visit. Quickly they pulled out the poisoned comb, and Snow-White opened her eyes.

'You must promise,' they pleaded, 'that you will never, never open the door while we are away. We cannot always be certain of returning in time to save you.' And once again Snow-White gave her promise.

And once again, far away in the palace, the Queen was asking her mirror who was the fairest in her kingdom. And the mirror answered:

> *You were the fairest to be seen,*
> *But Snow-White in the forest green*
> *Is still more lovely than the Queen.*

At this reply, the Queen trembled with rage and jealousy. Retiring to her secret room at the top of the palace, she began to prepare a poisoned apple. It was the most wonderful-looking apple, and she knew that none would be able to refuse it. She knew, too, that a single bite would be enough to kill.

Satisfied with her work, the Queen disguised herself as an old, cheerful farmer's wife, and set out once more for the cottage of the Seven Dwarfs.

'I dare not let you in,' Snow-White called from the window when she saw her. 'My Seven Dwarfs would never forgive me.'

'But they are such beautiful apples,' the make-believe farmer's wife said in her softest voice. 'And I have one here that will taste as sweet as honey. See how red and crisp it is. Are you afraid to take even one bite of it?'

Snow-White leaned far out of the window and her eyes were bright as she stared at the apple.

'If you are so afraid to taste this harmless fruit,' said the wicked Queen, 'watch me; I shall take a bite, and then you may have the rest.' And while Snow-White watched, she took a bite from the side of the apple—the side that was not poisoned.

Thinking the apple was harmless, Snow-White could not resist the delicious fruit, but no sooner had she sunk her teeth into the rosy-red fruit than she fell senseless to the ground.

The wicked Queen let out a hideous laugh. 'White as snow. Red as blood. Black as ebony. You are truly dead this time, and the Dwarfs can do nothing to save you.'

She turned away and hastened back to the palace. At last the mirror gave her the answer she desired: there was none more beautiful in the kingdom than herself. On hearing this, her jealous heart knew peace again.

What despair there was in the cottage that night when the Seven Dwarfs returned home. There was nothing they could do to bring Snow-White back to life again, and for three days and three nights they wept without ceasing.

'We must bury her,' they said at last.

But instead of putting her in the cold, dark earth, they placed her in a glass coffin so that passers-by might stop and admire her beauty. And each Dwarf took it in turns to mount guard.

Time passed. Snow-White, as lovely as the moment the Dwarfs had first seen her, seemed to lie peacefully asleep, her long black silken hair spread over her shoulders. The Seven Dwarfs stayed faithfully on guard, day and night.

It chanced that a young and handsome Prince came riding through the forest. When he saw the glass case and the lovely Snow-White inside, he fell in love with her instantly.

'Let me take this glass coffin away,' he said to the Dwarfs. 'I will give you any treasure you ask in return.'

'We would not sell this coffin for all the treasure in the world,' replied the Dwarfs.

But the Prince would not accept their answers, saying that if he could not continue to gaze upon Snow-White, he would surely die. At length, the Dwarfs, out of pity, said that he might take the coffin away.

The Prince ordered his servants to carry it on their shoulders and bear it back to his palace. But on the way, the servants stumbled, tilting the coffin. With a sudden jerk, the piece of poisoned apple that was lodged in Snow-White's throat fell from her lips. At once she was alive again.

'Where am I?' she asked as she pushed open the lid; and the Prince, overcome with joy, took her in his arms.

'Do not be afraid. You are safe, and I love you more than

anything in the whole world. Come with me to my father's palace, and we shall be married at once.'

To this, Snow-White could only answer 'yes', for the Prince was the most gentle, most handsome youth she had ever set eyes on.

'But first,' she cried, 'we must tell my dear Seven Dwarfs.'

And so, mounted on the Prince's splendid white horse, they returned to the cottage to say goodbye to the Dwarfs, who could scarcely speak for joy at the sight of them.

Soon it was time to set off for the palace, where they made plans for the wedding. So happy was Snow-White that she even sent an invitation to her wicked step-mother.

> *Magic mirror on the wall,*
> *Who is the fairest of us all?'*

the Queen asked, when her invitation came. And the mirror answered:

> *Thou hast beauty which is fair,*
> *But Snow-White's beauty is more rare.*

At this, the wicked Queen, overcome with jealousy and rage, fell into a fit from which she never recovered.

THE SHEPHERDESS AND THE CHIMNEY SWEEP

Perhaps you have a cupboard somewhere just like the one in this story. It is, of course, very old and very black—black with age, great grandmamma will tell you—and the carvings on it look like flowers which have no names.

The cupboard that I am telling you about was also very old, and it was black with age, and the carvings all over it looked like flowers, flowers which had no names. It had something else besides the flowers—tiny stags' heads out of which sprouted long antlers. And strangest of all, between the antlers of one of these heads, sat a little man.

The children of the house called this little man General Goatylegs because, you understand, he had the feet of a goat, and two little horns that stuck out from his head, and a long beard. He also had a grin; no matter which way you looked at him his mouth stretched into this wide grin. And if you didn't look at him, why then, he took the chance of staring at a round table that stood under a long mirror.

On this table there rested a dear little porcelain Shepherdess. Her hair was as golden as ripe corn; her dress was trimmed with sky-blue ribbon bows and her hat with spring flowers. On her dainty feet were pretty green slippers, and she carried a basket.

What a strange fellow the Shepherdess had for a companion. Can you guess? A little Chimney Sweep also made of porcelain, but black as coal dust and not a bit handsome.

The Shepherdess and the Chimney Sweep had been together on that table for a long time, though they were still quite young. They loved each other and they respected each other, perhaps because they knew that they were both made of the same delicate, fragile porcelain.

Three times as big and also made of porcelain was the old Chinaman who stood a little distance away; he would nod his wise old head whether it was 'yes' or 'no' he meant to say.

The pretty Shepherdess had no way of proving it, but she accepted the old Chinaman's word when he said that he was her grandfather. And more, because of this relationship, she had to do whatever the old Chinaman said.

One terrible day, General Goatylegs asked for the Shepherdess's hand in marriage. He did not ask the Shepherdess herself, but the old Chinaman who claimed to be her grandfather. And the old Chinaman gave a kindly nod, which meant, 'Yes certainly, I am delighted.'

And he was, for he said to the little Shepherdess later that day, 'I have given you to General Goatylegs to be

his wife. He will make you a first-class husband, and you will be known as Madam Major-General-Commander-in-Chief-Goat-Feet, which is his full title. Just think, your home will be inside that splendid cupboard where all the silver is kept.'

'No, no!' cried the little Shepherdess in deep distress. 'I don't want to be shut up inside that dark cupboard. Why, I have heard he has eleven porcelain wives shut up there already.'

'Then you will make the twelfth,' the old Chinaman told her, 'and tonight the wedding takes place.'

And with these words, he nodded his head once and went to sleep.

The pretty little Shepherdess began to cry until she remembered her Chimney Sweep.

'You can help me,' she sobbed. 'You must help me to run away.'

'Of course I will help you,' the little Sweep told her. 'We shall escape together; I have a sound trade and I can take good care of you.'

'But how can we get down from this high table? We have been here so long.'

'I will show you,' said the Sweep. 'It can be very easily managed, and if you watch me carefully you will see just where to place your feet. My ladder will help you too.'

It was a difficult climb for the dainty little lady but at last she was safely on the ground beside her Chimney Sweep.

Just as they were preparing to run out of the room they saw that something very strange was happening to the cupboard. General Goatylegs was jumping up and down in a perfect frenzy of rage and the stags were stretching out their antlers in an alarming way.

'They're running away, they're running away!' General Goatylegs shouted, in the hope of waking up the old Chinaman. 'Stop them, stop them!'

The Shepherdess and the Chimney Sweep grew so

confused and frightened by all the noise that, instead of
running out of the room, they hid in the bottom drawer of
a chest under the window sill.

What strange company they found themselves in, for a
puppet show was taking place when they arrived. And
there were the ladies, diamonds, hearts, clubs, spades,
drawn from several packs of cards, sitting in the front row
fanning themselves with flowers, while behind them sat
the knaves, and they all had two heads, exactly as you see
them on playing cards.

The Shepherdess and the Sweep watched the stage. The
play was all about two young people who loved each other
but were never allowed to marry. This made the Shepherdess
cry so much that the Sweep took her outside again very
quickly.

From the floor they could see the old Chinaman fussing
about on the table above their heads.

The Shepherdess was so frightened at the sight of him
that she dropped to her delicate, porcelain knees.

'Don't give up so easily,' the Sweep whispered. 'I have

an idea. We can hide in that big jar in the corner. We shall be among the roses and the lavender and if the old man sees us we can throw water in his eyes.'

'That jar was once engaged to my grandfather,' the Shepherdess whispered back. 'It was a long time ago but they remain good friends. No, there is nothing left for us but to go out into the wide, wide world.'

'Do you really mean that?' The Chimney Sweep looked at his beloved anxiously. 'The world is wide indeed, and we shall never again be able to return to the places we know.'

'I know,' said the Shepherdess, 'but I do mean it.'

'Well then,' said the Sweep, 'the very best way out into the wide world is by the chimney. Will you be brave enough to climb up through the chimney with the soot all round you? We'll have to climb a long way up until we come to the hole which opens on to the world.'

'Yes,' said the little lady. 'I will follow wherever you go.'

It was dark inside the chimney—so dark that the little Shepherdess cried out in fear, but she followed her loved one bravely, and they went on climbing up and up and up. Every now and then, the Sweep would stop and show her the very best place to put her tiny porcelain feet.

244

What a long, long climb it was! How tired they both were when at last they reached the very top.

'I can see the sky!' cried the Shepherdess. 'And there are the rooftops of all the houses. What a wide, wide world it is! I never believed it could be so big.'

And she put her tiny head on the Sweep's shoulder so that he would not see how fast her tears were falling.

'It is far too big,' she whispered at last. 'I cannot bear it. How nice and safe it was down there on our table beside the mirror. I shall never be happy again until I am back there once more. If you love me truly you will take me back at once.'

In vain, the brave Chimney Sweep tried to reason with her. He reminded her of her stern old grandfather and of General Goatylegs and the black cupboard with the eleven porcelain wives. But his Shepherdess only sobbed the louder, and nothing he said could make her change her mind.

So, at last, they made their weary way back down the dark, steep chimney. What a terrifying journey it was, for climbing down was just as hard as climbing up.

'Let us rest here for a minute,' said the Sweep when they

reached the ledge behind the mantelpiece. 'If we listen hard enough we might hear what is going on inside the room.'

But there was no sound at all. Everything seemed very quiet and peaceful, and at last they both dared to peep through a crack in the wood.

'Look! Look! The Chinaman is on the floor!' exclaimed the Chimney Sweep.

'He must have tripped and fallen down,' cried the Shepherdess in deep distress, 'when he tried to catch us. Oh dear, he is broken in three pieces. It is all my fault. Oh dear!'

And she began wringing her two hands in despair. 'We are to blame,' she cried. 'What shall we do now?'

'We'll go back to our table,' said the Sweep. 'And please don't worry. It is not as serious as you think. Your grandfather can be stuck together again, you know. When they find him they will take some glue and stick his legs on to his body; then they will stick on his head and make it very secure. It has been done before with people like us, you know, and the cracks don't show.'

'Well, if you say so,' said the Shepherdess looking a little happier. 'Then let us get out of this horrible chimney and go back to our table at once.'

So they did just that, and General Goatylegs was grinning much the same as usual when they finally came to rest.

'It was a lot of trouble for nothing,' said the Chimney Sweep at last. 'We are back where we started.'

'I wouldn't mind,' said the Shepherdess, 'if only my grandfather was himself again.'

'They'll fix him soon,' said the Sweep confidently. 'You watch.'

And very soon the old Chinaman was back in his old place, beautifully stuck together with glue so that hardly a crack showed. But there was something different about him. Nobody quite knew *what* until Major-General-

Commander-in-Chief-Goat-Feet started asking once again for the Shepherdess to be his wife.

'You seem very stiff and proud since your accident,' he began the next morning, 'but I must insist you tell me "yes" or "no". Do I marry her or don't I?'

The Shepherdess and her loved one looked anxiously at the Chinaman to see what he would say. Was he going to nod his head and say yes?

But the Chinaman did not nod. He couldn't nod any more because of the glue, and, of course, he was much too proud to admit it. General Goatylegs grew tired of waiting for an answer that never came and gave up asking for the Shepherdess's hand in marriage.

That is why the Shepherdess and the Chimney Sweep are still together and still most blissfully happy. One day they will have an accident and get broken, but that hasn't happened yet. Perhaps, when it does, there will be someone to stick them together again.

Let's hope so.

Perhaps you really do have a cupboard just like the one you have read about in this story. Perhaps—who knows?—there are, somewhere in the shadows, two small dainty ornaments. If they should happen to be a tiny Shepherdess with pretty green slippers, and a small Chimney Sweep as black as coal dust and not a bit handsome—treat them very tenderly. After all, they went through a very exciting and dangerous time together.

THE GOLDEN GOOSE

Once upon a time an honest woodcutter had three sons, one of whom went by the name of Dummling, which is to say Simpleton. There was no doubt that Dummling was well named. Everything he did turned out badly, and his two elder brothers treated him with the utmost scorn.

Sad to say, so did his parents. 'We have a fool for our youngest,' his mother would often sigh, and she would give him the burnt end of the cake or loaf or whatever she happened to be baking at the time.

One day the woodcutter asked his sons to help him cut down a tree in the forest.

'I'll go,' said the eldest son, and he picked up his axe.

'Then take some of this raisin cake and a bottle of wine,' said his mother fussily. 'You'll want something nice to eat after you have cut down the tree for your father.'

Dummling watched his brother stride off into the forest. He knew that none of the family would ever suggest that he do something useful, but Dummling had such a merry nature that he was soon whistling cheerfully.

Meanwhile, the woodcutter's eldest son had reached the tree that was to be cut down. Just before he set to work, he thought he would try the cake and have some wine. He was about to eat when he saw a little grey-bearded man coming towards him.

'Good-day to you,' said the little man. 'It's a long time since I had anything to eat or drink. Will you share your cake and wine with me?'

'That I will not,' said the young man. 'The very idea. If I even give you as much as a bite of this cake—why then it means all the less for me.'

The little grey-bearded man disappeared with never a word in reply. But when the clever woodcutter's son began to hew down the tree, his axe slipped and cut his arm, and he was forced to return home.

'Let me go,' said the woodcutter's second son the next day. 'I will certainly take more care.'

'Very well,' said his father. And his mother said, 'And here is some delicious fruit cake that I baked only this morning. Take it, and this bottle of wine. You'll want something nice to eat after you have cut down the tree for your father.'

The second son picked up his axe and strode off into the forest, and Dummling watched him go, wishing in his heart that his father had given him the chance.

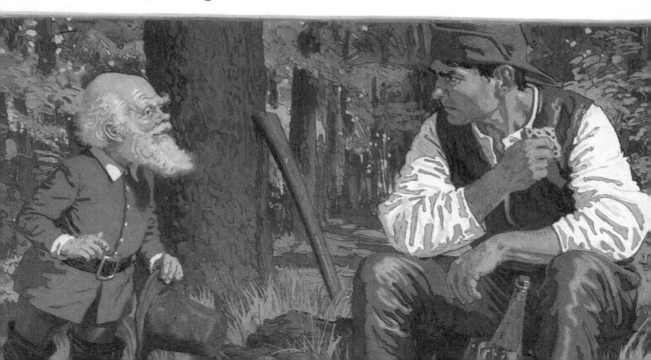

When the second son reached the tree, the same grey-bearded little man appeared. 'It is a long time since I had anything to eat or drink,' said he. 'I beg you to give me a bite of that cake you are bringing out, and a drink of the wine.'

'Certainly not,' said the young man. 'I shall be hungry enough after I've cut down this tree to eat a dozen cakes. Be off with you.'

The little grey man vanished, and the woodcutter's son had a bite of the cake and then attacked the tree with his axe. But after the first blow, the axe slipped and cut his leg so badly that he was forced to give up working and had to limp all the way home.

'Now, father,' said Dummling, 'with my two brothers unable to help you, what do you say to letting me go and cut down that tree for you?'

'You'll never do it, Dummling,' said the woodcutter. 'You're too much of an idiot.'

Dummling, however, would not take no for an answer. He begged so hard that at length the woodcutter said, 'Go then, if you must. You'll learn sense when you cut yourself.'

'And you had better take something to eat,' said his mother. 'There's a piece of old cinder-cake in the cupboard and a bottle of sour beer. Take that if you want to.'

Whistling merrily, Dummling picked up his axe and went off. When he reached the tree, there was the same grey-bearded little man waiting beside it. 'It's a very long time since I had anything to eat or drink,' said he. 'Will you share what you have with me before you begin work?'

'Indeed I will,' said Dummling. 'I'm only sorry it isn't something more tasty. But all I have is a piece of cinder-cake and a bottle of sour beer. You're very welcome to both.'

But when Dummling unwrapped his cinder-cake, he found, to his astonishment, that it was rich plum cake. And when he opened the sour beer, it tasted like sweet wine.

'Well,' said the little man after they had eaten. 'There's

no doubt you have a generous heart. Now I'll do something for you. Over there stands an ancient tree. Take that axe of yours and cut it down. You'll find something of interest there among the roots.' And so saying, he vanished.

Dummling scratched his head for a while wondering what he should do. Then he took his axe and cut down the old tree. To his amazement, there, among the roots, sat a goose with golden feathers.

'Well,' said the woodcutter's youngest son. 'Well, well, well!' And he picked up the goose, tucked it under his arm, and set out for the nearest inn.

When he reached the inn, Dummling made up his mind to spend the night there, for it was already dark. The innkeeper's three daughters stared at the goose curiously, and when Dummling told them its feathers were of purest gold, the girls could scarcely contain themselves.

'If only I had just one of those wonderful feathers,' the eldest thought, 'I could buy all the dresses I want.'

She made up her mind to take one if the chance came. And come it did, for quite soon Dummling put his golden goose on the table and went outside for a breath of air.

The innkeeper's eldest daughter seized hold of the goose—and found herself stuck fast.

'I thought you might try to get a feather for yourself,' said the second sister coming in. And she took hold of her sister to pull her away. She too was stuck fast.

When the youngest came running up to find out what was happening, her sisters cried out, 'Keep away. Don't try to touch us.' Too late! The girl, thinking that she was missing something, grabbed hold of the second sister. And she too was stuck fast.

When Dummling returned, he picked up the golden goose and, with never a glance at the three girls trailing behind, went up to his room. So that night Dummling had the innkeeper's daughters for company.

In the morning he set out for the town with the girls trailing behind him. Whenever Dummling turned right, the girls turned right too. When he stopped, they stopped. When he went on, they had to follow.

Their cries of distress were overheard by a parson, who came after them to see what the matter was. Peering at the procession in a short-sighted way, the parson began to lecture the innkeeper's three daughters for chasing after a young man. And with the best intentions in the world, he

took hold of the youngest girl's hand, only to find that he could not let it go.

Presently, as the strange procession crossed the field in front of the church, it was spotted by the parson's sexton, who rushed out to him.

'You have forgotten the christening at twelve,' cried he. 'Don't go off with these people, parson.' And the good man grabbed hold of his parson's sleeve, and, of course, was held fast.

'Mercy upon us,' exclaimed the parson, struggling to rid himself of the sexton, and at the same time free himself from the innkeeper's daughter. 'Help! Help!'

His shouts attracted the attention of two peasants who were working in the far corner of the field. They rushed up. One of them grasped the sexton's long black coat while the other took hold of his companion's smock.

Dummling, with not a backward glance, continued on his way, and behind him, hopping and skipping and stumbling, came the innkeeper's three daughters, the parson, the sexton, and the two peasants. When he reached the city where the King had his castle, Dummling saw a notice bearing the words:

WHOEVER MAKES THE KING'S DAUGHTER SMILE WINS HER HAND IN MARRIAGE.

'Well, well,' said Dummling to himself as he studied the royal proclamation. 'So the King has a daughter who cannot smile. I must see about that!'

As luck would have it, the King's daughter was sitting at one of the castle windows when Dummling came into the square. At the sight of the young man with the golden goose tucked securely under his arm and his seven unwilling companions trailing behind, all stuck fast, one to the other, the King's daughter began to smile.

'The Princess is smiling,' whispered some of the crowd who gathered each day under her window. 'What a miracle!'

'No, no, she laughs!' cried others. And it was true; the Princess was laughing. In fact, she laughed so much that the King thought she would never stop.

'He wins! He wins!' shouted the delighted crowd. And they pushed Dummling forward. 'He must marry the Princess.'

No sooner was Dummling inside the castle than the spell broke, and the innkeeper's daughters, the parson, the sexton, and the two peasants were free to return home.

Dummling was brought before the King. The King was far from pleased at the idea of having a poor woodcutter's son in the family, so he said, 'There is just one more task you must perform before the marriage with my daughter can take place.'

'What is it?' asked Dummling.

'You must bring me a man who can drink a whole cellarful of wine,' said the King, humming and hawing.

'I will see what can be done,' said Dummling. And he left the castle and went straight to the tree in the forest where he had first met the little grey-bearded man.

There on the tree's stump sat a short fat man with a very sad face.

'What's the matter with you?' asked Dummling.

'I have such a thirst,' said the man, 'that I could drink the sea dry. A barrel full of wine would suit me . . .'

'Then come with me,' cried Dummling. 'I have a means of satisfying that thirst.' And he led the man into the King's cellar.

By the end of the day the thirsty man had emptied every wine barrel in the cellar.

'The wine is drunk,' Dummling told the King. 'And I have come to claim your daughter's hand in marriage.'

The King frowned heavily. The more he thought of this simple fellow as his daughter's husband the less he liked the idea. So now he said, 'There is just one more thing that must be done. You must find a man who can eat a whole mountain of bread.'

'I will see what can be done,' said Dummling. And he left the castle and went back to the forest. There by the tree stump stood a tall thin man with a very sad face.

'What's the matter with you?' asked Dummling.

'I have such a hunger,' said the thin man pulling at a leather belt that spanned his waist, 'that I could eat a mountain. Already this morning I have devoured a hundred rolls, and look at this belt—it goes twice round me . . .'

'Then come with me,' said Dummling. 'I think I can satisfy you.'

And he led the man to the mountain of bread that had been freshly baked by the King's order.

The man faced the bread and began to eat. He ate without stopping, hour after hour, and by the end of the day the mountain of bread had vanished.

'The mountain of bread is eaten,' Dummling told the King. 'And now I shall take the Princess for my wife.'

'Not so fast, young fellow,' said the King. 'You must

find me a ship that will sail on land as well as on water. Do that, and my daughter is yours.'

This time Dummling made no reply. He ran from the King's presence, out of the castle, and into the forest. And there, on the tree stump, sat the little grey-bearded man himself.

'You are the only one who can help me,' said Dummling. And he told the little grey man what he wanted.

'Very well,' said the little man. 'I have helped you twice already for the sake of your kind heart. Now I will help you again.' And he gave Dummling a ship that could sail on land as well as on water.

When the King saw Dummling sailing across land in his ship, he knew he must keep his promise. So Dummling the simpleton married the beautiful Princess and, in time, became King himself. And a very good King he made.

THE RED SHOES

Over the hills and far away there once lived a little girl called Karen. She was so poor that she did not own even a pair of shoes.

One day the shoemaker's wife took pity on Karen and made her a pair of shoes out of some red cloth. They were not proper shoes, but Karen was very proud of them.

Shortly after this, Karen's mother died. Karen wore her red shoes to the funeral. She was all alone in the world; her mother had left her nothing, and soon her clothes were in rags. This sad state of affairs might have continued for ever had not a rich, lonely old lady noticed Karen.

'I'll take her home with me,' said the old lady. 'I'll care for the motherless child and bring her up properly.'

Karen gladly went with the rich lady. 'She must have noticed me because of my red shoes,' the little girl decided. And from that moment she thought a great deal about them. But the shoes being of cloth soon wore out.

'I will buy you another pair of shoes,' said her adopted mother. 'Let us go to the shoemaker today.'

Now, the lady was very old, and she could hardly see. She wished to buy black shoes for Karen so that the girl could wear them to church. But Karen, once she was inside the shop, had eyes only for a pair of red shoes placed high up on a shelf.

'I'll have these,' she said. The shoemaker blew the dust off them and said they were cut out of the finest leather.

'They fit perfectly,' said Karen. 'Please let me have them.' And the old lady agreed because she did not see that the shoes were bright red.

Karen wore her shoes every day. She wore them even on Sunday, even on her first communion Sunday. This meant that all the people in the church saw them. The bishop himself saw her red shoes.

When they came out of church, a burly one-legged soldier in a tattered scarlet uniform nodded to Karen. To the old lady he said, 'Dust your shoes, madam?' The old lady permitted him to do this.

'Mine too, please,' said Karen, holding out her foot as the old lady offered the soldier a silver piece.

'My, what pretty dancing shoes!' said the soldier as he wiped the dust from them with a piece of rag. Then he stroked the red shoes with a rough, weather-beaten hand.

Karen's feet went tap-tappity-tap on the cobblestones. The old lady was waiting for her to climb into the carriage, but Karen's red shoes carried her round and round the graveyard. In and out between the headstones she danced, over the mounds of green grass, and back again to the path.

If the waiting coachman had not run after her, I daresay she would be dancing there still, but he caught her and lifted her on his shoulder and put her in the carriage.

When Karen was safely indoors, two maidservants tugged at the red shoes until they came off, and Karen's dancing feet were still at last.

For more than a week Karen did not wear her red shoes. At the end of the week the old lady fell ill, and who better to take care of her than Karen?

The old lady grew steadily worse. A nurse came in every day, but she expected Karen to sit quietly in the sick-room for some of the time.

'Your mistress will die soon,' the nurse whispered one evening. 'Will you sit with her, Karen?'

Karen looked at her shoes on the shelf, bright red and highly polished. Then she looked across at the old lady. For a whole week she had thought of nothing else but wearing her red shoes that night to the village dance. She looked back at the shoes and could not resist them. She took down the shoes and put them on.

Out of the house she ran and into the village hall. She began to dance. She danced and danced. But long before it was time to go, the red shoes danced her out of the hall.

Into the woods they danced Karen; and when she tried to turn right, they turned left; and when she tried to turn left, they turned right. Through the woods and fields she sped in her red shoes. Whenever she tried to rest, she

seemed to see the one-legged soldier nodding and laughing. And over and over again she heard his voice saying 'Pretty dancing-shoes! Dancing-shoes! Dancing-shoes!'

How frightened Karen was! All through the night her dancing feet carried her along, and all through the next day. She was so tired she thought she would die; her shoes had grown on to her feet and she could not remove them.

At last Karen found herself in the churchyard, and there she saw an angel, shining white, tall and stern. 'Dance on, red shoes,' he said in a voice like thunder. 'Carry this vain and foolish child to the ends of the earth . . .'

Karen sobbed in her fright, but the red shoes carried her away from the church and far away from the angel. Over the hills they danced her until she came at last to a small stone cottage, the home of a sword-maker.

'Come out, come out!' Karen called. 'I cannot come in. Come out and cut off my dancing feet with your sword.'

The sword-maker came out with his sharpest sword, and Karen danced up and down before him, saying, 'I thought more of my red shoes than of being good. I cared more for my red shoes than for my dear old lady . . .'

The man raised his sword and cut off her feet, and the little red shoes went dancing away by themselves—over the hills and into the dark deep forest.

'Make me a pair of wooden feet,' Karen begged the man, 'and give me a pair of crutches. I will go back to the church and tell the angel how sorry I am.'

The sword-maker out of pity granted her request, and Karen hobbled away down the hill, across the fields, and through the woods until she came to the churchyard.

The tall, shining angel was no longer stern; he smiled at Karen and Karen smiled back at him. 'I have paid for my pride,' she whispered. And the angel nodded.

Karen went into the church where she felt peace such as she had never known before. As she knelt there, she forgot the red shoes that had caused her so much despair, and she smiled and was happy.

HOP O' MY THUMB

Once upon a time there lived a woodcutter and his wife who had seven children—all of them boys.

The woodcutter and his wife were so poor that sometimes they did not know where to turn to for money. Their children were growing so fast they were always hungry.

The youngest son, however, was the one who gave his parents the most anxiety; it is true he ate very little, but this was because he was so small. Indeed, when he was born he was only the size of his father's thumb, and that is why he was given the name of Hop O' My Thumb.

One winter the snow lay much longer on the ground than ever before, and as a result the seeds did not grow. By the time it was spring a great famine had spread across the land, and quite soon the woodcutter had nothing to give his family. All his savings were gone, and there was no food in the larder.

'We can no longer feed our children,' the woodcutter told his wife one night as they sat beside the empty grate. 'When our boys come down in the morning for their breakfast there will be nothing to give them. My dear, there is only one thing to do. We must take them into the forest and leave them there. Perhaps some rich man will find them and look after them better than we are able to do.'

His poor wife wept and wrung her hands at the very idea, but at last, as the night wore on, she agreed to her husband's plan. After all, anything was better than to watch her children die of hunger.

The woodcutter and his wife had raised their voices as they argued this way and that, and little Hop O' My Thumb had heard everything they said, for unlike his brothers he had not been asleep. For a long time he lay thinking what would be the best thing to do. As soon as it was light, he got up, dressed quickly, and crept out of the cottage.

He had made his plan, and this is what he did. He ran to the little stream that flowed past the cottage, and there he filled the pockets of his jacket with tiny white stones. Then, smiling to himself, he sped back to the house, and was in bed and pretending to be asleep when his mother called him.

'We are going into the forest,' his mother told him. 'We shall take all of you and you must help your father to gather firewood, for there is no money to buy any.'

The boys were so excited that they quite forgot their

hunger, and very soon they all set out, the woodcutter leading the way. The forest was dark and lonely, but the woodcutter knew every twisting path so well that quite soon they were right in the very deepest part.

'I will cut down the small tree,' said the woodcutter, 'and you boys must collect all the branches and tie them into bunches. Work hard and don't play about.'

With that he felled the tree with his axe, and set his seven sons to work. While the boys darted here and there, intent on gathering up as many sticks as they could, the woodcutter nodded to his wife, and swiftly and silently the two of them stole away.

Presently the boys began to shout and call for their father, thinking that he was playing some kind of game with them. But when he did not appear, they grew frightened and anxious and began to weep bitterly.

Then Hop O' My Thumb said, 'There's nothing to fear. I know the way home. All we have to do is to follow the trail of white stones.'

And when his brothers still seemed to doubt him, Hop O' My Thumb repeated what their father had said the night before, and told how he had filled his pockets with stones and dropped them, one by one, on the way.

So Hop O' My Thumb led his brothers through the deep forest and along the winding paths until at last they reached the cottage.

'Perhaps we shall not be very welcome,' Hop O' My Thumb whispered. 'Let us wait awhile outside and see if we can hear what they are saying.'

It so happened that when the woodcutter and his wife had arrived home early that afternoon they had found ten silver coins waiting for them. This was in payment of a debt that they had long forgotten about. At the sight of so much money the woodcutter's wife wept for joy. She started to rush to the butcher to buy meat for herself and for her husband and for her seven sons, until she remembered that she would never see the boys again. Then all her joy vanished, and she began to sob.

'My sons, my poor little sons!' she exclaimed tearfully. 'What would I give to have them safely back home. Perhaps, by now, they have been devoured by wolves. Woe is me! Woe is me!'

This was all Hop O' My Thumb needed to hear. He pushed open the door and ran to his mother, his brothers at his heels.

'Don't cry, Mother, here we are!'

What joy and happiness there was in the woodcutter's cottage that night, and what a feast they all had as they sat round the table. And so it was every night while the money lasted, for there was always something to eat for supper, and very often for breakfast and dinner too. But ten silver coins don't last for ever. The day came when all the money was gone and the larder was empty of food. Once again the woodcutter was overcome by despair, and that night he told his wife that he was going to take the children into the forest again and leave them there.

Just as they had done before, the woodcutter and his wife raised their voices. Hop O' My Thumb again overheard his father's plan.

'I will do what I did before,' he thought to himself. 'As soon as it is light enough I will go to the stream and fill my pockets with little white stones.'

But when he got up at the first light of dawn he found the door locked and bolted, and the bolts were too heavy for him to draw back. Sadly Hop O' My Thumb crept back to bed. Now he must think of another plan.

Before setting out for the forest the woodcutter gave a small piece of bread to each of the boys for breakfast. Hop O' My Thumb, at the sight of the bread, began to smile. He could leave a trail of breadcrumbs behind him as his father led them into the forest.

This time the woodcutter took his sons to another part of the forest, choosing small hidden paths that the children

would never discover for themselves. And once again he cut down a tree with his axe and set the boys to work. Then, taking his wife by the hand, he stole away.

The brothers were not so upset when they found they had been left alone. 'Hop O' My Thumb, show us the way home,' they cried.

The tiny boy immediately began to look for the crumbs he had dropped, but he could not find a single one, for the birds had flown down from the trees and eaten them all.

'It's no use,' he said at last. 'We really are lost. We shall have to try and find our way out of the forest without any help.'

As he spoke, the wind made the trees creak and moan all round them. And after the blustering wind came torrents of rain that beat down on them and turned the brown earth into muddy pools.

The boys squelched through the mud, helping each other along as best they could, but often falling down. When darkness fell, they were no nearer home, and Hop O' My Thumb climbed a tall tree to spy out the land.

'I can see a light shining in the blackness,' he told his brothers as he joined them again. 'We must try to reach it. Come on!'

They were all so tired that they could scarcely put one foot in front of the other, but Hop O' My Thumb kept urging them forward until at last they came upon a house. And there in one of the windows a candle was burning. Hop O' My Thumb knocked on the door, and it was opened at once by a woman who smiled at them and asked what they wanted at that time of night.

'We are lost,' Hop O' My Thumb told her, 'and so cold and wet. Please may we come and shelter with you? These are my six brothers.'

The woman's smile faded at his words, and with tears in her eyes she exclaimed, 'You poor little dears! You don't know what a terrible place this is or you would

not ask to come in. A giant lives in this house, and there is nothing he enjoys more than boys, roasted or boiled.'

'Alas! Alas!' cried Hop O' My Thumb with a glance at his trembling brothers. 'But we are so tired. What can we do? If you send us away we shall surely be devoured by the wolves. I - I think we would rather be eaten by your husband.'

The good woman was so moved at the sight of the seven children that at last she said she would take them in.

'Perhaps I shall be able to hide you away when the giant comes home,' she told them, and then she invited them to sit down by the fire, over which she was roasting a whole pig on a spit for her husband's supper.

Just as the brothers were beginning to get warm, there came a thunderous knocking at the door. The giant had returned. Quick as lightning his wife whisked the boys under the bed and went to open the door.

The giant did not stop to greet her. Instead, he roared for his supper and stumped over to the table. The young pig was pink and but half-cooked, but he was too ravenous to wait, and presently his wife placed it on the table before him and he began to eat.

Suddenly, with his mouth very full, he began taking great sniffs, turning his head this way and that. 'I smell fresh meat!' he roared.

Timidly his wife answered, 'That must be the veal in the larder: I'm keeping it for your dinner tomorrow.'

Taking no notice of her the giant bellowed again, 'I SMELL FRESH MEAT!' and he got up from his chair, made straight for the bed, and peered underneath it.

'Ah! Wretched woman,' he shouted. 'Here is meat enough for my three friends who will feast with me in a day or two. Did you think you could trick me?'

And with that, Hop O' My Thumb and his brothers were dragged from their hiding place. They screamed and kicked, begging for mercy, but as this giant was the most cruel and greedy giant that ever lived, he simply laughed

at them. With one hand he held all seven, while with the other he picked up his knife and started to sharpen it on a huge stone.

'What is the point of spoiling your supper?' the giant's wife said quietly. 'The pork is growing cold. Why not leave the boys as they are until the morning?'

Grudgingly her husband dropped Hop O' My Thumb and his brothers on the floor.

'Oh, very well. See that they have a good meal,' he ordered. 'The plumper they are the better they will be for eating.'

The giant had seven young daughters. They were comely girls by giant standards, but they were true daughters of their father, and far from lovable.

All seven daughters slept together in one enormous bed, and each wore a little golden crown on her head. In the same room stood another enormous bed, and it was to this that the giant's wife sent the boys after she had given them a good meal.

As they entered the vast bed-room, Hop O' My Thumb saw the seven giantesses with their seven gold crowns.

'It would be just as well if we wore these fine golden crowns

and the giant's seven daughters wore our caps,' Hop O' My Thumb thought cunningly, 'for who knows what the giant will do in the night. Surely he will not harm the heads that bear the golden crowns.'

And so, after the giant's wife had left them, Hop O' My Thumb jumped out of the huge bed, and in less time than a sparrow's cheep had placed the golden crowns on the heads of his brothers and himself. The sleeping giant's daughters had the caps in exchange.

Long before it was light, Hop O' My Thumb heard the giant's heavy step in the passage; the bedroom door swung back. Trembling, Hop O' My Thumb held his breath as the giant entered the room and strode over to the bed. Scarcely daring to blink, he waited as the giant's thick fingers fumbled in the dark. He felt them press heavily on his golden crown and heard the giant grunt, 'Crowns of gold! Crowns of gold! This must be the wrong bed.' Muttering angrily, the giant lurched over to the other, and there felt on the pillows the soft shapes of the boys' caps.

'So-ho!' he growled. 'Here they are, the rascals! Now to work.'

And without more ado he slew all the seven daughters and stuffed them into a sack that he slung over his shoulder. Then, well pleased with himself and more especially because his wife knew nothing of his night's work, he carried the sack down to the cellar and went back to bed.

From his own bed Hop O' My Thumb waited, pale and shaking, until he heard from somewhere far down the passage the noise of the giant's snores.

'Get up quickly,' he whispered to his six brothers. 'Don't make a sound. The giant is fast asleep. If we don't escape now, we never shall.'

And with that, Hop O' My Thumb hustled his brothers over to the window. In a flash they had jumped out into the garden and were over the high wall and into the forest. They ran as they had never run before, on and on through the black night.

When morning came, the brothers were far away from the giant's house. It was just as well, for the first thing the giant did on waking was to call loudly to his wife. 'Stoke up the fire,' he shouted. 'There's some fine fresh meat in a sack in the cellar. I have a big hunger on me this morning.'

His wife did as she was ordered, for she was too frightened to do otherwise, but when she opened the sack she gave a piercing scream and straightway fell down in a dead faint. The giant rushed into the kitchen to see what was wrong.

At the sight of his seven dead daughters he groaned heavily.

'What have I done? What have I done?' he cried. 'These boys have tricked me. They will pay for this. Rouse yourself, wife, and fetch me my seven-league boots.'

Now the giant's seven-league boots were magic boots. When wearing them, the giant could cover vast distances,

so it was no wonder he set off like a violent gust of wind and in a moment was out of sight. But though he covered seven leagues in a single stride he did not catch a sight of Hop O' My Thumb and his brothers.

In fact, when the morning was more than half gone, the boys by a stroke of good fortune had found the right path and were almost in sight of their cottage.

'We are nearly home,' Hop O' My Thumb cried. 'It won't be long now.' But even as he spoke he saw the towering figure of the giant on the horizon.

'Quick, hide between these big rocks,' he ordered. 'In another moment the giant will be upon us.'

Seconds before the giant rushed past, the boys hid themselves.

But now the giant himself was feeling very tired and decided to rest before going on with his search. He sat down not very far from where the brothers were hiding and was soon fast asleep. The noise of his snores rumbled round the rocks like thunder claps, and when he heard them, Hop O' My Thumb got an idea.

'Make your way to our father's cottage,' he told his brothers. 'I'll follow soon.' Then he stole quietly up

to the snoring giant, and with great skill and courage gently pulled off first one boot and then the other. When he tried the boots on his own small feet, they shrank to his size. Being magic boots they could do this. Hop O' My Thumb hopped up and down with excitement as he saw a way to punish the wicked giant.

Back he went to the giant's house, and, of course, he reached it in no time at all. The giant's wife was surprised to see him, but as she had been crying all the time her husband had been away, she was quite glad to stop and have a talk with Hop O' My Thumb.

'I have seen your husband,' the boy told her, 'and he is in great danger. He has been captured by a fierce band of robbers and they are demanding all his treasure. If I do not take back the gold, the robbers will kill him.'

The giant's wife threw up her hands in horror and, being a good wife, went immediately to the giant's treasure chest and brought out several bags of gold.

'Here, take these,' she said to Hop O' My Thumb. 'The robbers will be satisfied with so much wealth, and my husband's life will be saved.'

Laden down with the gold, the boy sped merrily homewards, and there were his father and mother and all his six brothers waiting on the doorstep to greet him. When the woodcutter saw all the gold he knew that never again would he have to worry about feeding his growing family.

As for the giant, he was never seen again; it is thought he was eaten by wolves.

It is said of Hop O' My Thumb that he went to see the King at the Palace and was given the important position of royal postman—which was not surprising when you think of it! For who else could visit the far corners of the kingdom with the speed of lightning? And from then onwards—thanks to his seven-league boots—little Hop O' My Thumb became BIG in importance, and all his family came to live at the Palace and share in his good fortune.

JORINDA AND JORINGEL

There was once a witch who lived in an old castle. This castle was a lonely place, standing as it did in the middle of a dark forest. The witch kept herself amused, however, by changing herself into a big black cat during the daylight hours.

The witch was known for miles around for her cruel ways, but even so, many a young girl who ventured within one hundred paces of her castle came under her evil spell and was instantly changed into a bird. Sad to say, there were no less than seven thousand birds kept in wickerwork cages inside this dreadful old castle.

One day two young people wandered, hand in hand, into the forest. Their names were Jorinda and Joringel, and their only happiness was to be together.

'Some say an evil witch lives somewhere in this forest,' said Jorinda as she and Joringel sat down on the grassy bank. 'We mustn't wander too far from the village in case we fall within her spell.'

Joringel laughed as he peered up at the blue sky through the trees. 'Who cares!' he cried boldly. 'Nothing can harm us; we are too happy in our deep love for each other.'

Presently a cloud masked the golden sun, and Jorinda shivered and sprang lightly to her feet. 'Then let us explore,' she said.

Lost in their happiness of being together, they wandered on and on through the forest until suddenly they saw before them an old castle. It was the witch's castle, and immediately Jorinda was changed into a nightingale.

Before Joringel could utter a single word, out of the castle stepped a crooked old woman with a nose as long as a broom handle and eyes as red as fire. She caught the nightingale in her hand, and disappeared within the castle walls again.

Rooted to the spot with horror, Joringel stayed all night in front of the witch's castle. In the morning the witch, before changing herself into a cat, came out and spoke to him.

'Be on your way, young man,' she croaked. 'Your lady-love is lost to you forever.' And she chuckled grimly, wagging her claw-like finger in his face.

Joringel could not bring himself to return to his own village; instead, he offered himself as a shepherd to a farmer on the far side of the forest. For many months he spent every free moment he had in walking round and round the

witch's castle in the hope of seeing his captive Jorinda.

One night, as he lay sleeping on his rough bed of straw, he dreamt of the castle and of finding a flower, blood-red in colour and with a pearl of great beauty at its centre.

In his dream Joringel took this flower to the witch's castle; at the touch of the flower, the strongly barred door flew open, and when he found himself in the room of the seven thousand birds, he had only to touch them with the flower and they changed back into maidens. But long before Joringel reached the cages that held the nightingales, he woke up . . .

Trembling with excitement, Joringel lay there; he was wide-awake now, but the memory of the blood-red flower was as vivid as if he were dreaming about it all over again. Unable to think of anything but his dream, Joringel gave up his work as a shepherd and set out to find the flower.

For days and nights he continued his search until, at last, he stumbled upon it in the corner of a field only a short distance from the forest. Blood-red in colour, he saw that at the flower's centre was a glistening dew-drop which looked, for all the world, like a pearl.

Gathering it to himself, Joringel carried the precious flower carefully until he came to the witch's castle. The heavily barred door flew open at a touch of the flower, and the youth, guided by the sweet singing of the birds, soon found himself in the room where they were kept prisoner.

The witch herself was there, feeding the birds from a sack of stale breadcrumbs. When she saw Joringel, her eyes blazed fire and her tongue spat poison, but she could do him no harm because of the magic flower that he held.

From one cage to the next Joringel wandered in a hopeless kind of way, for all the nightingales looked alike. Suddenly, out of the corner of his eye, he saw the old witch take hold of one of the cages and hurry to the door with it.

Giving a triumphant shout, Joringel spun round, caught the old witch by the sleeve, and touched the nightingale inside the cage with his blood-red flower. Instantly Jorinda,

more beautiful even than he remembered her, was standing by his side.

Then Joringel touched all the birds in the vast room with his magic flower and changed them back into maidens. When this was done, he touched the old witch herself, and she turned into a screeching owl that he immediately placed in the stoutest of the cages.

When this was done, and the maidens sent on their way, Jorinda and Joringel, hand in hand, went back to their own village where, shortly afterwards, they were happily married.

As for the castle in the forest, some say that with the passing years it became a gnarled old tree so bent that no bird would nest in it—except for one screeching owl. Well, that is what some say, but you can never be absolutely certain of the truth; it all happened so long ago.

LITTLE RED RIDING HOOD

Once upon a time there was a little girl with golden hair and big blue eyes. Nobody knew her real name—except her Mummy and Daddy and Granny. Everybody called her little Red Riding Hood, because wherever she went she wore a red cape and hood.

Red Riding Hood lived in a very pretty cottage at the edge of a big wood, but she never went to the wood alone because of a big bad wolf who had his den there.

'Red Riding Hood! Red Riding Hood!' her Mummy said to her one day. 'What do you think? I have just heard that Granny is ill. Oh dear, what can we do to help?'

Red Riding Hood was very sad when she heard her Granny was ill. 'Granny lives on the other side of the wood,' said she. 'It is a long, long way by the road, isn't it?'

'It is indeed,' said Mummy, 'but I cannot go myself today. Besides she would like to see you, Red Riding Hood. She loves you so much.'

'Let me go then, Mummy,' cried Red Riding Hood.

'Poor Granny! Let's take her lots of good things to eat. That will make her better.'

'Very well,' said Mummy, 'I shall fill the basket with eggs, jam tarts, thick honey, and a pound of fresh creamy butter. If you hurry, Red Riding Hood, you will get there long before tea.'

'I will carry my basket very carefully,' Red Riding Hood promised, 'and I won't put it down anywhere.'

Then she kissed her Mummy and ran quickly down the garden path. 'Perhaps it won't matter if I take the short cut through the woods,' said she to herself, as she hurried along.

Have you ever been in the woods on a summer's day? Red Riding Hood almost forgot about her sick Granny as she skipped among the toadstools and over the green grass.

Red Riding Hood's dancing feet carried her swiftly along, and she was not afraid of anything. She sang a song; it was a funny little song about a Squirrel in a Top Hat and a Hedgehog which had lost all its prickly spines.

Then Red Riding Hood remembered her Granny and she stopped singing her happy song.

'Grandmamma is sick,' she told herself. 'I mustn't chase butterflies, and I mustn't sing any more. I must hurry, hurry, hurry through the woods.'

But, alas for little Red Riding Hood, her song had reached the ears of the big bad wolf who lived in the woods. The wolf was sly and cunning and always hungry. It was a long time since his last meal.

'Ah-ha! So-ho!' said the big bad wolf as he watched Red Riding Hood pass. 'Ah-ha! So-ho!'

The wolf waited for a moment. Then he ran very quickly through the bushes so that when Red Riding Hood reached the big tree, he was already there.

'Good-day to you,' he said, in a very soft voice—soft, that is, for a wolf. 'What a pretty little girl you are, and what a big basket you have. Now, I wonder, what is in the basket? And where you can be taking it?'

'The basket is for my Granny,' said Red Riding Hood.

'Ah-ha!' said the big bad wolf. 'And I suppose you are on your way to your Granny?'

'Yes, I am,' said Red Riding Hood. 'You see, my Granny is sick, and she must have nice things to eat.'

'And where does your sick Granny live?' asked the wolf, who did not dare to attack Red Riding Hood just then because there were woodcutters nearby.

'Just on the other side of the wood,' said Red Riding Hood, 'in a dear little cottage. She lives all by herself and she loves me very much. But I can't stop to talk.'

'Of course not,' said the big bad wolf with a very wide smile. 'Hurry along, my dear, I'm sure your Granny is anxious to see you. Where did you say the cottage was?'

'Not far—on the other side of the wood,' said little Red Riding Hood, 'but I really must be on my way—that is, after I have picked some flowers for Granny.'

As soon as Red Riding Hood was out of sight, the wolf set off in a great hurry. He knew a short-cut which would take him straight to Grandma's cottage, and he would be there long before Red Riding Hood.

Bushy-Tail Squirrel, the Singing Birds, and the two Long-Eared Rabbits watched him rush past like the wind. 'Where is old wolf going in such a hurry?' they wondered, but they didn't dare to ask him.

All Grandmammas are nice; Red Riding Hood's Granny was very good and sweet and kind. As soon as a little bird told Granny that Red Riding Hood was coming to see her, she began to feel better. Soon she felt strong enough to sit up in bed and do a little bit of knitting. And all the time she

was listening hard for Red Riding Hood's gentle voice.

'I hope she brings me a pot of honey,' said Granny to herself. 'A teaspoonful of honey after my nasty-tasting medicine will be far nicer than a peppermint.'

Grandmamma suddenly fixed her eyes on the door. She was sure there was someone outside.

'Grandmamma, Grandmamma, may I come in?' called the bad wolf in a voice as sweet as sugar. 'It's your own little Red Riding Hood come to see you.'

'Bless you, dear child!' Granny called out. 'How glad I am you are here at last. Yes, yes, come in.'

'The door is shut, dear Grandmamma,' called back the wolf. 'How do I open it?'

'Just lift the bobbin,' said the old lady. 'Just lift the bobbin, darling. I'm surprised you have forgotten.'

The big bad wolf licked his lips with his long flat tongue as he lifted the bobbin and pushed open the door.

It did not take very long for that bad wolf to gobble up Grandmamma. Then he wrapped himself in her shawl and fixed her nightcap behind his wicked ears and balanced her spectacles halfway down his nose.

'If I draw the blinds,' said the cunning wolf to himself, 'and keep well down between the sheets, little Red Riding Hood will suspect nothing.'

Then he hopped into bed and prepared himself to wait. Meantime, Red Riding Hood was hurrying along. Already the sun was gone, and there was a certain chill wind blowing which made her shiver.

'I shall give Grandmamma a nice hot water bottle to keep her warm,' said Red Riding Hood to herself, as she ran on. 'And I'll make her a strong cup of tea. We can eat some of the jam tarts, and perhaps have some toast with creamy butter on it.'

At last the cottage came in sight, and Red Riding Hood walked the last few yards up the path. Very gently she knocked on the door.

'It's me, Grandmamma, it's your own little Red Riding Hood,' she called out.

'Come in, my dear, come in,' called the wolf in a croaky whisper, which he hoped sounded like the voice of an old lady. 'Just lift the bobbin, dearie, and come right in. Your poor old Granny can scarcely wait to set eyes on you.'

'I'm coming, Grandmamma,' Red Riding Hood called back, and she lifted the bobbin and pushed open the door.

'Come right in, come right in, dear child,' said the wolf in a whisper. 'Come very close to the bed, my dear.'

Little Red Riding Hood smiled her sweetest smile as she came towards the bed. What a surprise Grandmamma would have when she looked inside the basket and found the pretty flowers she had gathered for her, in the woods. And how pleased she would be with the jam tarts, the pot of honey, the eggs and the creamy butter.

'That's right,' said the wicked old wolf, as Red Riding Hood tip-toed up to the bed. 'Come and give your Granny a big hug.'

'But Grandmamma,' said little Red Riding Hood, as she

came close to the bed. 'Grandmamma, what big arms you have got.'

'All the better to hug you with, my dear,' replied the wicked wolf.

'And Grandmamma, what big ears you have got!'

'All the better to hear you with, my dear,' said the wolf.

'And, oh Grandmamma, what big eyes you have got!'

'All the better to see you with, child!' said the wolf.

'And Grandmamma, what big, big teeth you have got!' cried Red Riding Hood.

'Ah-ha! So-ho!' snarled the bad wolf. 'All the better to EAT you with.'

And the big bad wolf sprang clean out of bed.

Poor little Red Riding Hood! Her basket fell to the ground, breaking the eggs and crushing the pretty flowers.

The big bad wolf was all ready to gobble her up.

'Help! Help!' screamed little Red Riding Hood. 'Help! Help! Somebody save me!'

Now it chanced that day that the brave, strong hunter was out in the woods. He had his gun with him; he meant to shoot a rabbit for his supper. The hunter was a friend of Grandmamma's, and he knew that she was laid up in bed.

'I'll just go to the cottage and find out for myself how she is,' the hunter said to himself.

But as he drew near the cottage, he heard a faint cry. It sounded like a cry for help—and, yes, it was coming from the old lady's cottage. The hunter began to run. He ran swiftly, his big hunting boots crunching over the grass. When he arrived at the cottage he went first to the window and looked inside. There was little Red Riding Hood, and there was the big bad wolf licking his lips with his long flat pink tongue.

The hunter made no sound as he stole back to the cottage door and pushed it open. He raised his gun.

Bang! Bang! Bang! The wolf clasped his big ears. Then he rolled over and over.

'Steady now!' said the hunter, in his deep kind voice.

The big bad wolf is dead. He can't hurt you now.'

'But—but he has eaten my Granny,' sobbed Red Riding Hood, running into his arms.

'We'll soon see about that,' said the hunter. And he took out his big knife and cut open the wolf.

And what do you think? Out stepped Grandmamma, almost as good as new, except that she wasn't wearing her white nightcap, shawl or spectacles!

So, all ended happily. The brave hunter stayed, and poured out Granny's medicine for her, and Red Riding Hood gave her a spoonful of honey after it. Then Red Riding Hood made a pot of strong tea, setting out jam tarts and cake, and Granny said she felt better already.

After tea, little Red Riding Hood hugged her Granny and promised to come again very soon.

Then she set off with the hunter to walk back home through the woods. And there was no big bad wolf to watch them go.

THE MAGIC TINDER-BOX

A proud soldier was marching along the high road. *Left, right, left, right!* He marched with his knapsack over his shoulder and his sword at his side. He had been in the war and was now going home. On the way, he met an old witch, dreadfully ugly, but smiling.

'Good evening, soldier!' said she.

'Hi there, witch!' said he.

'You are proud and your sword is strong. You are a real soldier, and I have a surprise for you,' said the witch. 'I can make you rich.'

'Go on talking, old woman, you make me curious.'

'Take a look at the old tree to your left. It's hollow, and inside, a passageway leads to a vast treasure. Climb inside, soldier-man, and find out for yourself. I'll tie this piece of hemp rope round your waist so that you can be pulled up whenever you say the word.'

'And what do I do once I am inside?' asked the soldier, dropping his sword.

'Search for the treasure, fool!' snapped the old witch. 'The passage is lit by a hundred lamps. You'll see three doors; the first opens into a room where stands a large chest, with a big dog sitting on top of it. The dog's eyes are like two saucers. But don't be afraid. Take this blue-checked apron. Spread it out on the floor and put the dog on it. Gather up as much money as you want. You'll find the chest is filled to the brim with copper coins. If, however, you prefer silver, then go to the second door.'

'What shall I find there?' the soldier asked eagerly.

'Another chest and another dog,' the witch told him. 'A chest stronger and bigger than the first, and a dog, terrible to behold, with eyes as big as mill-wheels. But take no notice of it. Put it on my apron and take as much money as you want. If it is gold that stirs your heart, hand-some soldier-man, go into the third room. The dog that awaits you there has eyes as big as towers. Don't be afraid. Put it on the apron, and it will do you no harm. Then take the gold, as much as you can carry, out of the chest.'

'Your voice creaks like an old rusty lock, but what you say makes good sense to me!' cried the soldier in high delight. 'But what must I do in return? Surely there must be some favour you crave?'

'No! Nothing! Not a farthing! Not a silver sixpence!' replied the witch. 'Just bring me back the old tinder-box

you find there. My grandmother left it behind when she went down there last!'

'Very well, witch! Shake hands on it. Put the rope about my waist. I am ready.'

And with that the soldier climbed into the tree and began sliding down the hollow trunk. Everything was just as the witch had described. He saw the long passage lit by a hundred lamps that shone like small suns. He saw the three doors and, without stopping to think, pushed open the first. There, in a vast room, a great dog lay upon a chest and, at the sight of him, rolled its eyes as large as saucers.

'Good dog!' said the soldier, and then he lifted the beast on to the blue-checked apron, just as the old witch had told him to do. Smiling with pleasure, he stuffed his pockets with copper coins and closed the chest.

Then he began to think of the next room where the second chest lay and, without stopping to think, he went to the second door and pushed it open. Inside, he saw the second dog with eyes as large as mill-wheels. This dog sat on a great, strong box, girded round with iron bands.

The soldier lifted the dog down, placed it on the apron, and opened the strong box. At the sight of all the silver pieces, the soldier gasped. Now he had no need to keep the copper coins that weighed him down and he threw them on the floor. Soon his pockets and knapsack were bulging with silver.

Then the soldier remembered the third door. The old witch had told him there was gold to be found. What a fool he was to waste his time on the silver! Away he rushed and, without stopping to think, pushed open the third door. The dog on the great chest had eyes as big as towers, and its head was going round and round like windmill sails. It was a frightening sight, but the brave soldier stood his ground. Saluting, he spread the blue-checked apron on the ground, lifted the dog on to it, and wrenched open the huge, strong chest that was girded by iron hoops.

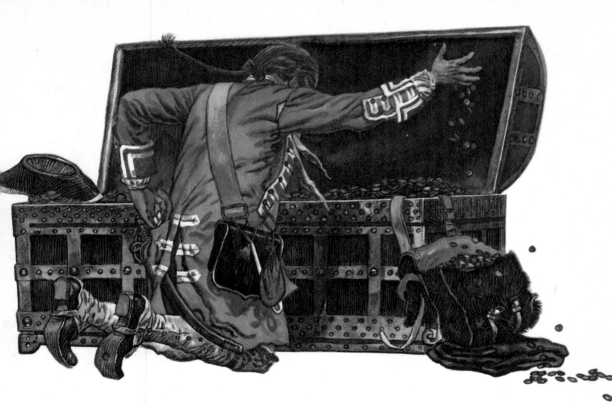

Gold! Never in his life had he seen such treasure! There were enough gold pieces to buy the whole of London with all its streets and houses.

The soldier emptied his pockets and his knapsack of the silver, and began loading himself up with the gold. He filled his cap and his boots as well as his pockets and his sack. Then he put the dog back on to the chest.

He moved slowly along the passage under the weight of the gold until he came to the bottom of the hollow trunk.

'Pull me up, old witch! Pull me up!' he shouted in a voice trembling with excitement.

'Have you got the tinder-box?'

'Dear me, no! The sight of so much treasure made me forget everything else.'

'Then go and get it,' the witch called back in an angry voice.

The soldier, grumbling to himself, went back along the passage, but it took him a long time to find the tinder-box, so weighed down was he by all the gold. Not until the old witch was satisfied that he had it would she pull him up.

'And what are you going to do with the tinder-box, old woman?' the soldier asked when at last he stood beside her.

'That is my business, soldier-man,' replied the witch. 'Ask me no questions.'

'Tell me what you are going to do with it or I shall draw my sword and kill you!' shouted the soldier, for by now he was beginning to want the tinder-box for himself.

But the old woman would not, and the soldier, with a grim smile, cut off her head.

So the soldier kept the tinder-box, and laughing aloud he slung the gold, which he had tied up in the blue-checked apron, over his shoulder, put the tinder-box into his pocket, and went on his way, whistling loudly as he set out for the nearest town.

No sooner was he there than he made for the best hotel. From now on he was determined to live like a prince. He asked for the finest room, and ordered a banquet to be set before him. But his uniform was so shabby and worn that the servant who came to look after him showed his astonishment. Well aware of his shabby appearance, the soldier went, as fast as he could, to the best and most expensive tailor in the town.

In next to no time, the poor soldier looked like a great gentleman, and quite a few of his new friends, thinking to flatter him, began talking to him about the king who ruled over the land.

'Such a noble king!' they said. 'And so fortunate in being blessed with the sweetest, most charming daughter— a true Princess.'

'I should love to see her!' exclaimed the soldier as he listened. 'She sounds a girl after my own heart.'

'Now, now, slowly does it!' his new friends exclaimed. 'She lives in a mighty fortress of copper that is guarded by high walls and towers. The king loves her so much that he takes every care of her. Do you know that there is a story going about that one day she will wed a common soldier? No wonder the king guards her closely!'

The soldier said no more, but he made up his mind that somehow or other he would see this lovely Princess.

The soldier began giving wild, extravagant parties that went on far into the night. He spent his money like water, and by the end of the month he was down to his last penny. He could scarcely believe it himself, but it was all too true. With no money to pay the rent of his expensive rooms he had to leave the hotel. He found a miserable attic and was forced to sell his fine clothes. All his new friends disappeared and the soldier found himself alone and unwanted.

One night—one very dark night—the soldier found he had no money at all, and only the old stub of a candle to light his room. Remembering the old witch's tinder-box, he took it out of his pocket and struck a light. Immediately the dog with eyes like saucers appeared before him.

'Master, what are your orders?' the dog asked.

'Funny thing, this tinder-box!' exclaimed the soldier, but he showed no fear. 'Your master orders you to bring him some money.'

No sooner had he spoken than the dog disappeared. But before the soldier had time to draw breath, it was back again with a bag of coppers in its mouth.

Quickly, the soldier learnt the secret of the tinder-box. If he struck it once, the dog with eyes like saucers would appear. Two strokes summoned the dog with eyes like mill-wheels, and three strokes brought the dog with eyes as big as towers. Each of the dogs would bring him as much as he wanted in copper, silver, or gold.

Now the soldier was poor no longer. Back he went to his

fine hotel and round him once again swarmed a host of
false friends. But the soldier could think of only one person
—the lovely Princess.

'Princess, Princess! Why is it not possible to see you?'
he asked himself over and over again. 'Everybody tells
me how beautiful you are. But of what use is your beauty
and your goodness if you are shut away in this copper
castle! Surely my tinder-box can help me.'

And with that he struck the box once, and the dog with
saucer eyes appeared before him.

'Do forgive me for calling you at this late hour,' the
soldier began, 'but if I could see the Princess who lives in
the copper castle for just one moment, I should be very
happy.'

The dog disappeared, but presently it returned, and on

its back sat the Princess. How beautiful she was! Truly, she was the most beautiful Princess in the world and the soldier was overcome. He could find no words, and the seconds ticked away until the moment was gone and the dog, obedient to his slightest wish, disappeared, taking the lovely Princess with him.

The Princess understood nothing of the soldier or his magic tinder-box, but she remembered what she thought must have been a dream. And she told her father about it when they were having breakfast together.

'It was such a strange dream, father,' she said. 'I was riding on a great dog with eyes like saucers, and this dog carried me a long way until we came to a room where a soldier was waiting.'

The king listened attentively. Then, frowning heavily, he left the room.

That same day he spoke long and seriously with one of the ladies-in-waiting, the oldest and ugliest of all the ladies in the castle, and the one he trusted most. 'When night falls,' he told her, 'hide yourself in my daughter's room. Do not sleep, but watch carefully and report everything you see.'

That night, while the lovely Princess slept, the lady-in-waiting kept watch, and at the stroke of midnight, she saw a great dog enter the royal room and on its back carry her royal mistress away from the castle.

Now, old and ugly the lady-in-waiting might be, but she was courageous and quick-thinking. Snatching up a pair of slippers, she wasted not a moment, but followed the dog and its rider out of the palace. Swiftly and silently she ran after them. When at last they came to the fine hotel, the lady-in-waiting, with great presence of mind, put a large white cross on the door through which the dog and the Princess disappeared.

Then, down the stairs she sped and along the streets so that she might report everything to the king as quickly as possible.

In the morning the king, the queen, and all the lords and ladies of the court set out in a great procession for the hotel.

'Whoever we find there will be punished by death,' said the king, and all the members of the court applauded loudly.

'My white cross that I made with chalk will show up on the door. In that way we shall know at once which one it is,' said the lady-in-waiting, very smugly.

But alas, once they were inside the hotel they found that every door was marked with a white cross. How could they know that the great dog of the tinder-box had done this in order to save his master from the king's fury?

'We have been tricked,' said the king on their return to the castle.

'We must think again,' said the queen. 'But I have an idea. Say nothing to the Princess of all this, but tonight I will persuade her to wear a tiny good-luck charm as she sleeps...'

The king looked rather puzzled because he was not so sharp-witted as the queen, but he watched carefully as she took her golden scissors and cut out a small square of silk. Out of this she quickly fashioned a little bag, and into this she poured very fine white flour. Then she made a hole in the bag, the tiniest prick.

'When the Princess goes on her travels tonight, the flour will leave a trail that we can follow,' she told the king.

It happened as the clever queen foretold.

Just as before, the Princess met her soldier, and the soldier, as he gazed upon her, knew that he loved her with all his heart. But he knew too that he dared not go into the castle, for he was only a soldier and not a royal prince.

Then the dog of the tinder-box carried the Princess to the castle, and neither the dog nor the soldier saw the trail of fine white flour that was left behind.

The next day, the king at the head of a small army came to the hotel and took the soldier away. He was thrown into a dark, cold dungeon and told he would be executed in the morning.

The soldier was in despair. So quickly had he been captured that he had not even had time to gather up his tinder-box. If only he could find some way to get it!

That night he did not sleep, and early in the morning he waited beside the barred window of his prison. He could see vast crowds pouring into the market square, and he knew that they had come to watch him die. As he stood by the window, a young boy came running past, kicking up his heels and shouting in excitement.

'Hi there!' shouted the soldier, as one of the boy's clogs flew off and shattered the window. 'Do me a favour, will you? I'll give you five shillings if you run to my lodgings and bring me back the old tinder-box you will find there.'

298

The boy hesitated, but five shillings was a lot of money, and after all he would not miss any of the fun. So off he ran and was soon back with the tinder-box. Scarcely had the soldier grasped it than the guards came and took him into the square, where the king sat on his throne. The queen sat beside him, and the entire court was in attendance.

'Grant me one last favour,' the soldier said to the king as he was pushed before him. 'Let me smoke my pipe before I die.'

'Very well, soldier,' said the king, who did not wish to appear hard-hearted. 'Your wish is granted.'

The soldier struck the tinder-box three times. Immediately the three great dogs appeared before him.

The king and queen turned white with fear.

'Save me!' cried the king. But the dogs had nothing to do. When he tried to stand, his knees wobbled so much he fell down. When he *was* able to stand, he grabbed his queen and ran away. So did all the soldiers.

From her turret window, the Princess smiled down on the soldier, and the soldier bowed low. In view of the presence of the three dogs, the crowds thought it best to cheer. The soldier called the Princess to his side, and she came, smiling. The next day they were married, and if I tell *you* they lived happily ever afterwards that will be perfectly true—though whether or not the soldier deserved his happiness is another matter altogether!

RUMPELSTILTSKIN

There was once a poor but boastful miller who wished to make his mark with the King.

'I have a daughter,' said he, when at last he found himself in the King's presence, 'who is as gifted as she is beautiful. She can spin straw into gold.'

'Indeed!' said the King. 'This news pleases me well. Bring her to the palace tomorrow and we shall see . . .'

When the miller's daughter stood before him the next day, the King put her in a room filled with straw. 'There is the straw,' said he. 'If you do not spin it into gold by tomorrow you shall die—and the miller with you.'

The poor girl was in despair. As the hours sped on she buried her face in her apron and began to weep. She was still crying bitterly when the door suddenly opened and a little man stood before her. 'What are all these tears for?' asked he.

'I have to spin straw into gold,' sobbed the girl, 'and I do not know how to do it.'

'What will you give me,' said the little man, 'if I do it for you?'

The miller's daughter unfastened from round her throat the golden chain that had been left to her by her dead mother and handed it to him.

'That will do,' said the manikin, and he seated himself in front of the spinning wheel. The girl opened her mouth wide at the sight of the straw being spun into gold; and when three reels were full of gold, and the straw all used up, she clapped her hands.

Early the next morning the King came in person to the room, and when he saw the gold he was surprised and delighted. He hid his astonished delight, however, by saying, 'I will have one of the bigger rooms in the palace filled with straw tonight. See to it that the straw is spun into gold by the morning.'

But as before, the little man appeared at midnight, and the miller's daughter dried her tears at the sight of him.

'What will you give me this time?' he demanded.

'Take this ring,' said the girl, and she gave him the gold band that had once belonged to her dead mother.

'That will do,' said the manikin, and he sat down at the spinning wheel. By daybreak six reels were filled with gold, and all the straw used up.

The King was even more pleased with the miller's daughter when he saw the gold. 'I cannot let her stop now,' he told himself as he eyed the gold greedily. So, aloud, he said, 'I am going to put you in a room that is bigger than the others. If you spin all the straw in this room into gold I promise to marry you.'

The miller's daughter was quite terrified when she found herself surrounded by so much straw, and as soon as she was alone she began to weep. As midnight struck, however, the little man appeared to her again.

'What will you give me,' he demanded, 'if I help you yet again?'

'I have nothing left,' sobbed the girl piteously.

'Then give me your promise that when you become Queen you will hand me your first-born.'

The miller's daughter dried her tears.

'The King will almost certainly kill me if he does not find gold in the morning,' said she. 'So I have nothing to lose.

Yes, I promise to give you my first child if the King marries me.'

At these words the manikin sat down at the spinning wheel and by daybreak no less than ten reels were filled with gold. Soon after he had disappeared, the King himself arrived, and his joy at the sight of so much gold knew no bounds. 'Tomorrow, we shall wed,' he cried, and he took the girl by the hand and courteously conducted her to the royal chambers.

The pretty miller's daughter married the King, and a year later she gave birth to a beautiful baby girl. So many things had happened to her that she had long ago forgotten her promise to the little man; it was, therefore, with surprise and horror that she woke up to find him in her room.

'Your child is but one day old,' said he, 'and belongs to me. Remember your promise.'

The Queen began to weep and wail and her tears finally moved the little man to pity. 'Very well,' said he. 'I will give you three days in which to discover my name. If, by then, you know what it is, you can keep the child.'

Wide-awake, the Queen lay all night puzzling over names. And when the manikin appeared to her in the morning, she said, 'I wonder if your name could be Caspar or Balzac or plain Jonathan?'

At each name the little man shook his head and grinned, and the Queen hid her disappointment. 'Come back to-morrow,' she said. 'I will have the right name by then.

After he had gone, the Queen called in her counsellors and they told her other names that she had not thought of.

'I wonder if your name could be Melchior or Sebastian or just plain David?' she said when the little man appeared on the second day.

At each name the little man shook his head and grinned, and once again the Queen hid her disappointment. 'Come back tomorrow,' she said. 'I will have the right name by then.'

After he had gone, the Queen sent out a royal messenger, telling him to go far beyond the hills in search of new names.

She waited anxiously for his return. When at last he stood before her, weary and travel-stained, she asked him how he had fared.

'I could find no unusual names,' said the royal messenger, 'though I traversed many miles, but on the homeward journey I lost my way in a dense forest. There, I came upon a little house. A fire burned in front of it, and round the fire pranced the oddest little man I have seen in a lifetime. He was singing as he hopped from one foot to the other.'

'Can you remember the song?' asked the Queen eagerly, and the messenger said, 'Indeed I can. It went like this:

> *Today I bake, tomorrow I brew.*
> *Soon I'll have the young Queen's child.*
> *How glad I am that no one knew*
> *That Rumpelstiltskin I am styled.'*

'That's it!' cried the Queen, clapping her hands.

Shortly afterward, the manikin made his third visit, and this time the Queen began, 'I wonder if your name could be Trimfoot or Shortleg or just plain Robert?'

'No, no, no!' shouted the little man gleefully.

'Then could it be Rumpelstiltskin?' asked the Queen gently.

The little man almost choked with rage. Then he shrieked, 'You know! You know!' and vanished in a cloud of smoke.

THE FLYING TRUNK

There once lived a merchant who was so thrifty that every gold piece he made was stored away for a rainy day. His savings grew until he was rich enough to buy up the whole town. Being of such a thrifty nature, however, he could not bring himself to spend any of his vast fortune and, when he died, it all went to his only son.

The son was as different from his father as jelly from stone. He spent his father's hard-earned money on every imaginable luxury and folly. He even played ducks and drakes with some of the gold pieces, and laughed loudly when he saw them sink to the bottom of the pond.

It was no wonder then that within the year the son had not a penny in his pocket—and not a friend in the world. He sold the last of his fine clothes to pay off his debts, leaving himself with nothing better to wear than an old dressing-gown and a pair of bedroom slippers.

As he sat in his empty room, a battered old trunk arrived from a distant relative. It bore a note that said, 'Pack up and go!'

'A very good idea!' said the young spendthrift to himself.

'And as I haven't a thing left to pack I'll pack myself.'

So the merchant's son jumped into the trunk and pulled down the lid. This was no ordinary trunk, however, for as soon as the lock snapped shut, the trunk took wing.

Away flew the trunk over the housetops. The young man settled himself as comfortably as possible as the trunk flew on—over the mountains and over the seas. Finally it came down in a country called Turkey, which the merchant's son, gazing through a peep-hole, easily recognised from the round shapes of the buildings called mosques.

The young man stepped out of the trunk, ready for any adventure. He dragged the trunk into some nearby woods and buried it under a heap of dry sticks and leaves. Then he set off for the city. As he strode along, his old dressing-gown flapped about his legs; this did not worry him unduly, however, for in Turkey many men went about in loose robes of one kind or another.

Presently he met a Turkish peasant woman. 'I see something that looks like a palace,' said he, pointing to a fine tall building with many domes. 'Can it be the King's palace?'

'Indeed yes,' said the woman. 'And the lovely Princess

lives there too. We don't see anything of her these days, for the King and Queen won't allow her to meet anyone.'

'Why is that?' asked the young man.

'Oh,' said the woman, 'some years ago she was crossed in love. Her parents do not want the same thing to happen twice.'

'I see,' said the merchant's son, and when the woman had gone, he turned back to the woods and unearthed his trunk. He seated himself on the lid and flew to the window of the palace's topmost room, where he guessed the Princess would be.

He found her sound asleep on her bed of pink satin, and instantly fell in love with her, for she was uncommonly beautiful.

Quite unable to stop himself, the young man knelt beside her and took her hand. He was kissing it for the third time when the Princess opened her eyes and stared at him in considerable alarm.

'Calm yourself, dear Princess,' said the young man. 'I have come to you out of the skies. I am a Turkish prophet, a man who appreciates rare beauty when he sees it. I offer you my heart.'

The Princess had never before met a Turkish prophet

and, in spite of her first fears, she began looking at the young man with favour, especially as he went on to praise her beauty in the language of the poets.

At last the merchant's son begged her to marry him, and the Princess said 'yes'. Then she added, 'But my parents, the King and Queen, must meet you first. They visit me in my room on Saturdays. Come on Saturday then, and be sure to have some story that will win them over, for they both set great value on a good tale.'

Then the Princess gave her suitor a handsome gold scimitar. 'Take this,' said she, 'as a token of my love.'

The merchant's son accepted the scimitar, and departed the way he had come—through the window on his flying trunk.

As soon as the young man was in the woods again, he buried his trunk as before, and set off for the city. Once there, he sold the gold scimitar for a fair sum of money and purchased a magnificent new gown, red in colour and embroidered with green dragons.

Well pleased at the way things were going, he returned to the woods where he set about composing his story.

When Saturday came, he flew off to the palace, and his appearance out of the sky was greeted with loud cheers from the court, and bows and smiles from the King and the Queen.

With a loving glance at the Princess, the so-called Turkish prophet seated himself, cross-legged, before Their Majesties, and began his story.

'There was once,' said he, 'a bundle of Matches. They had a position of some importance in the kitchen, for they sat on the high mantelpiece. Even so, the Matches spoke endlessly of their family connections . . .'

'I can understand that,' said the Queen. 'Family is so important.'

Pleased that he had captured the Queen's attention, the merchant's son then told the rest of the story; his witty way of talking about the Plates and what *they* said, and his description of the Fire Tongue's dance quite delighted the King, who knew nothing of what goes on in a palace kitchen after dark.

The merchant's son gave life to all the ordinary kitchen utensils, and finished his story by saying, 'As for the proud Matches, they talked so much about themselves that they grew overheated and burnt themselves out . . .'

'Well, it was a capital story,' declared the King. 'You can marry my daughter on Monday.'

And the Queen said, 'We will make preparations right away. I shall be honoured to have a Turkish prophet in the family.'

In his splendid red and green gown, the merchant's son looked every inch a prophet, and as he strolled through the streets on the Sunday many of the people bowed before him.

There was a great deal of singing and dancing throughout the capital that night; streamers hung from every window; and mountains of sugar-plums and turkish delight were given away among the crowds.

'Perhaps I had better do something myself,' thought the young man, who had not been able to give his future bride a suitable wedding present. And he went off and purchased a large quantity of fireworks with the money he had left over.

The sparkling and glowing fireworks made a very fine display especially as the merchant's son set them off while flying over the city in his trunk.

'Truly, he must be a great prophet!' all the Turks in the streets below exclaimed. 'How fortunate our Princess is to be marrying him.'

Of course, the merchant's son was much too high up to hear what the people were actually saying about him, so he made up his mind to return his trunk to the woods and walk back to the city. When he was down among his future subjects he would learn what they thought of him.

This time he buried his flying trunk carelessly, for he was growing too sure of himself. Then he walked briskly into

the city where he learned, to his pleasure, that the people thought highly indeed of the Turkish prophet.

Well satisfied, the young man returned to the woods, for he meant to call on his Princess that same night, and there was no way of reaching her except by means of his flying trunk.

What a terrible sight met his eyes; his trunk was on fire! In fact, it was almost in ashes. A spark from one of his own fireworks had dropped on to the dry sticks and leaves and set them alight. The flames had made short work of the leaves, and had then attacked the trunk, setting it ablaze.

Without his flying trunk, the young man was of no importance to anyone. He kicked the ashes and set off to wander through the country.

In time he earned quite good money with his stories, especially the one about the Matches burning themselves out in the kitchen; and the one about the Turkish prophet, his flying trunk, and the Princess who sat all day on the roof searching the sky with lovesick blue eyes.

THE FROG PRINCE

Once upon a time there was a King whose daughter was as fair as a summer's day. Beyond the splendid castle in which they lived stretched a spreading forest, and on the edge of the forest was a deep well.

It was here the young Princess loved to come, bringing with her the golden ball that was her favourite among her playthings. One morning, as she tossed the shining ball high into the sky, it dropped into the deep waters of the well and disappeared.

When the Princess saw what had happened, she began to sob loudly, as if it were the end of the world. Peering through her storm of tears down into the dark waters of the well, she was suddenly astonished to hear a voice coming, it seemed, from the depths of the well.

'What is the matter, Princess?' said the voice. 'You weep as if you were in great trouble.'

'I have lost my golden ball,' the Princess answered, looking all about her for the owner of the invisible voice. 'It is down this well and I shall never see it again.'

At this, a huge, ugly frog broke the surface of the water,

310

and the Princess saw that the voice came from the frog, for now it was speaking again. 'What will you give me if I bring back your golden ball?' it asked.

'Dear, dear frog!' exclaimed the Princess. 'Anything you want! You can have my finest dress, my richest jewels, even this gold crown that I wear upon my head. Anything —if only you will restore my golden ball to me.'

'I want none of these things,' said the frog. 'But if you give me your promise to love me, to let me sit with you at your table and sleep with you in your little bed, then I shall go down to the bottom of this well and bring up your golden ball.'

'I promise! I promise!' cried the Princess, but as she dried her eyes she thought to herself, 'What nonsense the frog talks. How can it hope for such things?'

The frog let itself sink to the bottom of the well, and presently it reappeared with the golden ball and tossed it on to the grass.

The Princess picked up the ball with a shout of delight and ran with it to the castle.

'Wait, wait,' croaked the frog hoarsely. 'You promised to love me. You promised I should be with you at your table. I cannot run like you. Wait for me!'

But the Princess ran until she reached the castle, and the frog returned sadly to the well.

The Princess soon forgot all about her promise to the frog; not for a moment did she expect to see it again.

One day, however, as she sat down to dinner, who should appear at the castle but the ugly frog. The Princess was the first to see the creature, and she ran to the door and tried to shut it.

'What is it? Who is out there?' demanded her father.

'Nothing, no one,' said the Princess quickly.

'Why have you turned so pale?' asked the King as she came back to the table and began to make a pretence of eating. 'Who was at the door?'

'I tell you there was nobody,' cried the Princess. 'Only

a horrible frog. It brought me back my golden ball after I had lost it in the well, and made me promise to let it eat at my table and sleep in my bed as a reward. The very idea is quite ridiculous.'

'But you promised,' said the King, 'and a promise must always be kept. Admit the frog and let it sit with you at the table.'

Scowling and tearful, the Princess opened the door and the frog followed her, hippity-hop, to the table. Then it hopped on to the table itself and begged to be allowed to eat from her golden plate. 'You promised,' said the frog.

'And a promise must be kept,' said the Princess's father, looking at his daughter sternly.

'How hateful,' whispered the Princess bitterly as she

pushed her plate towards the frog. 'I do not know how I can possibly take another mouthful.'

'Now carry me upstairs, and I will share your bed,' said the frog when the meal was over. 'It is no more than you promised.'

'No, no, no!' cried the Princess.

But the King said, 'A promise given must be a promise kept. Do what the frog asks.'

The Princess shivered visibly as she took hold of the cold, slimy frog and carried it up to her bedroom.

'Put me in your little bed,' said the frog. 'It is no more than you promised.'

But the Princess would not. Instead, she dropped the frog in a corner and flung herself weeping on her dainty white bed.

As she lay there with her eyes closed she felt the cold slimy touch of the frog who had jumped up beside her.

'It is no more than you promised,' repeated the frog.

With a cry of rage and horror the young Princess jumped to her feet, took hold of the frog by its legs, and hurled it against the wall.

As the frog hit the wall something strange and wonderful happened; it changed instantly into a tall, handsome Prince.

'We must be grateful to your father, the King,' said the Prince, coming towards her and taking her hand. 'It was because of him that you let me eat at your table and took me to your room. Your actions have broken the wicked spell that changed me from a true Prince into a miserable frog.'

Long ago, though the Princess knew it not, it had been written in the stars that she would meet and fall in love with the Frog Prince. And that is what happened.

After the wedding, a golden carriage, drawn by six prancing white horses, came to the castle to take the Frog Prince and his bride back to his own kingdom where they lived happily together for many years.

THE WOLF AND THE SEVEN KIDS

Once upon a time an old and very loving nanny goat had seven little kids of her own to care for. She loved them so much that she never liked to leave them alone in the cottage.

One day, however, she found that there was not enough food left for their dinner so, calling them round her, she said, 'My dear children I must go into the forest and get some food. Whatever you do, you must not open the door after I have gone. The wicked wolf of the forest might come. Be on your guard against him, for if he catches you he will eat you, skin, hair, and bones.'

'How shall we know him?' asked one of the kids.

'You will know him by his rough voice and his black feet,' Mother Nanny Goat said. And with that she picked up her shopping bag, opened the door, and went out.

It was not very long before a knock sounded at the door, and a voice called out, 'Open the door, dear children. Mother is back and has brought you each a present.'

But the seven little kids knew that it was the wolf because of his rough voice. 'You are not our mother,' they called back. 'Our mother has a soft gentle voice. You are the wolf. Go away and leave us alone.'

On hearing this, the wolf ran all the way to the market, where he bought himself a lump of chalk, knowing that the chalk would take the roughness out of his voice if he sucked it. Then he went back to the hut. 'Open up, dear children,' he called out in his new soft voice. 'Your mother has come back with the shopping, and there are cakes and sweets for all of you.'

But the seven little kids had seen the wolf's big black paws on the window ledge. 'You are not our mother,' they called back. 'Our mother does not have black feet. You are the wolf. Go away and leave us alone.'

On hearing this, the wolf ran back to the place where the miller had his mill. 'Give me some white flour,' he said to the miller. 'If you don't I'll gobble you up here and now.'

So the miller gave the wolf some of his white flour, and the wolf covered his paws with it. Then he went back to the hut. 'Open up, dear children,' he called in his soft voice. 'Your mother is back from the forest and has a new toy for each of you in her shopping bag.'

'Show us your paws,' called back the seven little kids. 'Then we will know if you really are our dear mother.'

At this, the wolf put his white paws on the window ledge. And when the kids saw the white paws they thought that it must be their mother. They opened the door and in rushed the wicked wolf.

Terrified, the kids tried to hide. One leapt into bed; another hid under the table; a third ran into the kitchen; the fourth hid in the blanket chest; and the fifth jumped into the washing-bowl. The sixth crept into the broom cupboard; and the seventh and youngest squeezed himself inside the grandfather clock.

The wolf found them all, except the youngest, and gobbled them up on the spot. Then, with his tongue hanging out and his tummy bulging, he left the cottage. After such a big meal, the wolf felt sleepy. And soon he had found a spreading tree in the forest, under which he fell fast asleep.

Not long after this dreadful happening, Mother Nanny Goat returned home. Imagine her surprise and shock when she saw the cottage door swinging wide open, and then the state of the cottage itself! The table was overturned; the bed was upset; water dripped over the floor; and the chairs were broken.

When Mother Nanny Goat found her voice, she began to call for her children. But not one of them answered except the youngest, who was still hiding inside the old grandfather clock.

Mother Nanny Goat hugged him tightly and listened to his terrible story of the wolf. How she wept! And the little kid wept too, in sympathy. 'Well,' said his mother at last, 'we cannot stay here in this place of sad memories. Let us try and cheer ourselves up by going for a walk in the forest.'

They had only gone a little way into the forest when they came across the wicked wolf. There he lay, under the tree, sound asleep and snoring so loudly that the branches above his head were shaking.

Mother Goat stared in horror at his bulging stomach, and as she stared it seemed to her that something was moving inside it. 'Gracious!' she gasped to her youngest. 'Don't tell me that my six children are still alive inside the villain. Quick, run home and fetch me my scissors and a needle and cotton.'

The kid obeyed, and when Mother Goat had the scissors, she snipped open the wolf's stomach. Out popped one little kid's head.

'So I was right,' she said joyfully, and snip, snip, snip, went her scissors, until, at last, all six kids were safely delivered.

'The monster must have swallowed you whole in his greediness,' said the nanny goat. And she hugged her children one by one. Then she said, 'Now four of you go and bring me some big stones.'

When this was done, Mother Nanny Goat piled the

stones into the wolf's stomach while he slept. Quickly and neatly she sewed up the slit, and with her seven kids hopping and skipping around her she returned home.

Just when the sun was setting, the wolf woke up from his long sleep, and feeling very thirsty made his way to a deep well where he could get a drink.

As he walked along the stones inside him rattled against each other, and the wolf cried:

> *What rumbles and tumbles*
> *Against my poor bones?*
> *It ought to be kids,*
> *But it feels more like stones.*

When he reached the well, he bent over to drink. But the heavy stones inside him made him lose his balance, and he fell into the well with a huge splash and was drowned. And that was the end of the wicked wolf.

ALI BABA AND THE FORTY THIEVES

Once upon a time, many, many years ago, there lived two brothers in the land of Persia. Their names were Cassim and Ali Baba. Cassim was rich through marriage, but Ali Baba was poor, and there was little love lost between the two brothers.

One day Ali Baba set out for the forest, driving his donkey before him. The day was no different from any other day for Ali Baba. He was a woodcutter, and, if his wife and family were to eat, he had to collect firewood daily and sell it in the market.

As it happened, however, this was a day Ali Baba would remember for the rest of his life. He had just finished loading his patient donkey when he heard the sound of galloping horses. Being a cautious man, Ali Baba quickly tethered his donkey behind some bushes and climbed a tree. The horsemen might be harmless enough but, on the other hand, they might be robbers, and the woodcutter was taking no chances.

'Hmm!' thought Ali Baba as he peered down through the branches. 'They are robbers, no doubt of it.' His sharp eyes missed nothing as the band of horsemen drew rein almost underneath the very tree in which he was hidden.

The men were richly dressed, and each carried a dangerous-looking scimitar at his belt. Their chief was tall, with cruel, dark eyes, and it was he who shouted, 'Wait until I give the word.'

To Ali Baba's amazement, the leader guided his horse to a massive slab of rock and uttered the words, 'Open Sesame!' Instantly the rock slab slid to one side, revealing a dark cave so wide that the horsemen entered four abreast.

'Four, eight, twelve,' Ali Baba began to count under his breath. When the fortieth and last of the robbers had disappeared inside the cave, the rock door slid into its former position.

'I'll stay where I am,' the woodcutter told himself. And he was wise, for, before long, the rock slab moved again, and out came the forty thieves.

After they had galloped off, Ali Baba slid down the tree and addressed the rock. 'Open Sesame!' said he in a voice that was scarcely above a whisper. And the rock obeyed.

Once inside the cave, Ali Baba almost forgot his fear at the sight of the treasure that met his eyes. Vast chests of gold and silver pieces, boxes of glittering jewels, rich silks, brocades, and furs. There was enough treasure to satisfy a dozen sultans, let alone a poor woodcutter.

Scarcely knowing where to begin, Ali Baba filled his pockets with gold and silver, added a few of the shining

jewels for good measure, and then repeated his 'Open Sesame!'

The rock obeyed, and Ali Baba found himself once again in the clearing. As fast as his trembling hands would let him, he untied his donkey, tipped out the firewood from the sacks that were slung across its back, and began filling them with gold and silver.

He made several journeys into the cave, but he was careful to take only a few gold pieces from each chest so that the robbers would suspect nothing on their return.

Then, well pleased with his unexpected good fortune, he made tracks for home. His wife had been anxiously waiting, for it was long past his suppertime.

'Don't reproach me,' said Ali Baba. 'Help me to bury this treasure under the floor while I tell you my story.'

'It would be a pity to bury the gold,' said his wife when she recovered from the first shock, 'without knowing how much we have got. I'll borrow a measuring cup from my sister-in-law and we can measure it before we hide it away.'

'Very well,' said Ali Baba, 'but keep a silent tongue in your head. If my brother Cassim hears of it he'll want the rest for himself, and then the robbers will be on to us.'

Cassim's wife was curious when the woodcutter's wife came rushing into her house asking for a measuring cup.

'I can't tell you anything,' said Ali Baba's wife. 'Just give me the measuring cup.'

'Wait here, then,' said Cassim's wife. And she went into the kitchen and rubbed the bottom of the cup with suet.

The next morning Ali Baba's wife returned the cup without noticing that a small gold coin had stuck to it. After she had gone, Cassim's wife rushed to her husband. 'Look at this!' she shouted. 'How can Ali Baba be as poor as he claims if he spends the night measuring out gold . . . ?'

'I'll find out,' said her husband, and he hurried off. When he got to his brother's house, he came upon Ali Baba replacing some bricks in the floor of his living room, and forced him to tell him the whole story.

'Treasure, you say!' cried Cassim, his eyes sparkling greedily. 'Then I'll take ten of my own donkeys and go to this cave right away.'

'If the thieves catch you,' said Ali Baba, 'it will be the end of you.'

But his brother pushed him roughly aside, saying, 'Don't expect a share of what I shall bring back.'

With his string of ten donkeys Cassim set off for the rock. So eager was he to get to the treasure that he gave no thought to the dangers. As soon as he had tied up his donkeys to the trees, he faced the rock and shouted, 'Open Sesame!' Instantly the huge stone moved to one side.

No words of Ali Baba's had prepared Cassim for the treasure he found inside the cave. Like a madman he rushed from one gold chest to the next. Then he came upon golden crowns studded with rubies, and diamonds the size of eggs.

Cassim was beside himself with joy. He wasted valuable minutes selecting the biggest of the jewels, and more

valuable time in pulling down the tapestries that lined the cave walls.

At length, when he was knee deep in silks and furs and his pockets and sacks were filled with priceless gems and gold pieces, he decided to leave. But what was the magic password? 'Open Barley!' shouted Cassim. But the rock did not move. 'Open Seeds!' he shouted again. 'Open Corn! Open Rye!'

And when the rock still did not move, he beat on the stone with his bare hands, crying, 'Open, I tell you! Open, open!'

Drowning his muffled screams came the sudden thud of horses' hooves, and Cassim knew the robbers were returning. Panic seized him and he ran deep into the cave searching for a hiding place. But the thieves had seen the donkeys, and as soon as the robber chief had uttered the magic words that the rock obeyed, they began searching the cave.

Cassim was soon discovered, and one of the robbers drew his scimitar and killed him. 'Let us cut him into pieces,' said their chief, 'and leave him here as a warning to others who might stumble on our secret.'

When this was done, the robbers rode away.

Cassim's wife waited in vain for the return of her husband, and when a whole day had passed and he did not come she went to Ali Baba. 'I will return to the cave,' said Ali Baba, 'and if he is there I will do what I can to save him.'

As soon as Ali Baba was inside the cave, he saw what had happened to his brother and he wept as he gathered the remains and bore them outside. He put them in a sack that he slung over his donkey's back so that he might take them home.

Ali Baba was now a man of some considerable fortune, for, besides his treasure from the cave, Cassim's widow asked him to take over her late husband's affairs, and he and his wife went to live in Cassim's house.

In this house there was a beautiful and wise young slave girl called Morgiana who had served Cassim with great devotion. To her, Ali Baba related the whole story.

'You will never see your master again,' he told her sorrowfully. 'And you must persuade your mistress to keep silent. If she talks the robbers will come, and we shall all die.'

'I understand,' said Morgiana, 'and I have thought of a way to make the townspeople believe that Cassim died from a sudden illness.'

Morgiana went in secret to the Street of the Shoemakers where she found an old man whose skill was known even to the Sultan.

'I have work for you,' she told him. 'But first let me blindfold your eyes so that you do not know where I take you.'

When this was done, Morgiana led the old man back to Ali Baba's house. 'You shall have two gold pieces if you will sew these clothes together in the shape of the man who once wore them,' she told the old man. And with the cunning of a craftsman, the old shoemaker stitched both Cassim's remains and the clothes into a man's shape again.

Morgiana gave the old craftsman his reward, and then led him blindfold through the dark streets until he was back home. In the morning Cassim was buried openly, and Morgiana let it be known her master had died suddenly the night before.

Ali Baba's secret was now safe from curious neighbours, and he began to lead the life of a rich but humble man. Rich because it was taken for granted that Cassim had left him everything, and humble because he had not earned his new-found wealth by his own labours.

It was not long, however, before the robber chief led his band back to the cave with more plunder.

'Our secret is known,' their leader shouted when he found Cassim's body had been taken away. 'Death to the man who knows it.'

He sent one of his men, disguised as a merchant, to see if he could find anything out in the town. By chance, the robber wandered down the narrow Street of the Shoemakers and came upon the old shoemaker as he sat cross-legged in front of his stall.

The old man's head was bent over his work as the thief stopped to talk with him. 'Tell me, old man,' said the thief, 'what goes on in the great city?'

'I know nothing of what goes on,' said the old man, 'except what is under my nose. And that is sometimes strange enough. Why, not long ago, I had to stitch a dead man's clothing together and himself inside it. Four pieces

did I join together with stitches as small as a gnat's eye . . . '

'Could you show me the house where such a deed was done?' asked the robber eagerly. But the old man shook his head.

'I was blindfolded,' he said simply. 'But if you care to blindfold me again, no doubt my feet will take me there.'

'Ten gold pieces,' cried the robber, 'if you will agree to such a thing.' And the bargain was struck.

Thus the old man, with a silk scarf over his eyes, led the robber straight to Ali Baba's house. The robber put a white chalk mark on the door and hurried back to his chief, who was waiting for him in the forest.

'I have found our man,' he reported, 'and marked the house with a cross of white chalk.'

'Then we shall go there this very night,' said the chief, 'and take our revenge.'

But in the afternoon Morgiana, returning from market, saw the white cross on her master's door and, suspecting it was there for some evil purpose, put a dozen white crosses on a dozen different houses up and down the street.

In this way the clever slave girl spoilt the robber's plan, and his fierce chief had him put to death. Another robber offered to see the old shoemaker, boasting that he would be smarter than his ill-fated friend. But though the shoemaker led him once again to Ali Baba's house, he was no more successful, for Morgiana spotted the red circle he had put on the door. Once again she marked houses up and down the street in exactly the same way.

The cruel chieftain had this second robber executed, and then himself went to the Street of the Shoemakers. Once again, on payment of several gold pieces, the old shoemaker allowed himself to be blindfolded; for the third time he found the house.

Having learnt his lesson, the leader of the thieves stayed long enough to memorise every detail of Ali Baba's house, down to the colour of the flowers in the garden. Then he returned to the forest.

The next day he disguised himself as an oil merchant and set out for Ali Baba's house, leading a train of nineteen mules, each of which had two great jars slung across its back. But only the first of the mules carried a jar that contained oil. In all the other jars were the robbers who, at a given signal, were to come forth and kill every man, woman, and child of Ali Baba's household.

Ali Baba received the false oil merchant with great courtesy and invited him to dinner, an invitation which the merchant graciously accepted.

'I will leave my oil jars in the courtyard,' said he, 'if you will kindly send one of your servants to tend the mules.'

When this was done Ali Baba summoned Morgiana and told her to prepare for an extra guest. Morgiana was pleased to see her master in such a happy mood, and, not wishing to waste time by going to market for oil, she made up her mind to fill her cruet with fresh olive oil from one of the jars in the courtyard.

To her horror, when she lifted the lid, she heard a voice from inside asking, 'Is it time?'

Recovering her wits, Morgiana whispered back, 'No, not yet,' and hurriedly dropped the lid. She went to each jar, getting the same question and giving the same answer. Finally she filled all her empty kitchen vessels from the real oil jar.

Now she knew, without question, that the oil merchant was in fact the robber chief, and that his men were hidden in the great oil jars.

As darkness fell Morgiana went into the courtyard again and again. She carried many kettles of boiling oil which she poured into each jar, killing all the thieves.

In the middle of the night the robber chief left his room and stole down to the courtyard to rouse his men. When none of them answered he lifted the lids of the oil jars and found them all dead. Fearful that he too would meet the same fate in the morning, he fled into the forest.

Alone and full of desire for revenge, the robber chief made yet another plan. This time he dyed his hair, cut short his beard, and took an empty shop next to one that Ali Baba had given to his son. The disguised thief soon made friends with his neighbour, and within the week was invited home. Suspecting nothing, Ali Baba invited his son's new friend to dine with him. But Morgiana, who waited upon her master, caught a glimpse of a dagger hidden away in the smiling guest's robe and instantly recognised him as the robber chief.

'Let me dance for our guest after dinner,' she said to Ali Baba, and her master gave his permission, knowing how much her dancing delighted his son.

After the meal, Morgiana changed into her most glittering costume, and with a jewelled dagger in her hand began her dance. Suddenly, without warning, she whirled towards the robber chief and plunged her dagger into his heart.

Horrified, Ali Baba jumped to his feet. 'Morgiana,' he cried. 'Are you mad? What have you done?'

'I have saved you, master,' said the slave girl calmly, 'from the only enemy you have in the world.' And she produced the robber's dagger to prove her words. Then she told her master the whole story, and Ali Baba wept tears of gratitude. 'Ask for anything,' he declared, 'and it is yours, for never had a master so loyal a slave.'

Before Morgiana could reply, Ali Baba's son said, 'May I speak for Morgiana? Make her a free woman so that I can ask her to be my wife.'

'It is done,' said Ali Baba.

So Morgiana and Ali Baba's young son were married, and, as a wedding present, Ali Baba told the happy pair the magic password to the cave in the forest—'Open Sesame!' For in time, all the treasure it contained would be theirs.

THE SHOEMAKER AND THE ELVES

Many years ago, long before you and I were born, there lived a shoemaker and his wife who fell upon bad times.

'Well, it has come at last,' the shoemaker said to his wife one night. 'I have enough leather for only one more pair of shoes.'

'You have worked hard all your life,' said his good wife. 'And you are as honest as the day is long. Leave the leather where it is and make your last pair of shoes in the morning. Come to bed and stop worrying.'

With a deep sigh, the honest shoemaker followed his wife upstairs to bed; after he had said his prayers, he fell fast asleep.

In the morning, when he awoke, his first thought was that today he would make his last pair of shoes. To his utter astonishment, when he went down to his work-room, he found the leather gone and in its place was a pair of shoes.

The shoemaker picked them up and examined them with the eye of a craftsman.

'Why, they are so well stitched,' he said to himself, 'that even I could do no better.'

That same morning, one of his richest customers passed

by, saw the shoes in the window, and was so taken with them that he offered the poor shoemaker four times their proper price.

With the money, the shoemaker was able to buy more leather—enough to make two pairs of shoes.

'You have had an exciting day,' said his good wife when her husband returned with the leather. 'Leave it here on the bench and eat your supper. There will be time enough in the morning to make the shoes.'

But when the shoemaker went to his bench in the morning he found the leather gone, and in its place were two pairs of shoes. These were just as beautifully made as the first pair, and were quickly sold for almost three times their value.

With the money, the shoemaker was able to buy enough leather to make four pairs of shoes. That night, not knowing what to expect, he put the leather on the table and went upstairs to bed.

In the morning, he found four pairs of shoes, stitched and ready. So finely made were the shoes that he could have sold a dozen pairs all in one morning. And, once again, the shoemaker had money to spend on buying more leather.

The same pattern of events took place day after day until the shoemaker grew rich. People were now coming from miles around begging for a pair of his shoes.

Sometimes in the evening the shoemaker and his wife would talk about the strange turn of fortune that had changed their lives.

'If only we could show our gratitude,' said his wife as Christmas drew near. 'Wouldn't it be nice if we could give our invisible friends a present for Christmas?'

'Indeed yes,' said her husband. 'But unless we sit up all night we shall never know who comes in secret to the workshop.'

'Then why not let us do that!' exclaimed his wife.

So that night, the shoemaker and his wife hid themselves

behind a tall cupboard and waited. Presently, as midnight struck, two little men came through the window, hopped on to the bench, and began cutting and sewing.

The shoemaker nearly gave himself away as he watched their tiny fingers at work. Never, in all his life, had he seen shoes so swiftly and finely made.

When their work was done, and the shoes neatly laid out in pairs, the elves vanished.

'So now we know,' said his wife after they had gone to bed and said their prayers. 'Poor little mites; they work so hard for us, and yet they look as if they can't even afford a stitch of new clothing . . .'

'It's all very strange,' said the shoemaker, 'but I would dearly like them to know how grateful we are.'

'I tell you what,' said his wife before she closed her eyes. 'In the morning I'll set to and make them each a nice warm vest and a shirt and trousers.'

True to her word, the shoemaker's wife got out her wool soon after breakfast the next morning. She knitted fast all day and, by evening, she had made two vests, two striped woollen shirts, two pairs of short trousers, and two pairs of long warm socks.

'There,' said she with a sigh of satisfaction, 'we'll put the presents out tonight instead of the leather. It's Christmas Eve, so they will understand that the presents are meant for them.'

When midnight struck, the two little elves appeared as usual. They seemed astonished when they could find no leather. Then one of them picked up the pink woolly vest, and the second tried on the socks.

Soon they were both fully dressed. In high delight, they hopped and skipped and danced round the room. And presently they began to sing. Their song went something like this:

> *Elves we are and fine to see;*
> *Too grand for cobblers, you'll agree.*

And with a final hop and skip they vanished through the window.

That was the last the shoemaker and his wife ever saw of them. From that moment on he made his own shoes. But he always had enough money for the leather and, being a good honest craftsman in his own right, he wanted for nothing.

THE DONKEY-SKIN

Once upon a time a rich and powerful King ruled over a country where all of his subjects lived securely in peace and happiness. His wife was so beautiful and so clever that he frequently marvelled at his good fortune.

As you might expect, this King and Queen lived in a splendid Palace, where they were surrounded by courtiers and servants. The Royal Stables were the finest in the world, containing numbers of swift, thoroughbred horses that the King greatly prized. But, oddly enough, his greatest treasure was a little brown donkey with lop-sided ears.

One day the Queen fell ill. Everything was done to help her, but she grew steadily worse, and when the doctors had given up all hope she called her husband to her bedside and said in a weak and trembling voice, 'My dear, I do not think I can live much longer. If you wish to marry again when I am gone, I beg you . . .'

The King interrupted her with tears in his eyes. 'You must not speak of such things. If you were to die, no one else could ever take your place as my wife.'

The Queen smiled at him.

'Oh, I do not doubt your love for me, but I beg you to carry out my last wish. If you meet someone who is wiser and more beautiful than I, you must marry her, for, although we have a daughter, the Kingdom needs a son and heir.'

The King agreed to her request, and a few minutes afterwards she died in his arms, leaving him so utterly wretched that no one could comfort him.

Day after day, week after week, the King mourned for his Queen. He shut himself in one room of his great Palace and, sick at heart, spent his time in weeping and lamentation. In great distress his courtiers watched him, and finally one of them ventured to remind him of the Queen's last wish.

Though much confused in mind, the King recalled his promise and set out to look for a wife. But he could find no woman to compare with his dead Queen, and he sank more deeply into despair.

One day his daughter Christabel came to him, and in his madness he took her for her mother, whom she closely resembled in beauty and grace. He imagined that he was young again and courting the golden-haired girl. He took her hands in his and begged her to marry him.

Christabel was amazed and grieved, for she could see that her father's mind was wandering. But being a good

daughter, and dutiful as well, she could not think how to refuse his impossible proposal without offending him or seeming to be ungrateful.

At last Christabel went to consult her godmother, the Fairy of the Lilac Trees. This wise fairy lived a short distance away. The path leading to her grotto was lined with lilacs and heavy-scented flowers that nodded and dipped to the Princess as she ran past. The walls and floor of the fairy's grotto were covered with coral and mother-of-pearl, so that the whole cave shone with a silver-pink light.

Christabel's godmother knew at once the reason for her visit.

'Child,' she began, 'I know what the King, your father, has asked you. But have no fear, for I will help you.'

Smiling with happiness and relief, Christabel replied, 'Oh! I knew you were the only person who could help me. What do you think I should do?'

'Go home,' said the fairy, 'and when the King again proposes marriage, make an impossible request. Tell him that he must give you a dress the colour of the sky.'

The Princess did exactly as her godmother had told her. But two days later, a messenger from the Court came to her and laid at her feet a box that held the most wonderful dress she had ever seen; it was a deep azure blue, as the sky is when you look up on a clear summer day, and it shimmered with silver and gold embroidery, as clouds shine and glow when the sun blazes through them.

Christabel rubbed her eyes in disbelief. The King had granted her wish. What must she do now? Only her god-mother could advise her, and, as soon as she was free, Christabel ran to the fairy's grotto.

This time the Fairy of the Lilac Trees advised her to let the King know that she wanted a dress the colour of the moon. Happy again at the thought that the wish could not be granted, Christabel returned to the Palace.

But the King was not discouraged. Two days later, a

wonderful silver-white dress, the colour of the moon, was laid at her feet. Christabel, acting on the fairy's advice, then asked for a dress like the sun, and for a third time the King granted her wish, giving her a gown covered with diamonds that dazzled all who looked at it.

'You must ask for the skin of the brown donkey with the lop-sided ears,' her godmother told her at last. 'The King will never bring himself to kill his precious donkey for you.'

But the King wanted Christabel for his wife so much that he could not refuse even this, though he wept as he gave the command to destroy the beast.

As soon as the donkey-skin was placed before her, Christabel knew that there was nothing else precious left she could ask for. She put the skin over her shoulders and fled from the Palace. All she took with her was a small gold ring that the Fairy of the Lilac Trees had placed on her finger when she saw her last. The Princess knew that she had only to rub her golden ring and she would have a trunk of her prettiest clothes.

The King, thinking that Christabel would agree to be his bride after she had received the donkey-skin, commanded that plans for the wedding feast be made. When he discovered that Christabel had left the Palace, he was heartbroken, and his soldiers were ordered to search for her.

Meanwhile, Christabel had wandered a long way. She looked so poor and ugly with the wretched donkey-skin on her back that, when she asked for work, the farm servants mocked her and sent her away. At last she came to a very small farm-house in a neighbouring kingdom. The farmer's wife had been searching for a girl who would do all the hardest and dirtiest tasks, and she agreed to take Christabel.

So Christabel was given a tiny room to sleep in, and from morning till night she was kept busy scouring and scrubbing, clearing the pigsty, and feeding the poultry. In addition, she had to put up with the rough farm lads who teased her because she seemed so plain.

'You should be called "Ugly Duckling",' they laughed. 'But with that funny old skin on your back, we would do better to call you "Old Donkey-skin" instead.'

One afternoon the Princess felt so sad and so tired that she slipped away from the farm-house. When she reached the river bank she sat down and began to cry. When she could cry no more, Christabel stared into the water and there she saw her own reflection, for the water was so still and clear that it acted like a mirror.

'How dirty and ugly I am,' Christabel sighed. 'How could I have allowed myself to grow like this?' And with that she leaned over the shallow bank and washed her face and hands. And now the river told her that once again she was fair and lovely.

'Let them call me Donkey-skin,' Christabel thought as she walked slowly back to the farm. 'At least, the King, my father, will not find me here.' And she pulled the old donkey-skin round her face and shoulders so that none should see how pretty she really was.

The very next day was Sunday, and when all the farm-

house was asleep, Christabel shut herself away in her tiny room, opened the magic trunk, and pulled out all her most beautiful gowns and her finest bracelets and necklaces. She put on her richest gown and then, taking the golden brush, she brushed out her long golden hair until it was as smooth as silk.

'How lovely to be a Princess again,' she said to herself, 'even if it is only for a little while.'

The very next day, who should come to the farm but the Prince of the kingdom, a gay, handsome young man greatly beloved by all the people.

'The hounds drew me so far into the forest,' the Prince told the smiling farmer's wife, 'that I lost my way. And now it is late. Can you shelter me for the night, I wonder, and bring me a bite of supper to eat?'

'You are more than welcome,' declared the woman, quite overcome with delight. 'And Donkey-skin will bake you one of her delicious fruit cakes while you are getting on with your supper.'

Donkey-skin, who had often heard of the wonderful Prince, was too shy to push herself forward—not that she was given the chance—and she shut herself in her little room after she had baked the cake.

Who knows what mysterious part the Fairy of the Lilac Trees played in all that was to follow? But it did come about that the Prince, having failed to find the farmer's wife to thank her for the meal, took to exploring the farm. And it so happened that he saw a light from underneath a door just close to the kitchen. It happened too that, being a gentle but curious Prince, he took a quick peep through the keyhole of this door, and there he saw—but of course you can guess—not Donkey-skin but Princess Christabel brushing her long golden hair with a small golden brush, and looking more beautiful than he had ever imagined any girl could look.

The Prince stayed only a moment and then went off to find a servant who could tell him about the lovely girl.

'Can you tell me her name? What is she doing here? Her beauty is dazzling like the sun! Who is she?'

Over and over again the Prince tried to find someone

who knew about the lovely girl in the dress of splendid satin who wore a ring on her finger and whose long hair shone like gold, but there was no one at the farm who had ever heard of her, and they looked at the Prince as if he had taken leave of his senses.

'A grubby young scullery maid lives in the small room near the kitchen,' the servants told him. 'She keeps company with bats by night, and by day she scours the pans and sweeps the floors. You can't mean old Donkey-skin, and we don't know of any other girls round the place.'

The Prince could not understand these answers, and after a time he went back to his Palace, troubled in mind and heart and so deeply in love that he could not eat. Night after night he tossed and turned in his bed, and his groans and moans brought the Queen, his mother, running to his side. On seeing how ill her darling son was, she roused the royal doctors. They came at once with hot pads for his feet and cold pads for his head, but neither

the hot pads for his feet nor the cold pads for his head did the slightest bit of good.

The Queen sat by her only son hour after hour, and in the morning, with tears in her eyes, begged him to tell her what had brought on this sudden and alarming illness.

'Mother,' whispered the Prince in a thin, weak voice, 'only one thing will help me. Send someone to Donkey-skin for one of her cakes and bring it to me.' And he lay back on the pillows, unable to utter another word.

The Queen looked round at the doctors and courtiers who were present and asked in amazement, 'Who is this Donkey-skin? Can anyone find such a person?'

'She is a peasant girl, an ugly little wretch,' one of the courtiers said at last, 'who is living at a small farm some miles away.'

'No matter,' replied the Queen. 'If my son wants to see her, we must let him have his way. Go straight to Donkey-skin, if there is such a person, and ask her to bake a cake at once.'

So a messenger was sent post-haste to the farm-house, and orders were given that Donkey-skin must start baking a cake for the Prince immediately.

Christabel was breathless with excitement when the royal command came that she should bake a cake for the Prince. Running to her room and disturbing the bats that were clinging upside down to the dark corners of the ceiling, she brushed her golden hair with her golden brush until it shone as if it were silk. Then she put on one of her beautiful dresses.

'He shall have the finest cake I have ever made,' said Christabel to herself as she put on the donkey-skin over her gown and ran to the kitchen.

Her thoughts as she worked tumbled over each other, and she failed to notice that her gold ring had fallen into the dough. Thus it happened that when the cake was ready for the oven, the ring was part of it!

When the cake was baked a beautiful golden brown,

Christabel gave it to the Queen's servant who had been waiting outside.

'Please can you tell me if the Prince is very ill?' she asked.

But the royal messenger could not bring himself to address a common servant girl. He accepted the cake in silence and, mounting his horse, rode swiftly back to the Palace.

The Queen was waiting anxiously to receive the cake and she carried it herself to the Royal chamber where her son lay pale and miserable.

'Your wish has been granted,' she said, gazing at him tenderly. 'Here is the cake that Donkey-skin has made. Will you take a slice of it now?'

Her words roused the Prince; he sat up in bed and began to eat, and as he did so, he all but swallowed the little gold ring.

His fond mother did not see him take the ring from his mouth and secrete it under his pillow, but she did see how his eyes were shining, and how a red flush stained his cheeks.

'Leave me,' the Prince said. 'I would like to be alone.' And as soon as his mother had left the room the Prince took the ring and gazed at it.

'This is the very ring I saw on the finger of the only girl I can ever love,' he said to himself. 'How can I find her again? I swear I shall marry the maid whose finger this ring fits.'

So many plans flashed through his mind that his fever began to mount again, and when the doctors were summoned, this time they declared that the Prince suffered from a disease that they could only describe as 'love-sickness'.

The Queen brought the King, and they both wrung their hands in distress as they looked down upon the Prince.

'My son, my dear and only son,' cried the King, 'tell us who it is you love so much. Even if she be the poorest and humblest in the land, your mother and I will gladly let you marry her.'

The Prince showed them the golden ring.

'My heart is set on marrying the one whose finger fits this ring,' he whispered. 'She who can wear this tiny ring

must have slender hands of great delicacy, hands which reflect the beauty and sweetness of her person.'

The King and Queen looked at the ring, and agreed that the owner of it would surely be of noble birth and refined taste. Then the King embraced his son and strode from the room. He called for trumpets and drums to be sounded throughout the city. Heralds were despatched to spread abroad the news that all young girls must go to the Palace to try on a ring. The girl who could wear the ring would marry the heir to the throne.

The princesses arrived first, followed by the duchesses and all the other fine titled ladies in their splendid carriages; but however much they tried, not one could push the ring on her finger. The ladies-in-waiting came next, twittering like birds about their hopes of becoming the Prince's bride, but their fingers were much too thick and they, too, went away disappointed.

Then the maid-servants tried, with no more success. At last even the scullery-maids and the little girls who looked after the sheep in their pastures were given a chance to try the ring, but their fingers were so short and so fat that they could not even push the gold circle beyond their nails!

Finally the Prince was told that all the girls from miles around had tried to wear the ring and that it would fit none of them.

'Have you fetched Donkey-skin, who made me that delicious cake the other day?' asked the Prince at length.

Only politeness stopped everyone from roaring with laughter at the very idea, but it had to be admitted that no one had thought of trying the ring on *her* finger.

'She must be brought here at once. It must not be said that anyone has been overlooked in this matter,' ordered the King, and he despatched two courtiers to bring Donkey-skin to the Palace immediately.

Christabel had heard the fanfare of trumpets and drums, and she had heard the proclamation of the heralds; she felt sure that her little golden ring must be the cause of all the commotion. How she longed to meet the handsome Prince; how she longed to present herself at the Palace—but somehow she did not dare. Imagine her joy and happiness when two royal courtiers came to the farm with the King's command.

'I will come at once,' said Christabel, 'but leave me alone a moment, please.' And while the royal courtiers waited outside, Christabel opened her magic trunk and took from it her lovely moon dress and put it on. But when the royal courtiers called out impatiently, she covered it up entirely with the ugly old donkey-skin.

The Prince greeted Christabel with great kindness, but he could not believe that he had ever set eyes on her before. How could this servant girl in the hideous donkeyskin be the adorable girl whom he had once seen through the keyhole?

'Are *you* the one who lives in the little room at the end of the passage near the kitchen? he asked, unhappy and ashamed that he could have made so foolish a mistake.

'Yes, Sire,' Christabel whispered. 'I am.'

'Very well!' the Prince sighed heavily. 'Show me your hand.'

From under the donkey-skin Christabel produced her small hand, so dainty and white that the King and the Queen and all the grand lords and ladies of the Court gasped in amazement. They gasped even louder when they saw how easily the ring slid on to Christabel's finger.

Suddenly the donkey-skin fell to the ground, and there stood the Princess, radiant in her beauty and joy. For a moment everyone in the room stood as if turned to stone. The Prince threw himself on his knees before Christabel, begging that she would marry him. The King and the Queen hugged her, and all the grand lords and ladies cheered.

But before Christabel could say a word, there was a flash of light, and the Fairy of the Lilac Trees appeared in their midst, filling the room with the sweet scent of lilacs.

Smiling, the Fairy told the court Christabel's story, just as I have told it to you here, and after she had finished, the King and Queen were even more affectionate, and the Prince was so moved by Christabel's adventures that he fell even more deeply in love.

Preparations for the wedding were put in hand. Kings and queens and even emperors from countries far and wide were invited to the ceremony. Some came in splendid carriages drawn by high-spirited horses; some were carried on the strong shoulders of native bearers; and from the East the rulers came mounted on huge elephants, or borne on the backs of great, smooth, striped tigers.

But the most magnificent of all the guests was Christabel's royal father. Now, as he realised how foolish and ill he had been, he found it in his heart to wish her long life and happiness for the rest of her days.

After the wedding, the Prince's father bestowed his own crown on his son, and placed him on the throne. With Christabel as his Queen, the new King ruled wisely and well for many years, and the joy and love they felt for each other spread, like ripples on a pond, throughout their happy kingdom.

LITTLE IDA'S FLOWERS

Ida loved flowers so much that it made her sad when their heads began to droop.

'Look at the flowers,' she said to the old gardener when she met him. 'They are so tired they can't hold up their heads.'

'Of course they can't,' said the gardener, and he tapped his nose to show that he was thinking. 'I expect they have been to a ball up at the castle and worn themselves out.'

'What!' exclaimed little Ida. 'Are you trying to tell me that the flowers go dancing?'

'Most certainly they do,' replied the gardener. 'Whenever the King goes back to his winter palace, the flowers take over. Two of the finest red roses sit on the throne, and the other flowers, the tulips and carnations and the yellow iris—so many of them I would have to make a list—spend the nights in dancing.'

'Really!' exclaimed little Ida. 'Do the flowers in our garden know what is going on in the palace, I wonder?'

'They do,' said her wise friend. 'They don't exactly speak

to each other as we do. They make signs, you know. If you watch that nettle over there you will see him bowing to that pretty carnation. He's probably telling her he loves her.'

'How splendid!' said Ida. 'When I get back to the nursery I will put all my tired, faded flowers into Sophy's bed. Then they will be fresh enough to go dancing when night comes.'

Sophy, who was Ida's best doll, was not very pleased to be taken out of her pretty pink bed and placed in a drawer. But Ida spoke firmly to her. 'It is only for one night, Sophy dearest,' she said. 'And look how tired my poor flowers are. If they rest in your bed they will soon be strong again.'

And she placed the drooping flowers, which had stood in a vase on the book shelf all day, in Sophy's bed and pulled the quilt over them up to their heads.

When it was time for Ida herself to go to bed, she looked long and carefully at the tulips and hyacinths standing in two pots on the window sill. These were her mother's flowers and she had not dared to put them to bed too.

'I expect you will be going to the ball later on,' she whispered to them before she jumped into bed. 'I do hope you have a lovely time.'

Ida fell asleep thinking about the flowers. When she

awoke it was still dark, and the house was very still and silent. 'I wonder what my flowers are doing now?' Ida thought. 'I would so love to know.'

And presently she got up and crept towards the nursery door. There were her flowers, dancing round and round to the music of the nursery piano, which was being played by a tall yellow lily. Its long face made Ida think of her own music teacher, who always nodded her head whenever she hit a black note.

The flowers danced beautifully, holding on to each other by their leafy arms. As Ida watched, one of her mother's red tulips went over to Sophy's bed and invited the tired flowers to join in. And soon they, too, were dancing as gaily as the rest.

Then Ida saw Sophy sitting up in the drawer and looking very much as if she wanted to dance. But none of the flowers looked in her direction. Sophy coughed and wriggled about until she fell out of the drawer and landed with a bump on the floor.

Ida was pleased to see that it was her own poor tired flowers who picked Sophy up. They thanked her for lending them her bed, and they invited her to dance with them. This Sophy did, most elegantly, and the full moon shed its bright silver light on her pretty face as she danced around.

Suddenly the door opened and in came some of the flowers from the royal gardens. The King and Queen of the Roses, with golden crowns on their heads, led the procession of poppies and peonies, sweet peas and marigolds, and, last of all, a group of shy delicate violets.

'Oh,' gasped Ida. 'Oh, oh, oh! How beautiful they are. I never dreamt...' And she gave a huge yawn.

Ida waited until all the flowers had been presented to the King and Queen, and then she crept back to bed and fell fast asleep as soon as her head touched the pillow.

In the morning the first thing she did on waking was to go and see if her flowers were still in Sophy's bed. Yes, there they were, but they looked even more faded than they had looked yesterday. 'I think,' said Ida, 'that I will put you in my best box with the painted birds on it, and bury you in the garden after breakfast.'

And this is just what she did. With the help of her two cousins who came to play with her, little Ida buried her dead flowers, and the two boys shot their arrows over the grave. 'I'm not really sad,' said Ida after the funeral. 'I know I shall see my flowers again next year, and they will look more beautiful than ever after their long sleep.'

HANSEL AND GRETEL

There was once a poor woodcutter and his wife who were very, very poor indeed. The woodcutter had two children by his first wife, a boy called Hansel and a girl called Gretel.

Hansel and Gretel did all they could to help their father and stepmother. Hansel tied up the bundles of wood which their father brought from the forest, and Gretel made the beds, and washed up the cups, saucers and plates.

The woodcutter longed to provide for his children, for he had a kind heart, but he knew he was coming to the end of his savings. Soon he would have no money left, not even enough to buy bread.

One night, when the children were upstairs in bed, his wife said to him, 'Husband, we have scarcely a penny left. There's not a drop of milk in the house and very little bread.'

'It won't always be so bad,' said the woodcutter. 'Be patient, wife. Things will get better soon.'

This only made his wife angry. 'That's what you always say, husband,' she screamed. 'If we could rid ourselves of the two children, we could manage to keep ourselves alive for a little while longer.'

The poor woodcutter exclaimed in horror at the very

idea of losing his children, but his wife went on. 'Early tomorrow morning we must take them so far into the forest that they will never find their way home. I tell you, husband, it is the only way. We'll give them a slice of bread each and perhaps someone will find them and take care of them.'

The more her husband protested, the more angry his wife became. Her loud voice soon reached the ears of the two children, and presently they woke up and crept to the top of the stairs to listen.

'Wife, wife! It is a terrible thing to do!' they heard their father say at last. 'But I cannot hold out against you any longer. Very well, I agree. We shall take them into the forest in the morning.'

Hansel squeezed his sister's hand. 'Don't be afraid, Gretel,' he whispered, as they stole back to their room. 'I'll think of something, I promise you.'

'What can we do?' poor little Gretel cried, when she was safely back in bed.

'We must pretend that we know nothing of their intentions,' Hansel said. 'I've thought of a plan already.'

As soon as the cottage was silent, Hansel crept down the

stairs in his bare feet. He turned the key of the back door and ran outside into the garden.

A big silver moon hung in the sky, shedding its light over everything. It lit up the pebbles at his feet, and Hansel stooped down and began to gather them up, one by one.

The round white pebbles were all part of the plan which Hansel had made. If his plan worked, the shiny pebbles would help him to lead his sister safely through the big forest.

As Hansel filled his pockets with the pebbles, he went over his plan again and again. In the morning, he would take the pebbles with him when they all set out for the forest. Then he would drop them, one by one, as they walked along.

'They will never notice what I am doing,' he told himself hopefully. 'They won't guess that I am laying a trail of pebbles which will lead us safely back home to the cottage.'

Hansel was so pleased with himself that he forgot to be sad. After all, his father had not really wanted to leave them alone in that dark forest.

'When they have us safely home again,' he thought happily, 'they will never try to send us away again. Then perhaps our fortunes will change; my father will be able to sell his wood in the market if things get better.'

By now, his pockets were bulging with pebbles and, with a last look round, he scrambled to his feet and ran back to the cottage.

'I hope Gretel is awake,' he thought. 'I must tell her all about the pebbles before we set out in the morning. She will be so pleased.'

Hansel found his little sister tucked up in bed.

'Gretel, Gretel!' he whispered, as he emptied his pockets and hopped into his own bed. 'Are you asleep?'

'No, Hansel,' Gretel whispered back. 'How could I be!'

'Listen, Gretel,' Hansel whispered, 'tomorrow, when our father takes us into the forest, you must pretend to be happy. Don't cry or make a fuss. Everything is going to be all right. These pebbles will show us the way home,

no matter how far we go into the forest. Promise to be brave.'

'I promise,' said Gretel. 'I promise to be very brave, and I won't say anything about the pebbles. Of course I won't. Oh Hansel, are you sure your plan will work?'

'I'm positively certain,' said Hansel bravely. 'Now go to sleep. They are sure to waken us early.'

Hansel was right. Almost as soon as it was light they heard their stepmother calling them.

'Gretel! Hansel! Get dressed quickly. It's going to be a fine day and your father and I want to take you both into the forest where you can help to gather sticks.'

The woodcutter led the way into the forest, but this morning he did not laugh or make jokes. Instead, he walked steadily on until they were in a strange part of the forest.

Hansel lingered behind, dropping pebbles as he went, and sometimes his stepmother called out crossly, 'Make haste, Hansel. Why do you keep so far behind the rest of us?'

'I'm coming,' Hansel shouted back. 'There is so much to see that I forget to hurry.'

357

When they reached the very middle of the forest, the woodcutter said, 'Let us rest here. We have come far enough.'

'Very well,' said his wife. 'You children begin collecting brushwood.'

While Hansel and Gretel scurried this way and that gathering sticks, the woodcutter and his wife stole silently away.

Hansel and Gretel were so busy collecting sticks that they did not miss their father for a long time. Then suddenly Gretel cried, 'Hansel, Hansel, it is growing dark and we are all alone! I am so frightened.'

'Rest here for a while,' said her brother. 'There is nothing to be afraid of. As soon as it is light, we shall be able to see the pebbles. The pebbles will lead us safely home.'

'I'm not afraid,' said Gretel bravely. 'I'm not afraid, Hansel.' She sat down beside her big brother and put her head on his shoulder.

As soon as it was light, Hansel and Gretel set out to find their own way home. The smooth white pebbles shone in the bright morning sunshine and Hansel shouted joyfully, 'Come on, Gretel! I told you they would show us the way through the forest.'

When their cottage came in sight, the children started to run. They flung themselves at the door, and their father opened his arms wide at the sight of them.

'We must never, never do such a thing again,' he told his wife. 'How lucky we are that no harm has come to them.'

But his wife did not agree. Times were still hard, and with two hungry young mouths to feed she knew that they would soon go short again. So it was that one night, when there was only a stale loaf of bread left, she said, 'Husband, we must take the children into the forest again. This time we must make certain they do not return.'

The poor woodcutter protested loudly but he was no match for his wife. and presently he agreed.

As before, Hansel overheard everything. This time,

however, he found the back door locked and the key missing.

'Don't worry, little sister,' he whispered, after he had crept upstairs again. 'It is true that I cannot fill my pockets with pebbles, but our stepmother is sure to give us each a slice of bread. I will leave a trail of breadcrumbs instead of pebbles. Then we shall still be able to find our own way home.'

Early the next morning, their stepmother called them and told them to get ready. 'Here is a slice of bread for each of you,' she said, as they started out.

Hansel crumbled the bread as he went along, leaving a long trail of crumbs behind him. When, at last, they were deep in the forest his father built a fire. 'Rest beside the fire, children,' he said, giving them a sad look. 'Your mother and I will go to another part of the forest to cut wood.'

Hansel put his arms round his little sister, and soon they were fast asleep. When they awoke, their parents had disappeared and they were all alone.

'Don't cry, Gretel,' said Hansel bravely. 'By the light

of this moon we shall see the crumbs and they will lead us home.'

Alas, the birds had made a feast of the crumbs and not a single one could Hansel find.

Hansel did his best to comfort his sister. 'If we walk and walk we are sure to find a path we recognise,' he said. But though they walked for most of that night and the next day they were still hopelessly lost.

'Hansel! Hansel! I am so tired and hungry,' Gretel wailed. 'I'm sure I shall die...' As she spoke a pretty white bird suddenly appeared. It flew round them fluttering its wings, singing the sweetest song they had ever heard.

'Look, Gretel, it seems to want us to follow it. Come on, let's see where it will take us.'

The bird led them to the strangest cottage they had ever seen. It was made of gingerbread, cake and sugar. Gretel stared at the gingerbread house.

'Oh, do look, Hansel,' she cried. 'The roof is made of cake, and the window frames are icing sugar! Doesn't it make you want to eat and eat?'

'Yes, it does,' said Hansel.

And Gretel said, 'Let's help ourselves.'

With cries of delight, Hansel and Gretel ran towards the gingerbread house. 'Look Hansel!' Gretel shouted. 'The pieces of gingerbread break off quite easily. Oh, I am so hungry.' And with that she took a big bite of wall.

Just as Hansel was breaking off a piece of plum-cake roof, the door opened suddenly and an old, old woman stood there. Hansel and Gretel got such a fright that they dropped their cake. But the old, old woman smiled at them kindly. Then she hobbled down the steps towards them. 'Come in, dear children,' she said, taking them by their hands. 'Come and stay with me. I promise you shall eat to your heart's desire.' With that she pulled them up the steps and inside the house.

The children soon forgot their fears when they saw the feast the old lady spread before them. 'Eat up,' she said in her croaky voice.

Now the old woman was really a wicked witch, and she had sent out her beautiful white bird to lead the children to her cottage.

She was sorry to find that the children were so thin. 'I must fatten them up first,' she told herself. 'When they are nice and plump, they will make a tasty meal.'

Hansel and Gretel thought they were in paradise. They had soft, feathery beds to sleep in. Every morning, there was creamy milk to drink, rosy apples and honeycake to eat.

The old lady seemed to want them to eat and eat, and she would not accept any thanks.

'You'll please me best,' she said over and over again, 'if you eat as much as you can. There's nothing I like better than to see fat little boys and fat little girls.'

'We would like to stay with you always,' said Hansel, one day, 'but we would like to see our father again too.'

The old lady looked quite upset when he said this. She pulled him towards her and began to pinch his arms and legs. Then she muttered, 'Yes, yes, almost ready! Perhaps

one more day! You must eat a very big supper, Hansel. I have made a special apple pie for you both.'

Hansel did not understand why she liked fat children so much until the next morning. Suddenly, the wicked old witch seized him in her bony hands and, with a horrible chuckle, pushed him into a large wooden cage.

'There!' she cried. 'This is your home until I am ready to eat you.' With another deep-throated chuckle she pulled down the lid and hobbled away.

'Let me out! Let me out!' Hansel screamed.

But the witch only laughed. 'You'll stay there until it is my pleasure to let you out,' she croaked. 'And that won't be until you are fat enough for roasting.'

Gretel could scarcely believe her eyes when she saw what had happened to her brother.

'You might as well earn your keep,' the old witch growled at her. 'Fetch me water from the well, and then scrub the floor until it shines like a new penny.'

Poor Gretel! She grew more and more frightened as she listened to the witch's cruel words.

'I'm going to fatten him up properly,' said the witch. 'Then it will be your turn, child.'

In vain, Gretel wept and begged for mercy.

'Set us free!' she cried, 'and we shall never tell . . .'

But the wicked witch only laughed and rubbed her bony hands together. For the rest of the day she kept Gretel busy about the cottage.

'I must stoke up the oven,' she said at last. 'Go into the yard and fetch me a bundle of sticks.'

'But it's such a big oven,' said Gretel. 'Why do you want to heat the big oven?'

The witch chuckled. 'You'll find out soon enough. Now do as I say, while I give that brother of yours his last taste of cream cake and apple pie.'

Gretel did not know what to do. But she made up her mind that somehow she would try to save her brother.

'I must be brave,' she told herself. 'There must be some way I can save Hansel from the wicked witch.'

In the morning, the witch told her, 'Fetch me some

water and fill the kettle. I'm going to make some pastry
first—and then ...'

'And then?' asked Gretel fearfully. 'What next?'

'What do you think, stupid!' the old witch shrieked.
'Today I'm going to eat that brother of yours, be he fat or
be he thin.'

'No, no, no!' cried little Gretel desperately. 'Oh how I
wish we had perished in the forest.'

'You can save your tears,' said the witch. 'For they won't
do you any good. They won't melt my heart either, for I
haven't got one.'

After Gretel had fetched the water and filled the kettle,
the witch went on, 'Now, child, just creep inside the oven
and tell me if it is warm enough for my pastry.'

Gretel realised that the witch meant to roast her too,
so, with great presence of mind, she said, 'But—but I don't
know how to get in. I won't be able to feel how warm it is
unless you show me.'

The witch grunted impatiently, 'Stupid goose! Watch
me!'

With that she put her head and shoulders inside the
oven. This was the moment Gretel had been waiting for.
With a big shove she pushed the wicked witch right inside,

and slammed the oven doors shut. Then she ran to the wooden cage and let her brother out.

How they kissed and hugged each other for joy!

'There's nothing to be afraid of now,' said Hansel. 'Let's explore before we try to find our way home.'

Now the witch had lived for a very long time, and with the help of her wicked spells she had gathered together a great box of treasure. It was not long before Hansel and Gretel stumbled over the witch's treasure chest.

'Diamonds and gold pieces and rubies!' Hansel exclaimed as he opened the box. 'Oh Gretel, our fortunes are made.'

'It's—it's the witch's treasure!' Gretel said.

But Hansel replied, 'The witch is dead, and besides, witches don't have any claim on treasure. Treasure belongs to the finders, and we have found it. Father will sell all these precious stones.'

Then Hansel began to fill his pockets with the diamonds and rubies and other precious stones. Gretel put all the gold pieces in the pockets of her pinafore.

When they had taken all they could carry, they left the gingerbread house and ran into the forest. They walked for a long, long time until suddenly they came upon a wide stretch of water.

'We can't possibly get across,' Gretel cried, but Hansel said, 'Look, there is a duck. I think she will help us to cross.'

'Let's ask her,' said Gretel, and she began to sing,

> *Little duck, little duck, help us, do;*
> *Hansel and Gretel are waiting for you.*
> *There's never a plank or bridge in sight;*
> *Take us across on your back so white.*

On hearing Gretel's song, the duck swam towards them. First, she carried Hansel safely across the water, and then she came back for Gretel.

'Look,' cried Hansel, after they had thanked the good little duck, 'I am sure I know this path. We have only to follow it and it will take us home.'

'Let's run,' said Gretel. So off they went, running as fast as they could until their cottage came in sight.

'Do you think father will be glad to see us?' Gretel asked doubtfully, as they pushed open the cottage door.

'Of course, he will!' said Hansel. 'He didn't want to leave us in the forest.'

The poor woodcutter, whose second wife was now dead, shed tears of joy when he saw his two children.

'Wonderful! Wonderful!' he exclaimed, and he hugged them and kissed them.

'All your troubles are over,' Hansel said at last, and he emptied his pockets on the table. 'Look, father, we shall always have enough money now to buy food.'

'Look, father!' cried Gretel in her turn, and she lifted up her pinafore and all the gold pieces tumbled out of the pockets and rolled on the floor.

Then the woodcutter hugged his children all over again, and the cottage rang with their happy laughter.

THE GOBLIN AND THE STUDENT

There are good goblins and bad goblins, as you very well know. There are, besides, goblins who are neither good nor bad but careful as to which side their bread is buttered. This story is about one of these.

Having looked around, the Goblin, who knew on which side his bread was buttered, decided to make his home with a grocer in the town. By so doing, he made certain of his supper. Indeed, the grocer not only set out a bowl of his creamiest porridge for the Goblin each night, but went so far as to add a lump of butter to it.

There was also living in the grocer's house above the shop a poor Student; he was so poor that he could not honestly call anything his own except the few books from which he got his learning.

The Goblin knew the Student, and sometimes wished that he could share some of his learning, but the idea of living in a poor attic was too dreadful to bear thinking about.

One morning the poor Student came down to the shop to buy a few of the things that kept body and soul together.

Among his purchases was a small piece of hard cheese.

'Here you are, then,' said the grocer. 'I'll wrap it up for you.' And he tore a page out of a tattered old book lying on the counter.

As the Student waited for his change, his eyes fell on the book and he knew at once that it was a very old and very rare book of poetry that should never have found its way into a grocer's shop.

'Take back the butter and the sugar,' cried the Student in an eager voice. 'And let me have instead that book of poetry lying there. It's worth more than food to me.'

'Please yourself,' said the grocer. 'There is no accounting for tastes.'

Smiling happily, the Student took the book and went upstairs to his attic, leaving behind a puzzled grocer and an equally puzzled Goblin, who had heard everything from his place behind a box of soap.

'What is poetry?' the Goblin asked himself. 'How can poetry be more important than butter?'

That night the Goblin crept upstairs; when he reached the attic he looked through the keyhole to see what he could see. There was the Student as he had expected. He was reading aloud from the ancient book of poems.

'Words,' said the Goblin to himself, 'just words!' But, as he watched, something strange and wonderful happened. The Student was bathed in a soft light, like warm sunshine.

The light seemed to come from inside the book. So, too, did the wonderful tree that was beginning to grow out of the pages.

The Student read on, and the tree grew and spread until its fresh green-leafed branches were all about the young scholar. All about him, too, were flowers; and the sweetest music the Goblin had ever heard drifted round the room.

So entrancing was the sight that the Goblin almost made up his mind, there and then, to forsake the grocer and offer himself to the poor Student. Then he remembered, just in time, his porridge and the lump of butter.

The Goblin allowed several nights to pass before once again he ventured upstairs and put his eye to the keyhole. The vision was as beautiful as before, and the Goblin remained in the draughty passage for so long that he almost forgot where he was.

370

Even so, he could not make up his mind to forsake the grocer and make his home with the Student. Then, one night, as the Goblin lay half asleep behind the soap boxes, he heard a loud knocking on the shutters and a voice shouting, 'Fire! Fire!'

All in a moment the grocer came rushing into the shop to save his most precious possession—which happened to be the cash box. And his good lady tumbled after him, clutching her gold earrings.

The Goblin thought only of one thing, the old book of poetry. And as the grocer and his wife rushed from the shop, the Goblin bounded upstairs to the attic. The book lay on the bare wooden table, and, with never a glance at the Student, who was still only half awake, the Goblin snatched it and jumped out of the window on to the roof. He had saved the only treasure in the house that was worth saving.

Truth to tell, the fire burned itself out without doing much damage. When the panic was over, the Goblin, still clutching the treasure, which he had wrapped in his little red cap for safekeeping, left his place among the chimney-tops and returned to the attic.

'So be it,' said the Goblin to himself as he restored the precious book to the table. 'I'll make the Student my master and put up with the attic.'

Then he remembered his creamy porridge with its lump of butter, and, being as like to a human as a Goblin can be, he added, 'But I'll not give up the grocer completely. I'll visit him nightly—in time for my supper.'

THE UGLY DUCKLING

The old farmhouse was so well hidden from the road that if you hadn't known about it you would have passed it by. There it stood, grey-stoned and lonely, surrounded by green fields and marshy waters.

In a deep ditch, close to this farmhouse, a Mother Duck was sitting on her eggs. She had been there for a long time, and already she was beginning to wonder if her babies were ever going to hatch out. But when the sun was sinking low in the sky, one of her eggs cracked, and her first-born came into the world. He was quickly followed by his brothers and sisters.

'Quack, quack!' said Mother Duck, well pleased with her new family.

Now there was but a single egg left in the nest and this one was by far the largest. The tiny ducklings were beginning to try out their legs when, finally, the big egg cracked wide open and the last of the brood scrambled out. Mother Duck looked at her youngest in dismay.

'Quack!' said she. 'Quack! Quack! Quack! Surely he can't be one of mine. How ugly he is! How different from all the others!'

So, almost before he could flap his wings, the Ugly Duckling learnt what it was like to be unwanted.

Early the next morning, Mother Duck took her small family down to the pond, hoping against hope that the youngest of her brood would pass unnoticed.

'Now we shall see,' she said to herself, 'if he can swim, for if he cannot he will be no child of mine . . .'

To her surprise, the Ugly Duckling dived into the water fearlessly, and soon he showed that he could swim even more skilfully than his brothers and sisters.

'Upon my feathers!' exclaimed Mother Duck, 'he must be my own son. I shall have to make the best of him. Everything depends on the Dowager Duck and how she sees him.'

Alas, the visit to the Dowager was not a success. Being the oldest and most important member of the farmyard, the high-born lady duck always spoke exactly what was in her mind.

'I cannot truthfully congratulate you, Mother Duck,' said she, 'on all the members of your family when I see that your youngest is quite unspeakably ugly.'

Mother Duck did her best to look as if she had not heard these harsh words, and the poor little Ugly Duckling tried to hide himself away, but there was no escaping the scorn in the Dowager Duck's eyes.

This was only the beginning of the Ugly Duckling's unhappiness. All that day and all the next and for many days after, the poor little Ugly Duckling was chased and snapped at and insulted wherever he went. Even his own brothers and sisters took sides with his enemies.

The Ugly Duckling was so miserable that he wanted to die. Instead, he decided one day that he would run away. No one wanted him in the farmyard, not even his own mother. Perhaps in the big wide world he would find a friend.

He could not fly very fast or very gracefully, but somehow he managed to make his way over the hedges and across the fields and through the woods until he came to a great marsh. Here the wild ducks lived, and here the Ugly Duckling came to rest. He was so tired and so sad that he felt he could not take another step. So he made a little nest for himself among the tall reeds and went to sleep.

Dawn saw the return of the wild ducks. When they caught sight of the Ugly Duckling, they immediately began to question him:

'Who are you?'

'Where are you from?'

'Who is your mother?'

'Why are you so ugly?'

The Ugly Duckling tried to make friends with the wild ducks, but he was too shy and too frightened to make much headway. To his relief, they left him to himself and he stayed among the reeds.

One morning something dreadful happened. He heard two loud bangs, and there, quite close to him, two of the wild ducks dropped out of the sky to lie stiff and still on the ground. Trembling, the Ugly Duckling did his best to make himself invisible among the reeds as another wild duck dropped into the water. He saw a dog swim out of the marsh and carry the body away in his mouth.

'I must leave this place,' he said to himself. And when darkness came he set out in the direction of the woods.

The wind tossed him like a leaf from one side of the path to the other, and the Ugly Duckling could scarcely make any progress. He was almost ready to give up when he caught sight of a hut with its door swinging open. Inside, an old woman sat at a table, and beside her, one on each side, sat a cat and a hen. When the old woman saw the little duck, she said, 'Come in, Duck. You're not a drake, are you? You are very welcome to stay with us— that is, if you lay me an egg every morning.'

These were the first kind words the Ugly Duckling had ever heard in his life, and for the next three weeks he was very happy. The old woman treated him with great kindness, although the cat and the hen mostly ignored him. But the old woman was only pretending to like the Ugly Duckling. When it was clear that she could not hope for any eggs, she lost her temper.

'Useless bird, and ugly at that!' she shrieked at him.

And the hen added, 'You're too ugly to be accepted in this world. Why don't you try the next?' Which was a cruel and silly thing to say. But then most hens do cackle away, don't they?

At that, the Ugly Duckling knew without question that he had outstayed his welcome. The next morning, when the cat was still asleep, and the hen, who had never laid an egg in *her* life, had her head in a basin of corn, the Ugly Duckling slipped away.

There was none to wave him goodbye or wish him well, and sadly he walked into the dark woods feeling, as he had often felt before, that it would be just as well if he were dead, for no one wanted him alive.

With that thought in mind he journeyed a long way until, one day, he saw before him a small pond, and the sight of the water made him want to swim again.

Once in the pond, some of his loneliness disappeared. And as he swam and dived and swam again, he began to feel happier, as if strangely he had come home, though there was not a single one of his kind about. But now the wind was blowing cold and the leaves on the trees were turning to dusty yellow and brown. It was autumn, and soon it would be winter.

One night the little duck looked upwards into the sky and there, above him, he saw some wonderfully beautiful birds with long necks. They were flying easily, and they were so graceful that the little duck could not help giving a cry of joy as he watched them.

Very soon after that, the first snowflakes fell and a bitter icy wind blew across the land. The Ugly Duckling had no idea of what was happening to his pond, but one morning, when he awoke, he found that part of it was covered with a sheet of ice. Round and round he swam in the water that was left to him, but slowly the ice spread.

That night the ice closed completely round him, and the next day he could not move. For all the world it looked as if the Ugly Duckling were dead.

It seemed so to the farmer who, by chance, was passing

that way, but just the same he broke the ice and he carried the seemingly lifeless bird back to his home.

'He's not dead,' the farmer's little girl said when she saw the Ugly Duckling. And she wrapped him in a shawl and put him near the fire.

Soon after, the Ugly Duckling opened his eyes and the little girl fed him and made much of him. Not so her little brother. He shouted with glee when he saw that they had a real live duck to play with, and would not leave the bird alone.

The noise and excitement frightened the Ugly Duckling and he tried to flutter away into a corner. He was still so weak that his movements were clumsy, and he fell into a big bowl of milk. The milk splashed all over the table and the floor, and the farmer's wife began to scream.

The children shrieked with laughter and clapped their hands, and the duckling, frantic now with fright, dashed from one corner of the room to the other, upsetting everything that came in his way.

Then the farmer's wife fell into a rage and began chasing him with a poker. The room was a prison and the Ugly Duckling was the prisoner. Half-dead from fright, he made for the window that, luckily for him, was open. Somehow he managed to squeeze through and escape.

When some of his strength returned, the Ugly Duckling left his hiding-place behind the hedge, and made his way across the frost-covered fields and icy ponds. On and on he went, and the farther he travelled the heavier grew his heart. Often, in these lonely days of winter, the Ugly Duckling wished only to die, but something inside him drove him forward.

Then one morning he awoke to see above him a blue sky, and to hear, as he lay still, the lovely song of the lark. It was spring again, and fresh hope sprang up in the Ugly Duckling's heart. For the first time he had a great desire to spread his wings and fly, not flutter a few yards at a time, but really and truly fly.

At first the Ugly Duckling flew just above the ground, so uncertain was he of his own strength; then suddenly he found himself soaring—soaring upwards. Joyfully he spread his wings. Over the woods and the forests he flew until at last he saw beneath him a wonderful park filled with brightly coloured flowers and a lake of shimmering, silvery water.

The Ugly Duckling glided down towards the beautiful lake, and his heart leapt with happiness at the sight of the dazzling white birds that raised their long, graceful necks to greet him.

But his joy at the sight of the royal birds soon turned to fear. 'I am so ugly,' he thought desperately to himself. 'No one in the whole world has ever given me welcome. What will these royal birds do to me? They will surely kill me for having dared to come so close.'

And with that thought uppermost in his mind, the poor Ugly Duckling prepared himself for their attack as slowly the swans came gliding towards him. He lowered his head and stared miserably downwards into the shining waters. The lake was like a mirror, and reflected in it the Ugly Duckling saw an image so beautiful, so graceful, that he could not believe his own eyes. Surely it could not be himself mirrored there in the water! And yet who else?

By now the great birds, the swans, were surrounding him in welcome. Two caressed him with their beaks, while the others murmured, 'Welcome, brother!'

'Look, Daddy, the swans are saying hello to the new one,' cried the children who had come to the lake to feed the birds. 'Let's give him our nicest scraps, for he is the youngest and the most beautiful of all.'

The youngest and most beautiful of all the swans! The Ugly Duckling had found his true home at last. He lifted his long, graceful neck and returned the caresses of his new brothers. He thought he would die of happiness.

THE LITTLE MATCH GIRL

On a cold winter's night a little girl was seen wandering from one brightly lit shop window to the next. Crowds thronged the street, for it was the last day of the old year, and many wished to buy presents to take home to their families. The little girl had no proper family—only a father who did not care for her.

The child clutched her bundle of matches in thin hands, blue with cold. The biting wind tore at her ragged dress, and the snow-covered pavement stung her bare feet.

Soon the lights in the shop windows would go out, the people would go back home, and she would be alone. 'I dare not go back and tell my father that I haven't sold any matches,' the girl thought. 'I can't go home.'

At the end of the row of shops, two grey-stoned houses stood close together; it was here between the houses that the match girl found a place to sit. How she shivered as she crouched low, hoping to escape some of the falling snowflakes. 'I shall light one of my matches,' she said to herself at last. 'It will help to warm my hands.'

The bright warm flame glowed in the darkness, and the

little girl thought for a moment she was seated in front of a warm fire in a room filled with bright ornaments. Then the match burnt itself out, and her vision vanished.

When the child struck her second match, the wall itself disappeared, and in its place was a table laden with good things to eat; so much was on the table that the little girl scarcely knew where to begin. But as she stretched out her hand, the match burnt itself out, and the vision vanished.

Presently, the little girl struck a third match against the wall. As it blazed, she found herself gazing at a tall Christmas tree. A hundred white candles twinkled at her from its green arms. Presents, wrapped in silver and gold paper, were heaped round the beautiful tree, and the little girl knew they were all for her.

As she stared upwards, the tree's glittering star fell down from the topmost branch; it was like a star out of the heavens. And the little girl remembered how once her grandmother, the only person who had ever truly loved her, had talked about heaven before she died.

How wonderful it would be to see her grandmother again, the child suddenly thought as she struck her fourth match against the wall. The match blazed into life and there, caught in its dazzling flame, was her beloved grandmother, as young and as beautiful as she had once been in real life.

'Don't leave me, Grandmother,' whispered the little girl. 'I know you will when the match burns itself out. Stay with me. Stay with me.' And she began to light one match after the other in frantic haste. When the last match was struck, her grandmother opened her arms and clasped the little girl to herself.

The match spluttered and died, dropping from the cold, lifeless hands of the little girl. She was found in the morning —the first day of the new year.

'Poor little mite,' said one of the women in the small crowd that had gathered. 'She must have frozen to death.'

'Yet she looks happy,' said another, 'as if she had seen something wonderful before she died.'

JACK AND THE BEANSTALK

There was once upon a time, in the nicest part of the country, a tiny farm. Life on this farm was very happy. The farmer was poor but he was hard-working and kind. His wife was good and gentle, and his son, Jack, though perhaps not quite as hard-working as he should have been, had nevertheless a way with animals.

Who knows how long that little family might have lived together if the good farmer had not caught a chill and died. He left behind him a young widow who knew little about the workings of the farm, and a son whose wits were not too sharp.

At first they were not too badly off, but the day came when Jack's mother told him there was no money left— not even enough to buy them a loaf to eat next day.

'No money—none at all?' cried Jack in astonishment when his mother told him that he would have to go hungry. 'But Mother, I can't understand it. I know we have nothing much left on the farm except Milky-White, but we do have her, and she's the best cow in the whole of the land.'

'Milky-White has always served us well with her milk,'

384

said Jack's mother, 'but now she has no more milk to give. We shall both starve.' And the poor woman began to weep.

'We could sell Milky-White,' said Jack, and he too wept at the very idea, for he loved the faithful cow. 'I tell you what, Mother, I'll—I'll get a job.'

But alas, although Jack tried hard enough, there was no one who would keep him for longer than a day, for the truth was that he let his mind wander. This meant that he never did anything well enough to satisfy even the most kindly master.

'It's no use,' said Jack's mother. 'Whatever you say, we shall have to sell our dear Milky-White. Today is market day, and you will be sure to find someone at the market who will give a good price for such a fine cow. The money you get will buy us food for the next few weeks.'

So, very sadly, Jack brought Milky-White out of the barn. 'Don't worry, Mother,' he said. 'I shall take Milky-White to market and make a good bargain. I promise!'

Jack had only gone a little way when he met a quaint little man. 'Hello Jack,' said the stranger. 'Where are you going?'

'To the market to sell Milky-White,' said Jack.

'You look a smart young fellow,' said the little man. 'I'll tell you what. I'll give you the best of a good bargain.' And he pulled out of his pocket five oddly shaped beans. 'You give me that cow of yours, and I'll give you these five coloured beans.'

'What!' cried Jack. 'Do you take me for a fool?'

'These are no ordinary beans,' the stranger told him. 'Plant them tonight and they will tower into the sky by morning.'

For the life of him Jack could not resist this bargain. He took the beans and gave the little old man his precious cow.

'Mother will be so pleased,' he said to himself as he ran back home.

Poor Jack! His mother wept tears of rage when she heard what he had done. She threw the beans out of the window and packed Jack off to bed without a bite to eat.

The next morning Jack woke early. He lay still for a moment, feeling very sorry for himself. Then all at once he knew something was unusual about his little room.

'That's funny,' said Jack to himself. 'It's early morning and the sun should be shining in through the window. Instead, it's very nearly dark.'

Quickly he jumped out of bed and peered outside. There his eyes saw an incredible sight. A great tree had sprouted up in the night, and its topmost branches were so high that they reached into the sky.

'So the beans did take root!' exclaimed Jack, his eyes beginning to shine with excitement. 'And it's the beanstalk that is shutting out the sun. Its stalks are so close together they are like a ladder into the clouds. I must climb it at once before Mother wakes up.'

Full of excitement, Jack dressed quickly and, as quietly as a mouse, dropped from the window and began to climb.

Up and up he went until the village began to look like a tiny cardboard model.

The higher Jack climbed, the more excited he became. Now he was in a swirling white world of clouds. Presently

he reached the very top of the beanstalk and saw before him a long white road and a tall grey castle.

The woman who came out of the castle to greet him was so big and tall that Jack felt like a dwarf. 'Good morning, ma'am,' said Jack politely. 'Could you please give me a bite of breakfast?'

'Breakfast!' the woman cried. 'You don't know what you ask! My husband is a giant with an appetite for boys.'

But Jack's longing for food made him recklessly brave, and with great daring he took her huge hand in his.

'Please, ma'am,' he begged. 'Just a sup of that lovely porridge I can smell cooking in the kitchen.'

At last Jack got his way, and the Giant's wife took him down into her vast kitchen. 'If you hear my husband,' she whispered, 'hide at once. We shall have plenty of warning, for the whole place will shake and tremble under his feet.'

Jack had just finished his plate of hot porridge when the whole castle began to shake and tremble.

'Quick, hide!' whispered the Giant's wife. 'My man is returning.'

Jack lifted the lid of the great stone oven and dropped inside. From his hiding place he heard a mighty rumbling voice: 'Fee-fi-fo-fum, I smell the blood of an Englishman. Be he alive or be he dead, I'll grind his bones to make my bread.'

'No, no,' said the Giant's wife quickly. 'You only smell the bones of that young ox you ate yesterday. There's fine ox soup waiting for you. Now eat up.' The Giant was tired and hungry, and the smell of the food which his wife placed before him soon tempted him to forget his suspicions. After he had eaten, he called for his bags of gold, which he liked to look upon, and then, soon after, fell fast asleep.

When the loud snores told Jack that it was safe to show himself, he lifted the oven lid and crept out of his hiding place. Then he tip-toed noiselessly towards the table. The Giant snored on, and Jack, with lightning speed, snatched one of the bags of gold and ran as swiftly as he could up the long stone stairs and out of the castle.

Down the beanstalk he scrambled, shouting to his mother as he dropped the last few feet, 'Come, Mother, our fortunes are made.' When his mother saw all the golden pieces, she smiled and clasped her hands with happiness.

Now, everyone knows that money has a way of disappearing. Jack and his mother enjoyed the best of everything for some months—until the day came when all the gold had been spent.

'Don't worry,' said Jack, 'I will venture up the beanstalk once more. The Giant's wife is a most kindly woman and the Giant may have some more treasure that he can spare.'

So, once again, Jack set off up the beanstalk. Up and up he climbed. At last, there was the long white road stretching before him and at the end of it the Giant's castle.

Just as before, Jack persuaded the Giant's wife to receive him kindly and later to hide him when the place shook and trembled under the great heavy step of the returning Giant.

But this time it was not his bags of gold that the Giant called for, but his favourite hen, a hen which, to Jack's amazement, laid golden eggs.

'Why,' Jack thought to himself, 'if I had such a hen she would lay golden eggs for me, and we would never be in want again. I must have that hen.' So once again, when the castle echoed with the Giant's loud snores, Jack with great daring snatched the hen.

Alas for Jack, the hen objected strongly to being taken away from her master and set up such a loud squawking that the Giant was instantly aroused from his heavy sleep.

With a mighty roar of rage he leapt from his chair and set out in hot pursuit of Jack and the hen.

With the hen tucked under his arm, Jack ran as fast as he could down the long white road until he reached the beanstalk. The Giant thundered after him, but he was in such a rage that his own long legs and big feet tripped him up. He stumbled, and this gave Jack the time he needed to escape.

Down, down, down he climbed, with the wonderful hen still safely tucked under his arm.

'Mother! Mother!' shouted Jack, when he saw his mother waiting below. 'I've got a hen that lays golden eggs. We are rich again!'

But for a long, long time Jack's mother did not want to hear of her son's adventures or even to look at the clever hen that laid the shiny golden eggs.

'I wish you wouldn't climb that beanstalk,' she would say to her son over and over again. 'Oh, I know we are rich now and the cupboard is filled with good things to eat. But mark my words, Jack, one of these days you will want to climb that beanstalk again and that will be once too often.'

Jack did not like to see his mother upset, and so he gave his word that he would not climb the beanstalk.

Now that they were rich, Jack found the days were very long, for he had nothing to do. Sometimes he went to market to look for the queer old man and thank him for his five magic beans, but he could never find him. Sometimes he went all the way to London to sell a golden egg, but he felt lonely in so large a place and was glad to return home.

'I can't understand you, Jack,' his mother would say. 'You just sit there dreaming when other boys are out playing in the meadow or helping on the farm. I wish, sometimes, that we had never heard of that strange old man and his beans. I am sure we would have managed somehow.'

'You don't understand, Mother,' Jack said at last. 'I can't forget that strange world of giants away up in the clouds. Let me return just once more, I beg you, Mother, for the last time.'

'Very well,' said his mother, at last. 'You may climb the beanstalk just one more time, but I shall not have a single moment's peace until you are safely back home with me again.'

Jack's eyes shone with excitement as he began to climb up the beanstalk. 'I will speak to the Giant's wife,' he said to himself. 'Perhaps she will let me into the castle again.'

But when Jack reached the castle the Giantess was nowhere to be seen, and so he began to explore on his own.

Up and down and round about the castle and courtyard he ran, and in a little while he found an open door.

'If I find a safe hiding place,' he said to himself, 'perhaps the Giant will fall asleep while he is looking at another of his treasures.'

Jack crept down the long stone stairway and into the big room where the Giant always had his meals.

The room was empty, and Jack made up his mind that the oven was, after all, the best place in which to hide.

It seemed a long time to Jack before he heard the Giant's heavy step. Then he heard the Giant bellowing, 'Fee-fi-fo-fum, I smell the blood of an Englishman. Be he alive or be he dead, I'll grind his bones to make my bread.'

'Impossible, good husband,' answered the Giantess. 'I have seen no one near the castle for days. Come now, enjoy this fat, roasted pig that's just ready for eating.'

Jack shivered with excitement as he listened, and presently he heard the Giant say, 'Wife, bring me my magic harp.'

Soon the room was filled with the sweetest music Jack had ever heard. As he listened he made up his mind that he must have the magic harp at all costs.

It was very uncomfortable inside the oven, but Jack was sure that the Giant would soon fall asleep. And that is just what the Giant did. Jack waited until the Giant began to snore. Then he jumped out of the oven and crept towards the big table on which the magic harp rested.

As he grasped hold of the harp, to Jack's surprise and horror it began to call out in a loud voice, 'Master! Master!'

With a great roar of rage the Giant woke up and sprang to his feet. Up the steps he rushed after Jack, shouting, 'Thief! Robber! I'll grind your bones to make my bread!'

Jack ran on and on, through the long passages of the big castle and out into the courtyard.

Soon he was on the white road that led to the beanstalk. But the magic harp under his arm squirmed and wriggled and would not stay still. Every now and again it called out in its loud voice, 'Master! Master!'

'If only I can reach the beanstalk before the Giant,' Jack thought desperately, 'he won't dare to follow.'

At last he reached the top of the beanstalk and, with the wriggling harp under his arm, he sprang forward and began to clamber down. Seconds behind him came the angry Giant, who also flung himself forward on to the beanstalk and began to climb down after Jack.

Jack could feel the beanstalk shake and tremble under the weight of the Giant, but he did not dare to look back in case he dropped the precious harp.

Down, down, down went Jack, and after him came the Giant. But the Giant had never climbed down a beanstalk before, so it was little wonder that his huge arms and legs grew weary and he had to stop for a rest.

This gave Jack the chance he needed to scramble down the last few yards. When he reached the ground he shouted, 'Mother! Mother! Quick! Bring the axe.'

Jack's mother, on hearing her son's shouts, rushed to the woodshed for the big axe.

'The Giant is coming after me,' Jack gasped. 'I must cut down the tree.' And he took hold of the axe and swung it with all his might at the beanstalk. But the stem of the beanstalk was so thick that not even the Giant himself could have cut it right through at a single blow.

Again and again Jack swung the axe. The beanstalk began to tremble as if it had been shaken by a storm of wind.

'Stand back, Mother!' Jack cried. 'Stand back! This time the beanstalk will fall.'

The Giant roared in helpless rage as he tried to save himself when the huge beanstalk began to topple over. Crash! went the beanstalk; and crash! went the Giant.

That was the end of the beanstalk—and the end of the Giant. The hole he made in the ground just swallowed him up.

As for Jack and his mother, they lived happily together for many years. When they wanted music, there was always the magic harp to sing for them, and when they wanted money, there was always the wonderful hen and her golden eggs. What more could anyone ask for?

PUSS-IN-BOOTS

There was once a poor miller's son and a very clever cat—and they are mostly what this story is about.

The miller himself was so poor that when he died he had only his mill, his ass, and his cat to leave to his family of three sons. The eldest son got the mill. The middle son got the ass, and the youngest son got the cat.

'Of what use is a cat to me?' the miller's youngest son asked himself bitterly when he was alone with his cat. 'A cat won't make my fortune.'

'You may find me of very great use,' said the cat, just as if he had read his master's thoughts. 'I may surprise you yet, if only you will trust me.'

'Trust you!' exclaimed the young man scornfully. 'My two brothers have got the best bargains by far. What can you do to help me make a living?'

'I promise you,' said the cat patiently, 'that if you leave everything to me, and give me what I ask, I will help you to make your fortune.'

The cat spoke so earnestly and with such an air of confidence that the miller's son began to think that he might as well hear what his cat had to say.

'All I want,' went on the cat, 'is a pair of tall boots and a big sack.'

'I can't think why you should want tall boots,' said the young man ungraciously. 'But if you must have tall boots and a sack, then you shall have them.'

'It doesn't matter why I want them,' replied the cat. 'But I assure you the boots will carry me along at a great pace and be of great assistance to me in the plans I have for making your fortune.'

And with that the young man had to be content. The next day the cat had his sack and a fine pair of tall boots, and from that time onwards he was known as Puss-in-Boots, which greatly pleased him.

Puss-in-Boots wasted no time. Armed with his sack and wearing his fine tall boots, he set out for the woods, where he knew a number of plump little rabbits lived.

Before he settled down into a sham sleep, Puss filled his sack with sweet-smelling bran. Then he looped a string round the neck of the sack so that he could draw it tightly shut whenever he chose. All worked out according to plan. Soon after Puss had closed his eyes, a young and silly rabbit ventured inside the sack. Puss pulled the string and the rabbit was caught.

Puss set out immediately for the palace, and so important was his bearing that he was taken into the King's presence right away.

The King was a jolly fellow, uncommonly fond of rabbit pie, so naturally he was highly delighted when Puss-in-Boots held out the plump little rabbit.

'A present, Your Majesty,' said Puss, 'from my most noble master, the Marquis of Carabas.' This was the grand-sounding name Puss had decided to give his master.

Everyone, even a king, likes presents, and this King was no exception. He was even more delighted when Puss turned up the next day, and the day after, with pheasants and wood pigeons and more rabbits—all gifts from the noble Marquis, so Puss told him.

As soon as the King began to wish that he could meet this most noble, this most generous Marquis of Carabas, Puss set about making more plans.

'Do as I say,' he told his master one day. 'Hold yourself

ready to bathe in the river tomorrow. I will tell you the exact spot and the exact hour in the morning.'

'Very well,' said his master, 'but I wish I knew what it was all about.'

And he was still wondering when, on the morrow, Puss helped him out of his ragged clothes and pushed him into the river.

The cat had scarcely time to hide his master's rags under a big stone before the clatter of horses' hooves was heard. There, coming along the road at a rattling pace, was the King's royal carriage drawn by a pair of prancing horses.

Puss immediately began to shout at the top of his voice, 'Help, help, my honourable master, the Marquis of Carabas, is drowning! Help! Help!'

As soon as the King heard the familiar name, he ordered the carriage to stop. All in a moment the young man found himself being pulled out of the water by the King's servants.

Meantime, Puss had the King's ear, and was whispering busily into it. It seemed that robbers had taken all his

master's fine clothing. Could His Majesty provide new robes to cover him until he returned home?

'He shall have the best suit in the royal wardrobe,' vowed the King, and he sent his servant back to the palace to fetch it at once.

The miller's son looked so handsome in his new royal suit of clothes that it was not surprising that the Princess, who was accompanying her royal father, blushed a very pretty blush.

'This is the noble young man who has been so generous with his gifts,' said the King graciously. 'Let me introduce you, daughter, to the Marquis of Carabas.'

The miller's son bowed low, and if he felt great astonishment at his new title he had wit enough to hide it from his noble rescuers.

'You must ride with us in our carriage,' the King went on. 'It will give us pleasure to have you with us. We have much to talk about.'

So the young miller's son rode in the King's carriage, and he sat on a red velvet cushion beside the King's daughter, which made him very happy.

Meanwhile, there was no soft velvet cushion for Puss. His high boots were carrying him along so swiftly that he was by now far ahead of the coach, and that is just how he meant it to be. There was a great deal of work still to be done before his master's fortune was made.

Huge green meadows and fields of golden corn bordered the road, and Puss saw with his sharp eyes that he was passing through a rich part of the country. But he did not draw breath until he came upon some workmen by the side of the road.

'Good fellow,' said Puss, 'in a few minutes the King comes this way. Be certain to tell him that all this land belongs to my lord, the Marquis of Carabas. If you fail to do this, you will be chopped up into mincemeat.'

The men had no idea who the Marquis of Carabas was, but they could see that Puss meant every word.

'Of course, of course!' they answered. 'Whatever you say, Sir Puss. Just leave it to us.'

The rumble and creak of the King's coach warned Puss that he must be off, and so with one last fierce scowl he took his leave. The poor workmen had no time to think before the King's carriage was upon them.

'That's a fine crop in the fields around,' the King called out. 'Tell me, good fellows, who owns all this land?'

'Why, Your Majesty, the Marquis of Carabas,' answered one of the men.

'Indeed, indeed!' the King said, as he sank back on his red velvet cushion and the carriage continued on its way. Time and again, the King stopped his carriage to enquire about the lands he was passing through, and who owned them. Each time he received the same answer.

'The Marquis of Carabas, Your Majesty.' Puss had done his work so well that all the peasants and workmen for miles around were too frightened to say anything else. It was small wonder that the King began to think this handsome young man must be worth a fortune of no mean size.

'I daresay he lives in a very splendid castle,' thought the King.

The poor miller's son, of course, had neither castle nor palace to his name. But Puss had his eye on a very sizeable castle that belonged to a well-known Ogre in these parts.

By a lucky chance, this castle lay in the path of the royal coach.

The Ogre, as Puss well knew, had the reputation of being a magician. He was also, as it happened, the richest man in the land, and all the vast estates which the King had just passed through were his.

'So far, so good,' said Puss to himself as he sped across the castle drawbridge. 'Now to meet the Ogre!'

The Ogre rather kept himself to himself. However, when he heard that Puss-in-Boots had come on a friendly visit, he asked him to step inside.

Puss found the Ogre in his large dining hall where the table was already prepared for a meal.

'It's very kind of you to receive me,' said Puss-in-Boots, and his tone was very respectful and humble. 'I have heard of your great powers as a magician, and I felt I could not pass by your castle without calling upon you.'

'Indeed,' replied the Ogre, and the tone of his voice was quite kindly. 'I did not know my fame had spread so far and wide, but I must admit ogre-magicians of my particular brand are very rare, very rare indeed.'

'Of course they are,' said Puss, and his voice was warm with flattery, and his green eyes were shining with admiration. 'Do tell me, Ogre, is it really true that you can change yourself into any shape—I mean at the twinkling of an eye, so to speak?'

'Yes, yes, perfectly true,' replied the Ogre. 'At the twinkling of an eye, I can change myself into any shape I choose.'

'You mean—you mean,' began Puss, so full of admiration

and astonishment that it seemed he was quite overcome. 'You mean, Sir Ogre, that you could be a tiger or an elephant or a lion just for the asking?'

'Indeed, I do!' roared the Ogre. 'You have only to name any of the great beasts of the jungle. I assure you it is all the same to me. My powers are quite astonishing.'

'So they are, so they are!' exclaimed Puss as he suddenly found himself facing a large fierce lion instead of the Ogre.

'You see!' growled the Ogre from inside the Lion; and Puss, who was nearly frightened out of his boots, could only squeak, 'Yes, yes, I see.'

Presently, however, Puss began to get his courage back and some of his old cunning. 'Of course,' he began, 'I can quite understand how a great big Ogre can change himself into a great big lion. 'I doubt if a great big Ogre is clever enough to change into a tiny mouse!'

'Easy!' snarled the Ogre. 'I'll show you!'

With that he straight away changed himself into a tiny mouse, as Puss-in-Boots had hoped and planned he would.

The next part of the story is quickly told. With a snarl and a pounce, the cat leapt upon that tiny mouse and gobbled it up.

That was the end of the Ogre, and Puss did not spare him a tear. With a sly satisfied twitch of his whiskers and a last look around, he rushed away to the castle entrance.

How well everything was turning out for Puss! For there was the King stepping out of his coach with a view to enquiring about the owner of such a grand castle.

'Your Majesty!' cried Puss. 'Welcome to the humble home of my lord and master, the Marquis of Carabas!'

'What!' exclaimed the King. 'Does this fine castle belong to the Marquis as well as all these vast estates?'

'Indeed, yes,' said Puss, and he swept his plumed hat off in salute, as the lovely Princess and the miller's son appeared behind the portly King.

'Enter, I beg you,' said Puss. 'In the name of my master, welcome to Carabas Castle.'

404

'Very kind, very kind,' the King said. 'We accept your hospitality. Pray, lead the way.'

Puss then took the chance to whisper to his master that all was well and that on no account should he show any surprise.

The King was astonished at the richness of the castle, and when he saw the wonderful dishes already arrayed on the table, he could not hold back his praise; nor did he frown when he saw that his daughter and the Marquis had lost their hearts to each other.

'It is very plain to see,' said the King when at last the banquet was over and they were on the terrace, 'that you two young people have fallen in love. I shall be delighted, Marquis, to give my consent to the wedding.'

So the King's daughter and the miller's youngest son were married and lived happily ever afterwards. As for Puss, he lived in luxury all his days, and never chased another mouse except for fun and a little light exercise.

THE LITTLE MERMAID

Long ago, when the world was very young, the Mer-people had their kingdom in the deepest part of the ocean where the water was as blue as a cornflower.

One day the youngest of the Mer-princesses was gliding on the surface of the sea when she saw a large three-masted ship at rest on the still waters. The sight was strange to the little mermaid, for this was the first time she had been allowed to leave the Mer-kingdom, and she stayed watching until the skies grew dark with storm clouds.

When the sailors on board the ship saw the danger signs, they hastily furled the sails. But nothing they could do could save them from the fury of the storm when at last it came. Their ship was tossed like a cork upon the waters until, at length, her stout masts broke and she began to sink.

Fascinated, the little mermaid remained where she was. As the fine ship floundered she saw a young and handsome Prince fall overboard. 'He will reach my father's kingdom,' the little mermaid told herself, and she smiled. 'I shall have him for my own.'

Then she remembered something her grandmother had told her when she was very young, 'A human cannot live in the water.'

'I must not let such a fine young man die,' the little

406

mermaid decided quickly, and she dived down, down, through the cold dark waters until she reached the drowning Prince. Seizing hold of him, she pulled him upwards and swam with him to the shore.

Using all her strength, she dragged him to safety, and then turned him over so that his pale face was touched by the warming fingers of the sun. She stroked his brow and marvelled at the softness of his skin. And presently the little mermaid knew she was falling in love with this fine young man.

As the church bells began to ring, the young Prince stirred. The little mermaid longed to speak to him but, before he could open his eyes, some girls from the castle came down to the shore, and the little mermaid hid behind a rock. The girls ran to their Prince and, seizing her chance, the mermaid dived back into the sea, and so returned to her father's kingdom beneath the waves.

From that moment the mermaid could think of nothing and no one but her human Prince. In vain her sisters tried to make her play with them in their wonderful garden or glide, like silver fishes, through the spreading sea-plants. The Mer-princess asked only to be left alone with her thoughts.

At last one of her sisters guessed her secret. 'You have fallen in love with a human,' she teased her little sister. 'You know you can never marry him.'

The little mermaid did not answer, but that same day she spoke to her wise old grandmother, who knew a great deal about the world of men.

'Do men live forever?' asked the little mermaid.

'No,' said her grandmother. 'They live only a short time compared with us. But then they have souls. When their bodies die their souls go to a wonderful place they call "heaven".'

'We have no souls,' said the Mer-princess. 'We live for two hundred, maybe three hundred years—and then we become as the foam. Is there no way I can get a soul?'

'There is no way,' said her grandmother, 'except perhaps if an earth-man loved you so much that he made you his wife. And that can never be, for in the eyes of men we are ugly. They do not like our shining silver tails. Earth-men and earth-girls have two stilts on which to walk, which they call legs.'

The little mermaid went back to her garden to think about her grandmother's words. 'My Prince might learn to love me if I had two legs,' she decided at last. 'I will go to the witch of the whirlpool and ask her to give me two legs instead of a tail.'

The witch of the whirlpool was a creature living in a house made of dry white human bones and surrounded by shiny toads and fat snails.

'I know why you have come to me,' she croaked when the little mermaid stood before her. 'You want to be rid of your tail and have, instead, two human legs.'

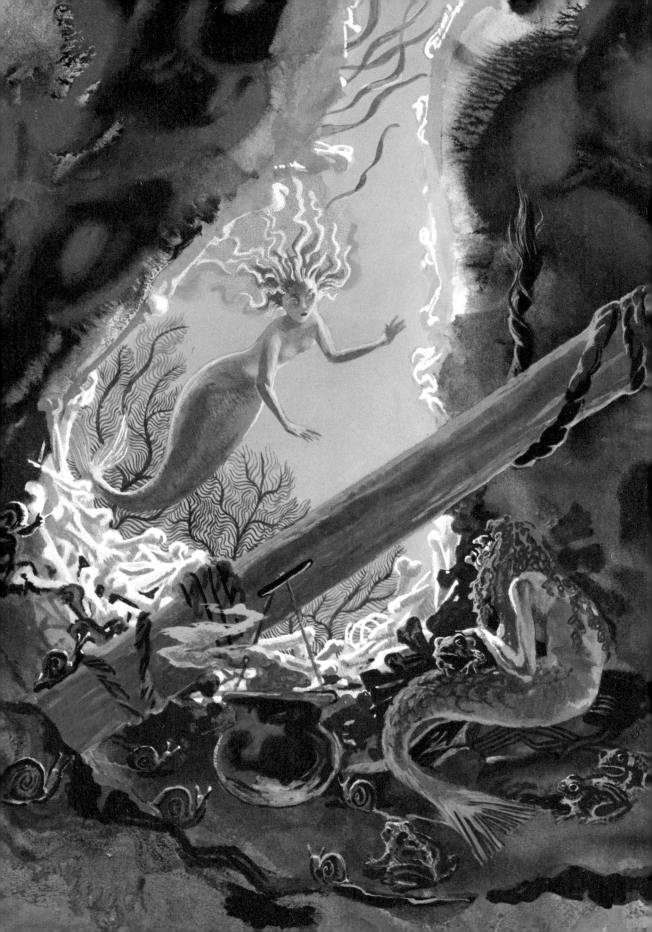

'Yes, yes!' cried the Mer-princess eagerly. 'Will you help me?'

'Your wish is foolish,' went on the witch, and she gave a shrill cackle that made her toads jump. 'You are even more foolish in desiring the young human Prince for a husband, and a soul that will go to heaven.'

'Will you help me?' begged the little mermaid again. 'I will pay any price.'

'My price is high,' said the witch. 'You must give me your pretty voice.'

'Anything,' said the mermaid, though tears filled her beautiful eyes at the thought of losing her voice.

'Very well,' said the witch, and she bent over her steaming cauldron. 'I will prepare a potion that you must take with you as you swim to land. When you reach the shore, drink it. Your tail will shrivel and disappear. In its place you will have two legs. Take heed, however! You will endure great pain. But you will be able to move and dance more gracefully than any human Princess.'

'If I have no voice,' said the mermaid as she watched the witch stir her cauldron until it boiled and bubbled, 'how can I tell the Prince of my love?'

'He will love you for your face and form,' said the witch curtly, 'if he loves you at all. But remember, he must make you his wife. If he marries another, your heart will break, and you will turn into sea-foam.'

When the potion was ready, the witch poured it into a small bottle and gave it to the mermaid, at the same time plucking out her tongue. The mermaid mutely accepted the phial and left the witch.

Before the sun set, she glided upwards through the dark waters until she reached the shore, and once there she drank the magic liquid, which stung and burned her throat like fire. So great was the pain that the little mermaid fainted away. When she opened her eyes, it was to find the Prince standing over her.

The Prince took her hand and led her to the palace; the little mermaid walked, as light as thistledown, by his side. So great was her joy that she scarcely noticed the sharp needle-like stabs that accompanied every step.

'Who are you? Where do you come from?' asked the Prince when they reached the palace. 'How beautiful you are!'

But the little mermaid could not answer. And the Prince told the ladies of his court to dress his little foundling in rich silks and to take care of her until she found her tongue.

So beautiful was the little mermaid and so gentle in her ways that the Prince found himself constantly wanting to gaze upon her. And as the months passed, he took her with him everywhere.

When he was tired and weary from hunting, he would ask her to dance for him, and though every step cost her dear,

the little mermaid danced as light as gossamer before him until he forgot his weariness.

'I shall never let you go,' the Prince vowed. 'Silent you may be, but you are as precious to me now as my own right hand.'

The little mermaid's eyes sparkled like stars at this, and when the Prince took her in his arms she trembled with happiness. Soon after this, the Prince told her that the King had asked him to go on a visit to another country across the sea.

'There is a beautiful Princess my father would like me to marry,' he said. 'But I would rather keep my heart free for you, little one. You shall come with me on the royal ship, and you shall be at my side when I meet this beautiful Princess.'

Alas, the foreign Princess was more beautiful than the Prince had imagined from his father's description. And as the mermaid watched them meet and walk together, she felt suddenly afraid of what the future would hold.

Soon the news was spread abroad that the Prince and the beautiful Princess had fallen deeply in love and would be married shortly.

'And you shall be our bridesmaid,' said the Prince, coming to the mermaid and taking her hand. 'I promise you that I shall care for you always.' Then he added, 'I am so happy. Tomorrow I marry the most beautiful Princess in the world. You too must be happy, little silent one.'

The mermaid turned away her head in sorrow, and the Prince left her so that he could go back to his Princess.

The next day bells rang throughout the city as the wedding procession was formed. The Prince walked hand in hand with his beautiful Princess, turning every now and then to smile at the little mermaid who, in a gown of silver and gold, held the bride's long train.

Once inside the church, the wedding service began, but the mermaid heard no word of it; she was thinking of what

would happen to her when night fell. After the ceremony came the dancing and feasting, and then the happy couple went aboard the ship that was to take them across the sea to the Prince's own kingdom.

The little mermaid went too, and the Prince asked her to dance for them. Her thoughts were filled with death as she danced, but no one watching would have guessed.

When the hour of midnight struck, the Prince and his lovely bride retired to their cabin, leaving the little mermaid on deck. As she stared down silently at the blue sea, her sisters from the Mer-kingdom came gliding out of the waves.

'It is not too late, little sister,' the eldest said. 'We are here to save you. We have been to the witch of the whirlpool and, in exchange for our hair, she has given us this knife. You must kill the Prince. His blood will fall upon your human feet and they will change back to a fish's tail.'

The little mermaid was happy to see her sisters again, and she picked up the knife that they flung on to the deck. 'I will do this thing and save myself,' she thought. And she stole to the Prince's cabin.

414

Her hand trembled as she stood there, ready to plunge the knife into his heart. But even as she raised her slender arm, she knew that his life was more precious to her than her own.

Far out to sea she flung the deadly weapon; then, with a sigh like the soft whispering of the wind, she plunged in after it, and was slowly dissolved into white foam.

The spirits of the air caught the foam and whirled it upwards out of the dark waters, and the little mermaid was suddenly herself again and no longer afraid. 'You will live with us, little one,' the spirits told her as they bore her upwards, 'for you have given your life for another. And there is no greater love...'

The spirits allowed the little mermaid to see her Prince once more. She was invisible to him, but somehow, as he gazed down at the sea, he must have felt her presence. The little mermaid kissed him gently, and her kiss was like the brush of a tiny feather on his cheek.

'Farewell!' the little mermaid sighed as the spirits of the air soared with her into the clouds. 'Farewell!'